THE CHANGELING

From Winter, Spring is Born

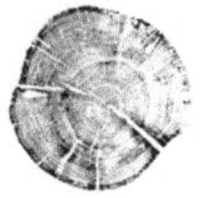

LY DE ANGELES

ISBN 9780645521405

Published in Australasia IMBAS PRESS

There is always more than one enemy

—The Great Mystery

You can't love alone. I know.

—Mercy Riley

We are—

wildwood and fen, hunter and hidden in holt

frost, rock-render and mist, heart of lake

mountain broken masts curraghs off inis mór

peat rain rot, blue fungi upon this forest floor

reindeer wolfhound boar wild horses

hen black bear orca and quiet after crying

tectonic plates to the chalk of conchearca

ash of volcano and stone out of brodgar

midnight sun rent arctic river wind's warning

mother ocean seals snow geese and dead mariners

bell of the red stag and map of my coastlines

piper of eagles and clan gathered for winter

drums of all people the roots of vast forests

what am I if we are forgotten bee swarm and owl head

tundra and bogland sídhe hollows of annwn

her mother, your brother, their lovers

and all of them come from us and will be us

bone stone shell ridge and lightning

        and everywhere you look

           you will remember, or you are nothing

ACT 1

1

SWEET DEATH

SPARROW

Blood makes petals in the snow. On nights this cold most of it freezes before it hits the ground. Poppy petals. Reminders of all the dead boys at Flanders. At Ypres. The men whose bodies she'd loved in her dreams and her fantasies, and how blown apart they'd been, with less than a second to register the tragedy of betrayal by those who sent them to this doom. Before they even had time to recognize how seemingly random violence mostly is.

She is Sparrow, a name she is known by out of a fondness for reminiscing, and to fool the nuns; something small to identify this snitty, hungry figure of a seeming-woman who is gamin and eldritch, almost childlike, but with blades hidden in the folds of seemingly soft flesh, hair like ice, eyes the color of honey and deep, like brackish pools of sorrow. She took to the streets when she escaped Our Ladys, to either make it because she is sufficiently strong and cunning or to be erased for her negligence at pretending to the garment of humanity. None of the faerie, the fáidh, have found her. And she believes the Mystery has forsaken her. Or is she, as is so often the case, distracted by her own intrigues? Sparrow is resigned, now. To becoming winter leaves. And dust, and the rubble of a broken heart.

She ghosts towards the night shadow of a six-foot-something high brick wall, wondering if the body she's wearing will bleed out before the whole story can reach some kind of resolution. Sorry, sort of, that she's been such a juvenile, playing *catch me if you can* with the slúagh whose job it is to track her. A hunt that no one, or nothing, would ever really want, but that some poor bastards have been tasked with. Well, she's evaded them so far. Left them lost, somewhere in the ice of the labyrinthine alleyways that will kill a body, unprepared for this kind of cold, for the desperation of those who live in the squats, and how ferocious they get when in need of whatever is their necessary poison. Down here, around the southside.

Sparrow believes they'll eventually find her because of those petals. But belief can be stupid.

Like breadcrumbs, she thinks, a throwaway line from a story-gone-wrong, that was just as biased and futile as her own cynicism. Breadcrumbs that Hansel figured were a clever idea when the pebbles didn't solve the problem set up by hunger, meant to help him and his sister find home again after the shit-show between their father and his new wife. Like always. What he'd been duped into believing was home, but that had been, instead, a brutal place of lies and intimidation. Just like the news. Like power taken, for power's sake alone. Breadcrumbs meant to be a means to find the way to come back from the old woman's cottage in the forest should she be the witch of evil intent the church made her out to be. Somebody should warn kids about birds.

She snorts what would have been a laugh, had it been a sound and not frozen air.

Sparrow didn't realize when she ran away so long ago now, that she'd have to pass through mythworld; through the towering giants that form the First Forest, that shrouds Forgotten Lake, that is also, in legend, Hy Brasil. That she'd become the focus of all these creatures. She had been so flippant. Simply made up her mind to live in flesh for a while. She had not, at first, known that the slúagh, batshit bad bullies, like two-legged raptors made of teeth and fog, and fitted out to appear like human men, would come, once her scent was discovered, where she had landed, in New Rathmore, the city's stink concentrated to a point of suffocation for those assuming the guise of mortals. She didn't know that the slúagh had been assigned the task of bringing her to the Monstrum or taking her out for being the witness to what had happened to those children in the institution. So now that she *is* aware, she runs.

They shoot. Miss the vital organs. The arrow, instead and maybe luckily, penetrating her shoulder. It passes right on through. She is weak and jaded, but her pursuers will be kicking themselves for not enacting a clean kill or capture, and will know by now that they've fucked up. That she'll find herself a holt. She knows she should shift, become mist or something, but blood and pain, while in a mortal shape, have a way of distracting techniques that should have been as easy as lying. And now, as she slides to the snow, almost forgetting herself, almost dying like some silly victim, she would have patted her own back for evading the scent of those poorly qualified unseelie bogles if she'd had the wherewithal to have thought her escape through a little better.

She tries to be oblivious to the harm she's suffered already, and what she has had to do to endure, while, in truth, being breathtakingly aware that she will never evade this travesty.

Sparrow does not think she has outfoxed the slúagh. Forests are seemingly as doomed to the chainsaw as she is to annihilation by some unforeseen enemy.

2

꜀꜀꜀ꟷꜜꜜꜜꟷ

TRICKSTER

DÉJÀVU DELACROIX

Two-twenty in the wee hours before dawn and the ice bomb locks the city down.

It's minus twelve degrees. The roads are a disaster of black ice. No social services getting through to deliver soup and coffee. No extra blankets. Not tonight. Maybe not any night soon. The broken dead all over the city, in back alleys, antiquated apartments where the heating failed three days ago, old people, poor people. They'll be found in the late spring. A body just has to make it through one night at a time, in this. That's the only way.

Here, in the sheltered corner of the abandoned bakery left to rust, its former purpose dissolving into some destiny as landfill, Déjàvu Delacroix is barely recognizable, even though most here know her face. She's rummaged through dumpsters for newspapers and discarded clothing, outfitting herself like a squat mountain. Giant of a woman, topping six foot. Keeping company with these discarded people. Men mostly. Silent, lost, belligerent men. Angry. Conspiracies, their only shelter from the facts of their failures. Their regret. The knowledge that they didn't love enough. Passing the goon between them, the pot, a lot of cigarettes. The day's begging money was spent on these off-switches. They keep as warm as is possible, hugging the ground around a forty-four gallon drum, flame cracking and spitting, savage with hunger, consuming packing-case wood and expertly busted up, discarded pallets that'd been abandoned down the side alleys, out back of shops and restaurants.

Laid out, all respectable, are two bodies frozen in a rictus of passion, identities that'll probably never be known to anyone. Seeming ordinary, just dead. They'd been found a few hours back, huddled together under that section of corrugated iron roofing that had fallen in, its back broken by the unprecedented snowfall. Discovered in a semblance of embrace. Warriors? Lovers, maybe? Their sweat, at the exertion of carrying the responsibility of staying alive into the futility of this little safe harbor, their doom. Bad mix, sweat and ice. Kills easily; them probably thinking they'd fulfilled their reason for having been born. Stopping to plan a way home, all so futile. *Sweet death*, it's known as. That innocent desire to just lie down. The exertion that becomes all too much. Stop, now, for just a minute or so. Maybe two of the pack from the unseelie court, silent hunters of Sparrow. And failing miserably. Screwed, because they'd promised the current regent that they'd hole her up, as hounds would; wear her down. Sparrow is certain of none of it. Her capacity to obscure a scent is beyond their skill at nosing her out. Maybe. She had thought she'd be alright, hanging loose from all those expectations. She'd born the daughter, hadn't she? Had hidden in that terrible place? Pretended to their shame and anonymity? Vanished, like haar in the morning of an infant spring. Never once considering the impact of her eventual testimony. Never wavering from a bottomless well of inherent justice.

Déjàvu relaxes, spread-legged on the bench—the only thing not looted when all these shops got themselves abandoned. In the relative snow-free protection of this part of the building where the roof still hangs in. She subtly guards Sparrow, silent and now-bandaged, who shares the dregs of her tobacco pouch with this monster of a woman, a possible ally.

The raggedy folk, silent and frost-breathed, watch for as long as they can remain interested, the fair-skinned, pale-haired stray, with the *shine*, who has wandered, half dead, into the flicker and haunt of the fire and been tended by the big woman. She should have been dirtier, thinks one. Should have been loved by her mummy, thinks another, remembering his own daughters from before he came back from Afghanistan a beaten man, dishonorably discharged for disobeying a command he knew to be obscene, having realized the whole debacle of a pretend-war was destroying the world a bit more every day. Knowing he'd been conned. Running from the nightmares but with nowhere to go except away from anyone who might care. Care is pity and that's worse than anything.

Should be me, thinks one of the thin girls, hiding her gaunt starvation beneath scruff and anarchy. Terrified of being recognized and dragged back to the facility.

Why do these people hang with Déjà? Because the older woman looks like she does, all muscle and angles. Even her tattooed knuckles are weapons. And why hang out with? What happens to the homeless girls who make the mistake of thinking it's okay to sleep at night? To be alone? Taken. Dog-companions abandoned. Them, left to howl with loss once the ketamine drains off their bodies. No one knows where those girls mostly end up, although one was found, like some raggedy, torn up doll, all blood and tendons and bone shards, unnamed and unidentified, down by the old wharf at the end of Copperhead Lane. Tied to a bollard by her shredded clothing. Left to bleed out.

Déjàvu hides the scarification patterns on her forehead beneath the hard, wool beanie, beneath a veil of perfectly symmetrical, individually defined silver and black dreadlocks, the fringe all blasphemous curls that shouldn't look this good on someone most people think of as just another rough-sleeper, maybe with a habit they don't know about because she never touches the booze. Some quietly presume she's a bouncer when she can get the work. Those markings, down her throat and along her clavicle are the deterrent, and etchings in ash, scarifications. Look closer and a body could just make out the map. Though no one could tell where that coastline is, where that chain of mist-and-spruce-covered mountains lie. No. To humans, it'd be damn-awful ugly on a woman, let alone one whose skin emanates light and depths, like oak. Disfigurements that got her thrown out of home, maybe? Or helped her survive. Foster care, juvie, locked up for looking at a cop with unreadable eyes? Or else marking her as someone you wouldn't rent a room to, even if she did have money.

She's here because of the killings. This darkest hour, even before the cold came; that paramedic and the cops call the dead zone time. It's when babies are stillborn, and old people die. It's when that woman's husband has fallen into a drunken stupor and, with all the might left in her unbroken arm she does him in with a hammer because she knows she won't survive another beating and neither will her kids. It's when the runaway opens the window and shimmies down the drainpipe, and hitches on down the highway, taking a risk every time a ride pulls over.

Déjàvu's not her real name, of course. Creatures like her don't have names. They're like bridges between what was and what could be. Potential friends, possible enemies. They check in, as humans, from time to time, because the gifted, like Sparrow, have a destiny that can fix a hole in the world, that somebody, probably a riddling joke invoked by Madoc Morcant, the up-and-coming bad boy of the unseelie court, the Monstrum, purposely pickaxed, intent on fulfilling some monkishly whimsical narrative of his own making. Like *World of Warcraft* or some other mindlessly violent attraction. Or else somebody fool enough to order a forest cut down, not thinking about what and who might live there. Things of that ilk and dumbness.

And Sparrow's saying nothing. Seemingly amnesiac. A ruse, of course. A mother bird protecting her nest, dragging a wing to distract the predator. It's always tricky when folks don't remember where they come from. Or pretend not to. Interrogation and prying don't work on faeries like Sparrow. It turns them onto junk and despair. They forget to be vital. Turpentine, or cheap tricks to pay for a habit because they don't cope with the cruelty of humans. Lot of these people around fires like this one, all over the country tonight. Heck, all over the world, truth be told. But Sparrow's fresh still. Like seawater crammed with bull kelp and a clean salt tang, somewhere off the shore of Clew Bay. Déjàvu can smell her, like a piece of preciousness or an unused razor.

Déjàvu's true nature was once the *water* of many rivers; many seas both inland, and off a vast and invaded Atlantic ocean. In her true shape she, or it, if one is rude, into objectification of otherkin, was a river, too long, too wide, too deep to even imagine anymore; too long in the mortal world but that's a necessity in times like these. She was once upon a time a vast piece of magic from when the world first breathed life, but nowadays (because they've learned they have to hide) they're remembered only as some old-person story. She's ox-strong. Like as not she could rip a truck in half if the mood took her so, in that sense, Sparrow's intuition is as clean as she is capable of being.

The question is, why is Sparrow here in the deserted, deadly district of New Rathmore at all? Why does she need protection? *Does* she need protection, or is this some kind of evasion? To a degree, over hushed whispers, Déjàvu is aware of an enemy, or enemies. Creatures out of mythworld that want what? That secret's yet to fully unfold. And it's too complicated for her to explain yet, so Sparrow confides part of the truth through the medium of graphite and paper.

Because the stories Sparrow draws, with just those pencils she keeps hidden in the deep inside pockets of her hoodie, come to pass.

Happen. Sparrow has *the sight*, the gift of comprehending an event before it happens. She expresses what she knows through art.

She depicts each murder and victim, despite the horror of her visions, days before the event. She's always right, and before Déjàvu, nobody has seen her sketchbook. Not anyone human that is. It was known to critters in the human world a while back. Rats and bats in the night when she'd sit under the streetlight, tongue between her teeth in concentration. Pigeons during daylight hours. Blackbirds. Cats on walls, seemingly sleeping. That's what she's doing now, and Déjàvu doesn't ever look at the faces, cause she knows just about everybody, and it'd be shocking, somehow, to see a death on the page afore she'd seen a body.

The word spread to the wisdom-holders of mythworld, certain beings out of legend, forever remaining out of sight through necessity and disbelief, that Sparrow escaped Our Lady of Perpetual Sorrows Mother and Baby Home and is now in the world of ordinary people. She needs attending to because she's not supposed to be working the *draíocht* (magic) just in case the tormentors, like from the days heavy with church persecution, began again. Sparrow was supposed to witness the swap of the mortal newborn with the changeling, make certain no one saw, and protect the human baby. To ascertain that the procedure was performed flawlessly. She has now, however, a destiny of her own here amongst mortals.

A major hubbub broke out across sky and sea, mountain and mythworld. A mighty conjecture of legendary beings convened. Night Mares came. Pleasant Dreams ceased sanguinity and took a serious turn, Enbarr de Manannán, the white horse from the sea, from the wild west coast off Weary Bay, sent envoys, night owls, known to call a body's name predicting their death a week or two before (so's to give them a chance to make peace), turning *when* into resolution. Well, they came as thick as crows and as murderous as ravens. People of every species, conspiring with mist and fog and hoarfrost giants who have heard tell of this one little chit of a woman, her drawings and her rebellion, all potentially damaging to their secret interference in world affairs.

The speculation about what could happen if predestination was ever realized as real unnerved the calm season and caused a cold like no one human had ever known. Déjà, however, is where she's supposed to be.

Oh, they all know. Sparrow's fate. If any of the unseelie catch her. She'll end up a slab of meat rotting in some derelict place, or else someone will burn her hands off, so she can't pick up a pencil again. No. She'll be dead. As dead as they are all going to be if nobody works out how to stop those responsible for the cruelty at the maternity home.

Come morning the world is blinding. Snow, mist, sky. But there's green a little further from the heart of the city. Snowdrops understand change. Humans have forgotten that springtime comes around eventually.

3

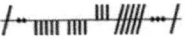

MONSTRUM

MADAWG MORCANT

Morcant is thirty years, going on ten thousand years, maybe. His true name is Madawg Morcant, but he doesn't use it for the simple reason no one in New Rathmore can say without it sounding like they got a cockroach down behind their back teeth, so he's known as Mad Dog Morgan. He appears young. A lie. He's been to the other side of the city and now he's sniffing the air along Napier Lane where in milder days, and before the lockdowns, it had been a hub. Bohemian impoverished savvy and exotic, with market stalls and scents of Lebanese and Chinese cooking, marijuana, incense, and other, less pleasant, unidentifiable scents hinting at decomposition and neglect. This part of town is best for hunting the ones he likes to fuck and forget, discarded like flotsam. He catches the subway every so often, from somewhere to here, no one watching the ticket-scanner, or riding the line, even soft-eyeing messages to his ownsome hounds, all seemingly asleep, blurry, and loveable should he need himself a happy, jolly young thing likes a good pat. Before prey.

Morcant sniffs the ice in the air like it's lavender or jasmine or the mane of a sleeping, raggedy old bear. Something exquisite is rolling in from some hospital over on the west side of New Rathmore. Something odd. Music that he knows is magic but that is only on the wind that howls with sleet and threatens anyone stupid enough to try bravery. And because of the oddness, he desires it. He does that. With memories, with awe, with plans. Snorts 'em like thick lines of cocaine as likely cut with bathroom cleaner as old-fashioned plain white flour. But not like this. He hasn't smelled anything like this since before the cold came. Before the dark.

Who? Morcant is unsure. He feels as though the walls are closing in. The dark man those uppity bastards from Inishrún thinks will have a part in saving the world from the bane of human ineptitude. Art and music. Like him, an unseelie trapped in the surface world. Perhaps. He has that niggle in his scrotum he gets when he's in doubt; that happens when it's just him who wants conjecture to be fact. The scent of the stranger on this night of frozen air is exquisite, so beaten and silent, he has to hold his hands across his crotch to stop the thing there from distracting his attention.

Sparrow draws his scarred, white face in graphite pencil on black paper.

4

FOR THE WORLD'S MORE FULL OF WEEPING

MERCY

In the long-ago cobbles were living fire. They knew flight. They soared as savage liquid miles high into an infant sky. They splashed and splattered onto the grey-green liquid crust of a slowly awakening earth and sank. Plummeted deeply to within her labyrinthine young breast, five hundred million trips around the sun ago. All inexorably crystallized into an aware, interconnected family of ancient stone that, over many more millions of years, slowly swam, sperm-like, from the deep beneath, instinctually reaching for the warmth of the sun that had been but a legend to the younger stones.

They lived with mountains. At the base of the runic chatter of brooks and burns. The backbones of arctic forests where they slumbered through the deep cold only to embrace the sun of brief summer.

The abrupt wakefulness that disrupted the slow discourse between diverse and widespread clusters. This was when humans began quarrying them and their families, gouging them from the landscapes before forming them into intersecting lines for horse carriages to ride upon and it was, to the majority, quizzical. Sadly peaceless. Graceless without ill intent towards their captors.

In the centuries of late, cobbles murmured amongst themselves of this or that change, of the addition of buildings forged of molded and fired river clay, shaped in ovens into even more rigid, straight and intersecting lines, shackled together with ash and sand, each with their own legends and stories of the ancient of days.

Others, fresh kids on the block but old friends from within mother volcano, were the limes and gravel that formed concrete.

The cobbles had speculated amongst themselves, since being shaped and trapped by countless now-dead quarrymen, that one day they would understand why they had been so disturbed, why they could not have rested in their slow-moving habitats without thought for their silence.

Then Mercy Riley came. She had sat with them and whispered under her breath, *Hello people.*

When she laid her blanket down it was not simply to sit on. No. She consciously warmed the stones with the soft wool things that held the sun in them even on a shadowy afternoon.

The dried blood red bricks of the hundred year old wall that supported her torso were reminded of the river and the shore of the deep-bottomed lake. They will not always be one shop or another. They will scatter and know individuality.

'But,' Mercy says, resting her head against them, 'community is important. You can't love alone. I know.'

······ / ᵢ ·· ᵢᵢ //

IMBOLG

WINTER'S END

Twenty five year old Mercy Riley inhabits the pavement outside the 7-Eleven on Copperhead Lane, just before the corner of Wharf Road in downtown New Rathmore. The docks. She and the year old, hip-high brindle wolfhound pup named Revel. Grandson of Cullyn, the first of the spirit dogs to roam the city at the summons of two bright pennies, set spinning in a ritual as old as memory. The companions of a warrior woman named Scáthach who walked out of a legend to also challenge the air of this world. That was just over twelve years ago.

Mercy's pockets would have jangled louder, with more coin, had she marked out her territory deeper within the city center but being away from this bit of wind off the sea, the comings of the boats and the pleasure Revel gets from flocking a scavenging of gulls into a pale afternoon sky, would feel like death to them both.

She gets by.

Other women wander here sometimes, homelessly, bodies weighed down with worldly goods, their faces ruined by the reasons they are here. They inform her to stay awake at night. To keep moving. To keep to the lights because predators wait in the shadows. In the dark places. Hungry for the ones still pretty, or else paid to pick up those worth selling. Mercy heeds them out of respect but doesn't do as they suggest. Mercy isn't afraid of anyone. She isn't really homeless although New Rathmore is not home. She is waiting.

She couldn't be missed because of her distinctive appearance. Local people talk. Notice. Speculate in low voices. They'd been curious when she had first set herself up. She has a head shorn of all her hair, and skin as pale as porcelain. Her eyes are mismatched, one deep brown the other hazel, eyelashes and eyebrows so black they seem made of night. She is beautiful. With scars caused by acne that had been as severe as smallpox; the craters that pit both cheeks attesting to the lie that of you don't squeeze them they won't leave a mark.

Copperhead Lane, down by the derelict wharf, is New Rathmore's hidden treasure. Hundred year old brownstone buildings, the windows demure behind lace curtains, idly moldering towards abandonment, each apartment occupied. Mostly by people who lived here all their lives. The old women sweep the snow off the concrete. Sit outside on the bluestone steps every fine day smoking joints or small pipes of tobacco, drinking thick Turkish coffee and telling each other's fortunes in the dregs; cat-calling old men on their habitual way to play Backgammon in the warmth of the pub. Students and visionaries hang out at Dimity's Café, talking Lorca or revolution. A woman and her daughter, once from Birmingham, sell the best of meat pies anywhere from a stall beside a firelit ten gallon drum out front of their basement apartment. When spring finally arrives and thaws the dead the street will fill, more even than now, as the smells become more acute. That man who looks too young to know the trade will sharpen knives and scissors, and the spades and secateurs of gardeners. Foreign voices will hawk their produce, and the mouthwatering scents of barbecued lamb and garlic will vie with the background smells of seaweed, barnacled wood, and maritime fuel.

Many on Copperhead Lane and thereabouts are aware of who and what Mercy is. Not, however, the flower sellers or the old women, not consciously anyway, nor the kebab shop owners, or the baker, leaning into the frigid wind and making it alive to their job at the boulangerie at four in the morning. But the cats behind the windows know. And the puppies passing Revel, who are all desperate to play with one such as him. Rats in holts know and so do those on the docks waiting for the thaw. For the fishing boats. Certainly, the raven parliaments and their rookeries, and the families of mice under the floor of the 7-Eleven. Even the windows and streetlights know what Mercy is. Know who she knows.

A *shine* of a deeper time, a kind of ammil, mists the afternoons of this now very special early February day with the glow that each particle remembers of the first and forever forest when they too dwelt in or around Forgotten Lake. The place they know as Hy Brasil.

Dimity's Books and Café, City's Largest Collection of Second-hand Books/Scifi/Best Coffee, proclaimed in vivid colors on the sandwich board in the middle of the sidewalk. That's where Mercy and Revel hole up on the nights when the cold is too unforgiving. Even for her. And Dimity or Merrin, a goth witch with a long black braid and bright red lipstick, delivers Mercy coffee and breakfast every morning, just as soon as she settles on the cobbles. Because both Dimity and Merrin also know who and what this lodger is. They have history with the Travelers, and her love, Willie-the-Red is one of them. A faerie with a fiddle. They are woven into the tapestry of stories the people who ride with them and are no longer quite mortal, tell at the summer gatherings up north at the old O'Neil place. Merrin also knows, because Willie had whispered to her just before Mercy had camped at her post, that Mercy could be called upon whenever there comes a need. That there will come a need.

Beside Mercy's small bag of personal belongings is a rolled up yoga mat she found discarded that makes a comfortable seat if someone stops. Revel's bowl. Their blankets. A cardboard sign on which she's written *Homeless not Clueless*. She sits for hours on end, her hands in mittens with the tips chewed off, a book in one, tarot cards in the other in offering. Most people keep walking. A few drop coins into the beanie at her crossed ankles. Begging always gets her enough to feed them both at the end of the day, though. And once in a while enough to buy black nail polish.

Funny thing is, Mercy does tell the future with her cards. Disturbing future things. It is not her grace to see the bright joys, the contented love. She cannot predict emotions she has never known. And she's yet to meet a punter who comprehends the wild as she does. She'd recognize it straight off. Doesn't need tarot for that.

Occasionally a woman, it is always a woman, with a day to kill and a need to stay away from what was once home, curiosity born of desperation and a need to know hope, sits awkwardly on the folded up mat and shuffles Mercy's cards. Looks into her eyes. Only then does she realize her mistake. Mercy's eyes are not those of desperation. They are fathomless. Portals to knowledge that the passer-by won't want to hear. That is usually when they hand the pack back, the prophesy unspoken, the money freely given. Because the truth is, only the shy ones who've lost everything but who cannot look at Mercy straight in the face, get told the date of their death, when they'll get beaten up and why; the destiny of their daughters.

6

ONCE UPON A TIME

DO A RUNNER

Mercy was born up along the rugged, salt-scoured coast where Weary Bay offers the only harbor. In the crabbed little delivery room of Our Lady of Perpetual Sorrow Mother and Baby Home, perennial residence of nine nuns. The lowering dark place is a leftover detritus from earlier lives of pencil jabbing and hair-cutting-with-shears-make-em-suffer heyday, a barred, brown brick ever-suppurating wound, like a curse-bound ogre, up the road on the hill outside the village. The nuns had pulled her from her mother's body and into the world, like all the others, oblivious as to who this child would grow to become. Though none of the girls or women were ever supposed to leave.

Mercy hadn't known which of them was her mother. Never knew to be curious enough to ask.

Baby Riley, they'd called her for the first two weeks. Riley could be anyone here. Or no one. Named Mercy for the baptism, simply because it couldn't be put off. She had grown up within the fortress, unfortunate enough to be rejected for adoption every time. It was the eyes, people said. Unnerving. Neglect was the only relationship Mercy knew until she was thirteen. That and the humiliation experienced by all the rejected children. They were caned on the palms of their hands on a Monday by the nuns in case they sinned during the coming week, across their buttocks and thighs if they talked back or refused their share of laundry chores. Taught to read and write and sew and launder, other basic skills, while excellence and curiosity were punished mercilessly.

Every one of the girls and women had been brought, against their will, to that fortress, of primness and suffering. Sometimes because she was pregnant, sometimes because she might get pregnant. Occasionally because she was too pretty. Too old to find a husband or no longer wanted by one. Often because abuse at home became public knowledge and the church thought she would be better off put away. What a lot of grief. What sadness. Mercy heard stories and sometimes asked questions. Learned to ask even more explicit questions as she got older. The girls taught her things she could do to give herself pleasure. They were often at it with each other after lights out. No one had touched Mercy like that though. Thought too young. In the early days.

Mercy weathered many beatings from her tenth birthday because she didn't keep her mouth shut about the first priest to interfere with her. Nor the next when they sent the first away. It happened to other girls. The severity of their welts informed her. Their downcast eyes. It was never talked about, but Mercy knew. Shame does that.

Sometimes girls ran away. They left messages with friends, of hopes and dreams. Whispers after lights out were like clouds of soft bees throughout the dormitories. There were tears. Of joy. And maybe's. Always maybe's. If the escapee was not returned it was one more flint in the eyes of those remaining. Mercy learned that the world beyond this compound was lipstick and boys and the cinema and MacDonald's and cell phones. She knew about them from contraband magazines that got chucked over the walls sometimes. By old friends. By locals. Who knew? Cosmopolitan. Marie Claire. Woman's Weekly. Modern life.

Even from behind the high and mossy walls Mercy was able to smell the ocean. The brine of it. The clean of it. And always the call of gulls by day and plovers at night. She knew she belonged with the sea and would one day live closer.

Come twelve years of age, when her menstruation began and her face erupted in the first of the boils and the nuns called her a filthy girl she knew she would escape.

It ended up being easy. The food was delivered from Brokeshire, a city miles away that catered for institutions. The food vans came on Tuesdays. Mercy scored kitchen duties and gave favors to the older girls for the chance at the morning shift. She had been lucky. She was on her own when the bread delivery man came in. She whispered to him that she would do for him what the priests had made her do if only he'd give her a lift. He said he'd be happy to, but she'd have to cover her face because he didn't want to look at it while she was *down there,* and she'd promised. He made a covey for her in the back behind the racks. She hardly breathed while the nun unlocked the high iron-barred gate.

They drove for ages. Then the truck stopped. When the man opened the truck door Mercy used her feet. Shoved the bread racks at him with all her strength. Scrambled. And ran.

He followed her for a while calling out *coomeer ya fookin little cunt* at the top of his lungs, and to get back or he'd do this or that. Until his vitriol became as indistinct as the decibels of wind in her ears. She outdistanced him and ran down the hill towards the abandoned jetty at the edge of town, at such speed that it seemed to Mercy she had never truly known her legs.

Then she hid.

7

WEARY BAY

AND ICE, MAST-HIGH, CAME FLOATING BY
AS GREEN AS EMERALD.

Not a place to visit. Not even a place to travel through on the way to somewhere else. On the surface of things, that is. A bent little town with a post office, a Sizzlers takeaway food joint where the youth hang out pretending to be rappers or gangsters. From the corner of the road, winding up the hill to Our Ladys, to the war memorial in the park that overlooks the protected aspect of Weary Bay, named Seal Bay, is everything the local people need that they can't get a bus ride away in Brokeshire. The village is walled to keep the tide out. Or the people in. Currachs and fishing boats moored to iron rings embedded to the rock wall, safely inside the zig-zag, hand-hewn stone protection reefs. Manic when the tide is in, stranded on their sides, along with careless rubbish and the ribs of long-dead dinghies when at ebb. The skies are grey, either threatening rain or delivering it in horizontal sheets ten months of the year, or swathed in fog or mist, ghostly, ever-moving, an illusion of soil and asphalt. Anybody on welfare, and there is a hunger of them, is sooner or later diagnosed with depression and medicated. That's the end then.

That or the drink. Or they leave and are not heard from again. Suicide, a bigger and crueler solution as the years yawn.

The work on the fishing boats is done by the men. Work that, beyond the cloister of Seal Bay, is an ever-present roiling, white-capped, mountainous madness of black ocean. Legend has it the sea along this stretch of the coast is bottomless which is why none of the wreckage of the drowned ever washed up on the shore. No fisherman is ever buried in the graveyard up on the cliffside, only old men who've been mutilated, rendered unemployable and unforgiven for some seeming failure, and so stayed home to grieve that their father's living was denied to him. Mute with their fated impotence.

Tattery farms that scar the landscape are in some state of dereliction or ruin, those still working mostly running, shearing, and butchering sheep. The biggest, still occupied, is owned by Barney Rumford who runs his milking cows and drives the only Massey Ferguson for a hundred miles. Whose own and only son drowned at sea. His wife Janey is one of the town's psychics because she can predict events by reading the dregs of tealeaves in the bottom of a visitor's cup. But back in the old days, before the trouble with developers, Barney had hated it. She stopped for years. She suffers that she didn't use her talent, despite him, because to this day she believes she could have warned her lovely boy.

The pub and lodgings are owned by Henry and Alice Poe. They won't be locals until they're old. They came down from New Rathmore twenty years ago. Saw the ad for the hotel's sale in the paper, and it'd been cheap. He'd been an I.T. man and Alice, a commercial lawyer. Their daughters had gone, each doing well without the need for parenting, so Alice had suggested a sea-change. They'd bought Oonah out, old Jim Pemfrey's wife. Jim's memory loss had taken a severe turn for the worse and he was diagnosed with dementia. Then the incontinence had set in. He was moved away and Oonah'd never set foot in the establishment after that. Hated the grog. Devout Catholic. Still. Rumor had it she'd poisoned him to get it over with. Sell the lot off and take his money. But ill will and whispers always insinuated slander around small villages like Weary Bay when boredom is such a tyrant.

Those that do well, do very well. Have been here for generations. Clan together over seafood chowder at the pub and tell each other stories. Play music. Exchange hydro tips. Not one person anywhere in the vicinity is away or ill when the matches are on because Henry was savvy enough to put in a big screen plasma television.

The Catholic Church had dominated in earlier times. Ridiculous for such a small area. The trade in babies that were born at Our Ladys was sufficient reason for a diocese, back when Mercy was born, to keep the old building and nunnery maintained. Most of the town's inhabitants had attended mass every day. Except for the Poe's. Except for the Rumfords. Never discussed religion. Everyone knew what happened at the maternity home, but no one spoke of it openly.

Even when the place had been closed down to the public and the church had abandoned the now-profitless village, everyone had lied if asked by random tourists passing through. People were told that all records had been destroyed in a fire. And until the inquiry that occurred eventually, no one thought to challenge the untruth.

The thing is that Weary Bay, like Inishrún, the little island off the coast, holds secrets. Holds them dear. If the clergy had known of them nothing was ever admitted.

Once a year, after the first hoarfrost, the rolling, custard mists descend the mountains behind the village, the rowan leaves turn red and yellow of the birch's turning informs of the death of summer, the nomadic come. One kind of traveler. The kind with a lower-case t. Erroneously called *gypsies* but, as 'gypsy' they called themselves. To a tract of meadow land with one old and gnarly tree, referred to as *Úllcran Ciallmhar*, Woman, Apple Tree Wise, on account of the legend that once, in this place, there stood a mighty and magical apple tree forest inhabited by bards and seers, seekers and visionary mad people, its paths scattered with silver leading to other times and lost worlds. If that were so it is long gone. Except for one tree, still fruiting in summer, so ancient she could have lived for a thousand years or two or more. Spoken to as a person. Given offerings of bangles and meat. Said to have a druid trapped within, with all her knowledge imparted through the juice of her fruit. The gathering place just up the road from the village. The gypsies bring business to the region and have done for centuries. They come from all over the country, drive their horse-drawn vardos or big old cars pulling gaudy fancy caravans to the perimeter of the field, pledge unfailing allegiance to the tree before setting up butcheries and hearths. The young men ride horses into the river, bare-chested despite the cold, challenging each other, teaching the boys and girls, and flirting with the young women from other clans.

They stay for a week or two. With music and dancing and contraband anything. Bare-knuckle fighting with big money for the winners with all the regional lads from as far away as Brokeshire and Orm Bay to the north and east as far as Lorridge and Knockhaven and St Albanshire trying their luck. Usually a pointless effort. Horse dealing, foul weather or fine.

Fortunes are told, and the spring maiden is chosen from among the local girls, never their own. The mothers and aunts and grandmothers of Weary Bay and beyond relentlessly condemn the practice, but they've never managed to get it banned. Some things are just superstitious but crossing the ways of these visitors is sure to bring those savage storms that summon the beast called the *kraken* from the depths of the bottomless sea and drown the men, boat by boat, all season. Till the other Travelers, the ones to be afraid of, the ones to respect for their draíocht—magic—faeries also called the fáidh, or other things behind closed doors and in whispers, come and break the curse at All Hallows.

Crowned with apple blossom, Mercy's mother, fourteen years old and considered a woman, presented herself to the visitors, compelled by dreams and desire of a man whose face was so bright and intelligent it was impossible not to seek him out. Fate demanded rapture. Destiny. In the firelight of the encampment, she found him. A tough man with haunted, hooded, erotic eyes the bottomless black of a selkie, hair the same, in two long braids, with gold glinting at each exposed and lickable earlobe, proclaimed *king* for a year, even though he was of the forest and not one of them. The man who'd won all the fights. For this, their final night's stay, she'd been their springtime-made-manifest, and everyone danced for hours. Mercy's mother and that man had consummated the night in the bushes and the day after he and the Travelers all went away. Three months later, pregnancy confirmed, and the people who had taken her in as a foundling in a cardboard box, who had lied and said they were family, gave her over to the nuns of Our Lady of Perpetual Sorrow Mother and Baby Home where she disappeared, her future intended for deletion. Or so it was rumoured.

She'd escaped only a month after the birth of that child and the erasure of her infant's identity.

Barney Rumford delivers milk to the local shop every day. Up before dawn, his urns still cleaned and sanitized with iodine solution so people in the village never suffer from the thyroid problems of other towns, his milk is unregulated and so unpasteurized. And Sheena Healey, the only Marilyn Munro peroxide blonde in the village, loads her wares into her mum's old lorry every Friday night at six and delivers deep-fried chips, potato scallops, and battered fish wrapped in newspaper, to half the town in defiance of the fast food franchise.

Summer is always short, under the shadow of an ever-lowering autumn when the village prepares for the arrival of those other Travelers. A rare race that only fools denigrate as diminutive, winged silliness because, in the month leading up to All Hallows which the old people still call Samhain, stalls are dragged from sheds and mended. Awnings are stitched where the mice have chewed edges off for nests, turnips and gourds are harvested and carved in preparation for the Jack o'Lantern to sit on the doorstep or the window ledge, crafts made to sell and barter, and silverware, everywhere, polished of tarnish on the off chance a visitor would deign to knock on a door for tea.

The Travelers are only pausing for a while at Weary Bay, however. It is not their destination. They are to sail across the water to Inishrún for whatever it is they do there. The people in the village don't want to know. It is still thought of as the devil's business, but carloads of them have been coming and eating the pastries and drinking the Guinness and the *uiske beatha*, single malt whisky, at the pub for as long as anyone remembers. They also attend Tír naTsamhraidh; also pay homage to the now gnarled and skeletal winter tree, leaves dropping early, probably to give the druid some quiet time. They leave their vehicles parked there. Some put up their hand-painted, talisman-hung tents if they are a day or two early while they wait for Raurie Mór's boat, a black-sailed Hooker, to tack her way up from the summer coastlands because no other ship will take to the water during the dark months. The current has come. The rips. The Rosie Rua, *an bád mór* (big boat), forty four feet long with mainsail, foresail and jib made of calico in the old way.

Always impressive as she closes the distance to the mooring, more often than not appearing from the deep sea mist, maneuvering her sharp splendor, like something out of myth, around the curragh, small craft, fishing boats, and trawlers anchored in the vertiginous shadow of the cliffs that loomed into the cloud as ancestral guardians. And the seals. Seal Bay within the folds of Weary Bay is named for them. Rookeries exists amongst most of the cladachs along the rugged coastline with the great stone outcroppings. But they come when the Rosie Rua does, because some amongst them have relatives that walk on two legs.

8

>⊣—ı—ıı—////·ıııı·ıııı—<

DELIVERANCE

BLACK ANNIS

Mercy hid the better part of a day and a night, hungry and cold and without any plan at all. Hid well beyond the sea wall where traffic or pedestrians might notice her, perhaps ask questions. She had no idea if the nuns sent out hunters for runaways, but she thought they would, and Mercy was not of a look to blend in. Out amongst the dunes with their feathery grasses and the threat of plover attack. She clearly had not thought this through. Autumn had always been her favorite time of year. The miasmic bliss of things breaking down. The smoke in the air, the rot of leaves as they become earth. The air ripping at the scents that summer hid for so long, within her swift-moving, quickly-spent brightness. She'd heard squirrels in the rowan trees, the oak trees, all that remained of a once-forest. Heard them and heard owls. Heard ravens and rooks like at no other time of year. Knew their preparations. Could almost make out the words. And it never occurred to her that other people did not.

But by then, outside the cancerous walls, the only hint that autumn was her friend was the bull kelp gluggle, a noise she knew well as the shoreline summoned it into the shallows for warmth. And who are you, she thought, as the heads of seals came above the froth and roil, one after another, all scrutinizing the shore. Almost, she thought, looking right at me. Mercy felt afraid then. Not of the air, not of the grey of rain that plastered her hair to her head and fell from her eyelashes, not of the smells and sounds she had lived her life by, but of how little she knew. Cloistered and imprisoned, there was now no prison door, locked to keep her spirit in. The bigness of everything was overwhelming.

'You lost, *mo chroí*?'

Mercy near jumped out of her skin as she uncoiled towards the voice.

Black Annis was only five yards away. Had somehow managed to get this close without a sound, without a smell. Short and thin, her hair shaved into intricate swirling patterns, eyes the color of yellow, amber-dappled hazel. Faded tattoos on her chin. Leg-hugging dirty jeans and a duffel coat two sizes too large. Bare feet. Gloves with the tips cut off. She looked to be about sixteen till eye contact. Then it was anyone's guess. She smiled at Mercy in an attempt to calm her, but the exposure of teeth only frightened the girl more because Black Annis' incisors were longer and sharper than those of anyone she'd ever known at Our Ladys.

'Don't run,' Annis whispered. 'I can help. I know what you are, and I know where you're from.'

Mercy didn't move. Didn't know what to do.

'You feel pretty fucken stupid about now I'm guessing.' Black Annis frowned to hide her smile and squatted, holding out an ornate silver hip-flask. 'Here.'

'What is it?'

'Uiske beatha. Waters of life. It's medicinal.'

Mercy took the flask and unstoppered it. She smelled it and recoiled.

'You don't smell the fucken stuff, do you? You'll never get it down. Hold your breath and gulp it.'

Mercy did. And it almost sucked the air out of her lungs it burned so strongly. Eyes as wide as the wingspan of a lark, she recoiled from Black Annis in fear. For a moment. Until the whisky blasted through her bloodstream like bullets of sunshine. They both grinned and Mercy was no longer afraid.

'Give it here,' said Annis holding out her hand. 'One's enough for you. What's yer name?'

'Mercy.'

'Mercy. Is that a name or are you begging me for more?'

'Mercy Riley.'

'Ah. Well, I'm known as Black Annis.'

'Known as?'

'Sort of the same as having a name but I've never had a name, so I'm known as Black Annis. Semantics. I didn't think they taught you a fucken thing in the women's prison.'

'It's not a prison.'

'Then why did you escape? And what's the plan? Look at you. They'll find you. They'll take you back. Do you believe the shite they taught you about god, with a big *jee*, and his only begotten son then?'

'What?'

'The dead body and nails and the blood? And his mother being a virgin and all?'

'No.'

'Can you elaborate?'

'No.'

'Fair enough. I'm soft. You can come with me to the others. We won't dob you in.'

'What's *dob you in*?'

Black Annis wiped the lip of the flask with her gloved hand, taking a long draft, screwing the lid back in place and pocketing it, like a vanishing trick, somewhere deep inside the folds of her jacket.

'Tell the authorities where you are. We won't.'

'Where are we going and who are the others?'

'To the island soon enough. Up to our camp at the apple tree till then, make you disappear. Here.'

She pulled a knitted, dull blue, shapeless beanie from one of her pockets and thrust it forward.

'We'll go around the village but keep to my side. They won't come near without an invitation, promise you.'

Mercy covered her hair with the offering, stood, and brushed the sand from her uniform.

'Fer fuck's sake,' repeated Annis, frustrated. Unbuttoning her coat and tugging it off, revealing a thick shabby sweater that made the Traveler woman look girthy around her middle, but spindle thin everywhere else. She helped Mercy into the cave of each sleeve, putting arms around her and holding her close. Summoning a sensation Mercy did not recognize.

'And say goodbye to your relatives, *mo chroí*. It's not nice to be impolite.'

'What?'

Black Annis tilted her chin towards the still-curious heads of the seals bobbing up and down in the rolling sea, Mercy hesitant and confused.

'Just do it. Everything in its time and place, Mercy.'

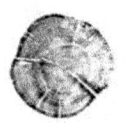

LOVE, THE LANGUAGE OF TREE, EARTH AND WILDNESS

ONCE UPON A TIME CONTINUED

The two made their way with the darkening sky that was inches above their heads. Clouds like islands rolled in from the western sea. The wind picked up and tore at Mercy, stinging her face with sand and danger. Who was she with? What was that about spells? What work of the devil had trapped her? Had she run away from that terrible place to become a victim of another evil?

She was mentally at war, yet she walked with Black Annis who did not slow her pace even when the sky broke and Mercy thought she would drown on the land. Not in her entire life had she been outside when it rained. *You'll catch yer death.* If there was washing to be brought in and the women were caught unawares it was left to the older penitents to brave a drenching. And some did die. Hacking their lungs out in the night. Whisked away by the nuns. Nobody said anything. Legend had it that when any of the women died they were returned to their families for a decent burial. Not true.

So, Mercy began to pray under her breath. 'Hail Mary full of grace—'

'Are you a liar after all, Mercy Riley?'

And again Mercy was afraid because of the flint and ice in the other's whisper.

'Sorry. Yer orrite. I won't hurt you,' Annis said quietly, head down.

She took Mercy in a great hug. 'You'll learn. Not your time to die. Might never be, neither. Almost there. Look now.'

Up ahead was a field with only one tree. Wide-limbed and skeletal. Almost human. Branches and trunk bearded in yellow and fire-orange lichens; moss, too green to be looked at for long, where the trunk met the soil. Couties in the lower branches. Every color. Some so old they were grey gossamer rags. And big old cars and mobile homes. A transit van or two that had once been rustless, some with windows in the back with faces in the shadows. A big old faded red double-decker bus with lace curtains and a riot of culinary herbs huddled inside oddly assorted wooden crates at the bottom of the back stairs. The vehicles formed a ring around the camp and a hearth still burned in the center of the open ground. One person, holding a wide black umbrella, sat in a director's chair, spread legged in an old man's pants, their gender eluding Mercy until a sleeve rolled up revealing a delicate wrist. This woman added split logs that caught the coals as they landed, sending up sparks and ash. Seasoned wood brought from elsewhere. She stoked at the embers and moved the already-steaming iron kettle deeper into the heart of the circle of stones.

The rain switched itself off as abruptly as it had dumped down. And as Annis and Mercy approached, one by one other people began gathering at the hearth. Nobody spoke. The woman holding the black umbrella closed it. She looked directly at Mercy.

Brighid appeared to be anywhere from forty to seventy years old. It was hard to tell as something seemed to adapt and change with every blink. Her hair, black as crows' wings, had been worked into intricate small braids every one of which ended with a bronze ring. Skin, as luminescent as pearl, a landscape of old scars and feathery lines of both laughter and grief. Patterned with faded tattoos of whorls and spirals, bird and beast of the forest, inked here and there with one story or another, all linked. Her forehead was lined with Ogham script as though that of an ancient parchment meant to be read before humans stood upright. Her eyes were as white as winter. Mercy wondered momentarily if she was blind. Only for a moment though as that pale gaze immediately pinned her. Trapped her so she could not look away.

'Brought your dinner back alive did you, Annis?'

'Stop it. She's frightened enough as it is. Mercy, this is Brighid.'

Annis pulled the beanie from Mercy's head in one fluid moment.

'See?'

'Oh,' and Brighid sat slowly upright. 'Unexpected, this.'

'What's happening please?' Mercy grabbed the ragged hat, feeling naked before the older woman.

'Gonna need spells to keep her hidden, see?'

'Where's she from?'

'I'm right here. You can ask me if you want to know anything about me.'

'That you are. And you're as wet as the sea. Come back when you're better prepared to speak to me.'

Feck, mouthed Annis, dragging Mercy towards the bus.

Mercy watched as ten or more people strode towards the fire in the company of dogs of every shape and size. The strangers exotic and peculiar. All of them. Mercy was ensorcelled. Something romantically familiar about many of them. They dressed like people in the picture books that had been read to her when she was small. Old books. Dick Whittington, At the Back of the North Wind and Dealings with the Fairies. David Copperfield. The Owl and the Pussycat, Puss in Boots, Cinderella, King of the Golden River. Mad mixes. Lace and jeans and top hats and earrings. Big leather coats and baggy pants with steel-capped boots or ones that went to the thigh that looked embroidered with stories like on a tapestry. All were tattooed in various stages of Brighid*ness*. Nothing like the women and men in Cosmopolitan. Marie Claire. Woman's Weekly. But they all smiled at her.

Annis, pulling at the front door of the bus, was beaten to it by the tall dark, dangerously beautiful man, in kneeless denim jeans and a thick Aran sweater under a ragged-cuffed pea-jacket. He dropped back the hood and stared, open-mouthed, at Mercy. His hair plaited into two braids, black and thick. The upright lines between his eyebrows made him look angry despite the unnerving depths of the irises of his eyes. He blocked the door. Then he rounded on Annis.

'Fookin stranger, is it? And a fookin child?'

'Feck off Raven. She needs help.'

'And I'm not a child so fuck off yourself,' brazened Mercy, her eyes glaring but her heart pounding.

'Keep her hidden lest the cops come sniffing about before we move camp.'

'Mind yourself, you,' Annis warned. 'Brighid's going to fix it so she gets unseeable.' She paused in her explanation when she realized what his scent meant. What those feral eyes mean. 'Please don't go again.'

'I never came back, Annis. It's a ghost, I am. Tell Hunter I'm sorry.' He pushed past, shouldering a pack and a bodhràn in a tattery leather case. He headed for the gravel in the distance. He left a smell in his wake. Loam, was it? Or peat? Or the pelt of some animal? Mercy didn't know what it was, but the effect shocked her. Her knees went liquid and she wanted to hold him. Knew, instinctively, he could keep her from harm.

Inside was like a home. With beds and side tables, suitcases and trunks, and mirrors. Lamps and a guitar and a piano accordion. A harp of old oak. Ornaments on shelves loaded with books. An astrolabe in a nook. Rolled up scrolls and bowls of jewelry that might or might not have been precious. Eiderdowns and ceramic ducks and cooking utensils, plates and cutlery, neat rows of boots at the back towards the stairs. Bottles of whiskey and plates of half-eaten food. A pile of newspapers. A radio.

'This is my section.' Annis pulled a leather trunk with brown corner supports from beside one of the mattresses. She opened it.

Nothing was folded. 'Pick what you like.'

'It's all a'tangle.'

Won't be, once you wear it, though. I don't want it back so I'm freely giving you whatever you choose.'

'I think you're weird Annis.'

'Met a lot of people like me in the fucken lour tower, have you? Enough to have an opinion, is it?'

'Don't be cross.'

'I'm not cross. I don't get cross. I've got a lot of work to do with you, you know. Strip.'

She threw her a towel. 'No one's coming. I'd smell em. So, do it.'

Mercy took off the water-heavy coat, and handed it to the faerie, who hung it over the railing that curved upstairs. Annis reached into the pile and grabbed jeans, a big grey sweater and a pair of woolen socks. 'What about these then?'

'Can I have some undies?'

'What?'

'Undies. Can I have some underpants and a bra?'

'A bra?'

She looked at the thin girl with the flat chest and the next-to-nothing hips and growled to prevent laughter.

'Got knickers. You alright with knickers?' And she opened the bottom drawer, of a set of drawers made of walnut wood with a fine polish and tiny brass fittings and pulled out panties. Slipper satin with hand-embroidered lace edging.

'I've collected them because I like pretty things. Never wore em. Never wear pretty things, like cats never eat the quarry they kill. By way of explanation, in case you need one. Just collect them. Here.' And she handed them to Mercy. 'Now get those bloody wet things off or you'll catch yer death.'

'Can you turn around or go outside, please?'

'Oh fer feck's sake.' But she turned her back anyway and pulled up a stool.

'What did you mean before about work to do?'

Mercy unpeeled the sodden uniform, pulled off the petticoat, unclipped the next-to-nothing cotton bra, slid off her underpants, and roughly dried her body as Annis thought about how to explain.

She sat on the stool with her back to Mercy and rested her head on her arms on the windowsill, contemplating. It would be dark soon. Time to go to the pub and play a few tunes.

'What do you believe in?' she asked, to break the silence.

'What?' Mercy fiddled, calculating. 'Nothing.'

She got the jeans done up and sat on the mattress for the socks as her feet were like ice. 'I do the prayers like I was taught and listen to all the stories they told us but no. Not a word of it. Things happened to me there.'

'What things?'

'Don't really want to say much but it meant everything they told me was a lie if they could hurt me for doing nothing.' She paused, seeing another pair of mittens the same as Black Annis wore. 'Can I have these?'

'Can I turn around so I know what you want?'

'Yes.'

'Yes.'

'I believe in badness,' Mercy continued, donning the gloves and flexing her fingers. 'How's that then? Is that a good enough answer?'

She bent double and rubbed at her hair till it stuck out at all angles.

Annis' mind was a whirl. At the way Mercy answered her. At the way she thought.

What have you got here then, ya fookin faerie? More interesting than simply a mortal, that was certain.

When they returned to the fire outside there was no sign of Raven. Annis knew he was trapped in a web of unreasonable love again and he always runs when that happens.

ALL THE BIRDS OF THE AIR

RAVEN

Pain. He tries to find consciousness. It is as elusive as the end of a rainbow. Whatever drugs they've got him on are almost good. But behind the morphine is all pain.

Open your eyes. Establish where you are.

Raven opens the eye that is not swollen shut. Searing white. Beeping. Trying to move but that is not an option. Instead, he raises a hand to the bandages around his torso. Cracked ribs. Lips glued together with his own goop. Turns to look.

On the chair beside his bed. Kind looking man. Ordinary looking. Not the sort of person hangs out where Raven does. A tough face but not needy. Not under an influence. Everything hurts.

'I'm here to help.'

Raven attempts to sit up and fails.

'Don't,' says the man.

Silence except for the beeps.

He tries again.

'Forget it,' says the man. 'I'll just talk. If you answer some questions that'll be enough. You okay with that?'

'Who are you, for a start,' whispers Raven through swollen lips.

'Henry Waubun. I'm a cop. Detective. Junior. A man was murdered beside you. What can you tell me of what you witnessed?'

Raven almost shuts down again.

'I'm not the enemy. Just tell me.'

Raven lies motionless in the sterile cubicle. He pretends he hasn't heard. He sighs and it hurts to sigh.

'What's your name? It helps to know.'

Raven feigns sleep. It isn't hard. The drug residue is a kindness.

'I'll be here when you come round.'

Raven knows who he is. What he is. He tries to forget. Doesn't use his true name because he knows there is an enemy, he just hasn't worked out who or what yet. Calls himself Birdie and has assumed the look of a man around thirty years old, when he is older than mountain time.

Underneath the wounds is a lean and hardened body, long, ragged dark hair, and hooded eyes that hold the secrets of otters and horses. Raven became intentionally lost six years ago during the food riots. That had been only his second beating, the first at the hands of hard men when he had been sentenced to prison. He'd been rescued after that, but not this time. Fists and batons, electric prods and capsicum spray by police in black, balaclavas hiding all but their eyes behind plexi-masks. More when they took him in. They'd also asked who he was. But by the time he came to consciousness he couldn't remember anything, for a while at least. Only the riots. Only the beatings. He never understood why they'd targeted him. Maybe it was his tattooing. Private security had been trained to profile certain appearances. The bosses of such still thought facial inking was for criminals or gang members. Left scarred and ambivalent he was released from the city jail that was overcrowded with other dissidents because the courts couldn't find a crime.

And then his *shine* was gone, and he would have to have thought too hard to recall what that was anyway.

The Travelers, especially his own clan anFiach Dubh, had never stopped hunting for him.

Nothing. No trace. Ranging across the world. All the clans searching. C'av'arn, the corvid queen of Bently Street High School. Every blackbird, rook and crow, of every city across the country. It was as though a day had swallowed him into its other side. And in a way it had.

Raven is not mortal. He doesn't remember that, either, anymore. He is hurt every time he lands in the wrong place at the wrong time, which is often, and because he is a loner he is at the mercy of whoever doesn't like his face. Which is a lot of people. Because Raven is considered beautiful by both men and women. An androgynous confusion. Ageless, fearless, arrogant. A target. Women try to seduce him but he isn't interested and they cannot understand. Men want to either fuck him or fight him. Raven has encountered both. Always violent.

He, like Mercy Riley, like Sparrow and Déjàvu Delacroix, is also in New Rathmore, but somehow he ended up way over to the west of the city amongst the tenements and the cinder block housing estates. The asphalt and gravel death at the end of a six storey dive, the ice dealers and the mothers without hope swallowing too much oxycontin. Refugees from war ravage, the slave trade, and madmen who would have their children blow themselves up for an ideal before the age of twelve. Raven is caught here. Wandering the streets, sensing. Trapped by empathy. His nature. In some ways Raven is the forest; the First Forest from which his brother, Hunter, strayed in the ancient of days. For love of a faerie, for love of a mortal woman. His heartland, a place known by many as Hy Brasil, but that is, secretly, Forgotten Lake, where Mystery still roams in abandon as hound, as hedgehog, as salmon, or whatever takes her fancy.

Hunter sought the Mystery's advice, in the perennial autumnal twilight of the silence and shimmer-mist of that place. Many times. She wouldn't help. Just said some things needed to play themselves out. He had maintained his milder tempest because she is always honest. She never makes sense till retrospectively.

Is he still alive? Just tell me that.

He *is* life, silly. Can't kill immortality no matter how hard someone tries.

You using him?

Don't push my buttons, Hunter.

The sky darkened. The sky never darkens at Forgotten Lake. And Hunter morphed back through time and space to join the faerie Travelers, on their way to Weary Bay before winter set in.

Raven wakes again. His mouth is a cesspit. Still hoping the morphine will kick in. It does, a bit. His body neutralizes toxins so the relief dissolves as fleetingly as a sigh. He always has to feel. He flexes his hands, clicking the clip on his index finger. Fluttering his eyes.

'Yes, I'm still here.'

Waubun pours water into a glass with a bendy straw and holds it to Raven's lips. 'You look like shit.'

'Oh, you think? Ow.' Raven sips the water, and the shape of his lips opens the crack. Fresh blood drips from his chin. Waubun takes the towel from the end of the bed and holds it to Raven's mouth.

'I'm leaking,' and he almost smiles but knows better.

Raven can't stay angry. That's another strike against him amongst the gangs and cruelty of his neighborhood. He walks most of the day. Rain or summer's heat. Except for the allotted computer time at the library. Jeans and that old, midnight blue Guns N' Roses hoodie, his head down, minding his own business until it isn't. Sensing his way to the trouble like a bloodhound. Getting in between the wailing child and his mother's boyfriend. Knocking on the door, five flights up, before the punches land hard enough to hospitalize her. Making his way along that alley to where the kid, seeming half his age, uncovers the fit pack he's stolen from his mother to show the others how to do what he's seen her do.

He can't always stop things. There's just too much hopelessness, too much anger and self-righteousness. Like cancer or head lice.

'You awake now?'

'What's the problem? I got beat up. Don't know anything, officer.'

'I'm a detective, you little shit. I've got a family. Two daughters. My wife never sees me. I'm here with you when I'd rather be home with them.'

'Sorry.'

'I have to inform you that I'm recording this conversation, you okay with that? Say yes.'

'Yes.'

Waubun relaxes and pulls his chair closer to the bed, leaning on the edge, switching the police-issue recorder to green. Raven observes through his good eye. When Waubun catches his gaze he will swear, later when so much goes to shite, that it twinkled with wit.

'Detective Inspector Henry Waubun. Time 21:13 hours, November 18, 2028. New Rathmore General Hospital. Name?'

'Birdie.'

Waubun waits. 'Birdie's a name?'

'It's my name, yes.'

'Okay Birdie, what's your last name?'

Raven stares straight ahead towards the window, dragging it out, doing what he's done so many times before. Attempting to sidetrack providing useless information.

'Got nothing,' he replies.

'Meaning?'

'No last name. Never have had. I'll be on your records from before.'

'Serious?' Henry pauses the recording device. 'Are you serious?'

'Check. Call in. I been arrested before. Nothing now, nothing then.'

Waubun speed-dials and puts the phone to his ear, identifying himself, wanting a record looked up. While he waits, he whispers *How old are you. What's your date of birth?*

Nothing there. Sorry, Raven mouths back.

'Yeah, got a man in New Rath ER been attacked. Calls himself Birdie without a last name. You got anything?' Both men remain in the silence of their own worlds and wait.

'Right,' he says finally after listening to the list of petty charges. He disconnects. Restarts the recorder.

'Birdie. No last name. No known date of birth. No fixed address. String of minor priors. So, Birdie, what happened this time and what else do you recall from yesterday?

'Got beat up.'

'No shit. Who by?'

'Never do know. It's a curse. I'm a target.'

'Look son—'

'How old are you, Henry?'

'Never mind, and don't be an asshole, I'm trying to help you.'

'Nothing, officer. Not a thing.'

'You got a phone, at least?'

'I keep losing them. If I get in trouble again, you mean?'

'Get some sleep, I'll be back.'

Waubun evades the faerie's range of vision and Raven sighs.

The man lied. There's no one to go home to. She left with the girls a long time ago. Seems his work kept him from one too many birthdays and he was absent from one too many school performances. Money isn't a father. Not a husband. Raven knows. He reads them all. The nurses with their banter, the doctors that don't really care. Other cops. The lawyers the courts appoint him. None of them know him. None of them want to. Is it different on the street? There's emotion. He can still read them all but... Passion. Savagery. Hope. Hopelessness. Reasons to fight and to fear. This is a language Raven understands. He just doesn't know why he is still alive. And, like Mercy Riley, he doesn't know other people can't do what he does.

The other language Raven understands is code. He can sometimes get up to three hours most days at the free computer port in the local library. He is unconscious of his use of coercion on naive people, not that all librarians are. But, again, he is disturbingly beautiful and the charm of a humble man is a potent spell. He'd first seen code manifest on screen by some kid whose fingers moved on the keyboard like electricity along a wire. He intuitively realized that the girl was creating a world. She was nine so he kept his distance in case someone thought he was a creep and sent him away, but he watched from across the room. Her mind worked magic and though she did not split the screen to display the images of her game, Raven learned it all. Her characters. Heroes and villains. Weapons. Temples and witches. Mages and jesters. Women in white who conquered adversity with stardust. Roads that led into dark forests and must be traveled with a passport made of dreams. Companions from some legend somewhere.

Dogs to dragons. Turreted fortresses and mushrooms that gave sage advice. Pumpkins and crystal coffins. It all made sense to him.

So, he taught himself. The sheer logic of it, beautiful. He's fluent at creating code that, if ever it could be drawn from its silence, would be music that no one has heard in this world. Not for a thousand, thousand lifetimes. Sequences of such complex peculiarity it is as though he has tapped into some kind of primality. If mathematics and the language of bytes are a forest, Raven speaks the language of hare and reindeer and, hence, can also express wolf tracks and the sound of water groggling onto the stones of the narrow gorge from deep within the rock strata. The hazy light from a gibbous moon. Wolverine dreaming and the high peep-peeping of a family of young eagles. The zwer as a covey of partridges take flight. Although he is unaware, he creates a concerto of Forgotten Lake, where the First Forest still edges down to the pristine clear water. Where the Mystery hears him and sighs with delight.

f. lll lll

RAVEN

AS LOVE CROWNS YOU

He hates himself for being mean. But she's shocked him. A child. What he sees. What happened. And even with it all, a *shine* of impossible beauty. Dauntless despite. It should not be. He ages five years between the bus and the fire.

He dishes up a plate of stew that's plopping like lava in an iron pot, a spatter burning his hand. His thoughts are momentarily distracted as he remembers the story of Gwion getting the *awen*, inspiration, supposed to go to the ugly kid. But then he's pulled back to the waif in the caravan. He sits broodily as far away from the others in the circle as he can get.

She's sunshine, he thinks, pretending to be like a normal person. He tries—a marionette trying to escape the strings—to hush the feeling. This terrible, utterly defensive behavior that strikes the fáidh out of nowhere. He does not understand. He knows he would do anything to protect her. To avoid this ache. Love that is utter. The reason he is capable of killing.

Hunter, tree-tall, a piece of the forest from the time before even the sídhe formed the first animals, let alone took on the appearance of humans, comes and squats beside Raven. Bark dark hair in long neat elflocks, piled high on his head. The sides of his scalp shaved to the skin, the patterns of knot-work and now-extinct species remembered into his flesh with ink in the long-ago. Dressed in many ragged layers as though every article of clothing marked a century of bards.

'Hmm.'

'Shut up.'

'For now,' he grins, showing white, white teeth and elongated canines.

'It's not funny, Hunter. I'm trashed.'

'And you'll still be twenty when she's dust. But you'll be protecting her for a reason, m'bonny.'

He stands and casts a long shadow across the meadow, even under the thick grey sky.

'Time I find out what this is about. Keep soft, Raven, orrite?'

'Yeah. Look at me.' And he holds out a pale, heavily veined hand that does not shake.

⫽—ɪɪɪ /ˑ ɪɪɪɪ ˑˑˑˑ

GYPSY MONEY

HORSES

Raven had been in prison years ago. For manslaughter. At a horse fair in France. Accidentally. Blow upon blow fell on the mare from the whip of the drunken owner. Lost a race. Lost him money. He spat and cursed, and Raven knew he would have her killed so he had reacted. Got between the man and the horse. The man was stunned. Outsider. Looking like he did. *Poofter*, he had said and turned the whip on the faerie. Raven had shoved his attacker and the man lost his footing and fell; his skull cracked. Dead.

Raven usually wore black. Said it didn't show the dirt. Jeans. Old boots. T-shirt under the long woolen coat he'd picked up in London in 1763, the fabric as clean as then, just faded to dark grey. Ratty black top hat. That was how he'd got the nomenclature of the corvid. Gold, *gypsy* money, glinted from the hoops at both ear lobes, night black hair in a long plait and dangling with raven, sparrow, and rook feathers, their quills dyed blue. Eyes fathomless with darkness. He'd been one of the first two-leggeds in the long ago and had once upon a time danced with mortals. When they knew him. Respected the vast forests and only killed to eat. He hadn't been amongst them forever it seemed. Even when people turned warped. When they cut down those forests to build cities. Went to war against each other. Not since a man used a harp string to strangle his brother out of greed.

He just couldn't do it so dwelt mainly in what woodlands remained. By his fire, playing his music with his low whistle or the bodhràn, with owls and hares and marmots as his audience. Fishing for salmon upstream of the rivers. Wandering the coast on the back tracks, exploring the limestone caves. Visiting ghosts. Climbing for gulls' eggs, his driftwood fires hungry haunts of blue, green, purple. Reuniting with the clans at Samhain on Inishrún, at Merrin's digs when they headed to New Rathmore for winter, up on Razorback Mountain for autumn, and every summer at the old O'Neil farm. Over time he visited other lands, other cultures. Seeking meaning and perhaps people with honor.

He'd been on his way to Paris to take passage across the ocean and home, for year's end, when he'd heard the mare call his name in desperation.

No one testified for Raven at the trial. Angry men accused him of wanton killing. The magistrate couldn't see it, despite the witnesses. But he sent the sídhe to prison for seven years all the same. For an androgynous beauty such as he that was a terrible fate, aging him a good three years biologically. When he was released, he busked the streets of the Fifth Arrondissement, oblivious of self and broken, until an artist named Jules took one look at the face beneath that battered hat and wanted to draw him.

She offered him lodgings in exchange for him sitting for her.

He'd asked what else she wanted and she assured him nothing. They shared her apartment for two years (and she learned all there was to learn about who and what he really is) until her distant nephew, misdiagnosed with schizophrenia because he saw the so-called dead and no one else could, looked like being institutionalized by his mother. He was one of the lost. Once again Raven crossed the ocean, taking with him a bodhràn Jules had bought, requesting he liberate Alan by teaching him the music.

Raven had found two people to trust. Jules and Alan. And many years after walking away from the boy, he'd found him again as a man, and they had become lovers for a while because love wasn't able to distinguish gender, for Raven. Alan took the Quicken brew, the mystical elixir. A reduction stewed from the berries of a mighty rowan that had never been found and had, because of it, never been cut down. It bestowed near-immortality on a previously mortal person. Of course, it couldn't stop a bullet but the Travelers and their human companions had learned ways to mostly avoid that. While Alan always loved Raven, he knew that none of the faeries could be held down or caged, so even though he continued to travel with the clans Raven did not, and Alan had understood. He understood everything. In many ways he was always Raven's leveler when trouble forced itself on one or more of them because Raven's draiocht is empathy. And when a perpetrator of cruelty was captured in earlier years it had been Raven who uncovered the madness. It had been Alan's presence alone that had stopped his friend from ripping that man's throat out.

13

CITADEL

THE ARTFUL DODGER

The Artful Dodger. Fifteen years old, maybe, give or take. Mass of greasy dull silver hair, bumfluff of a mustache of which he was most vain and hopeful. Thief. Food getterer. Nothing that will keep him alive past this year, most likely. Except he's always been fifteen. Additive addict. Sugary caffeinated, carbonated anything. Whatever it takes to keep him awake because the Artful Dodger never sleeps. His nights and days, when he's not recruiting, are for living within the old game *World of Warcraft: Shadowlands*. He's got past *Sanctum of Domination*, is now a revered knight of the Covenant of the *Night Fae of Ardenweald,* has utilized his training at Runecarving Memory, sufficiently to challenge, and best, the *Tower of the Damned*, and he's now close to level 22. There's pride in that. He is almost capable of smiling. He tries remembering how. But there is no one to care for his experience. For Artful. None who share his exhilaration. Plugged into their consoles to poison other people's code. Havoc making.

He shares the two storey warehouse known as the citadel, with ten hackers of varying ages from nine to fifty. All with exceptional, perhaps even wizardly skills in the online dark arts. Accommodation is free as are the consoles. Just do the work. Their benefactor is Madawg Morcant but because none of them have ever seen his name written down, and no one can pronounce it, they clandestinely call him Mad Dog Morgan.

At a distance anyone watchful enough could explain just how tall and elegant Artful's master is. His prematurely silver hair is barber-shop trimmed. He dresses in a well-cut suit over a spotlessly white T-shirt with quixotically scuffed steel-toed boots. What color are his eyes? No one knows. Distinguishing features? Not that anyone could have said because no one in the citadel dares be that watchful. Morcant enters from a basement elevator, wanders over to Tommy Ng's console, and leaves paper instructions. Tommy, whose heritage is Vietnamese, and who also plays the violin when he is solving a particularly gnarly crack, is the most artful of the dark webmasters. He pretty much runs this pack of geniuses but trusts none of them. He trusts no one except his owner because Mad Dog saved his life. Plucked him from the river he'd thrown himself into, intending to drown. Knowing the filth would kill him if the black water didn't.

Couldn't take the hunger and couldn't live with the fact the internet died.

Mad Dog. Morcant. So certain of himself. Of what he needed to live the life he had become used to before the world went dark. Knew he needed his savvy warriors and prided himself on this man's unflinching allegiance. That any one of his courtiers could trace anything, anytime, if it exists online. Hence the snail mail.

Mad Dog meanders from person to person, pale, delicate, gold and gemstone-ringed hands stroking the back of each neck seductively while leaning over a shoulder to peruse the work. An unspoken rule that no one ever sees his face. Don't even turn around. So other than the general idea of him he can never be identified by anyone if things come crashing down someday. He calls each of them *my child* in his soft-spoken, accentless and ageless voice. Asking each how they fare, putting money in a pocket here or a pocket there, letting whichever person scoring thus know that an extra job is in the offing, perhaps not as pleasant a one as sitting at a desk. Perhaps requiring a stiletto or a piano wire. Never anything as vulgar as a gun. Instructions are verbal only, especially if Mad Dog finds himself a new candidate from the streets.

This place is like a full pantry of exotic hoodoo to those that have been recruited. Dodger's world is now an age of abject poverty for the majority, with homelessness and food queues a block long. Petrol has long since dried up except for those who caused the problem. They pay a private, militarized security force to keep some semblance of peace while more prisons and compounds are built. They bask in helicopter rotor breezes, to the sound of rubber bullets and taser screaming on the streets of every major city across what had been known as the free world. To the distress of real police.

From the outside you'd think the factory was abandoned, the welded-mesh security fencing impenetrable. All the windows are boarded up and the entrance is only visible to those who know the way in and out. But if you listen closely, which nobody does because there are no pickings here for even the hungriest, you can just make out the smooth hum of generators. Anyone exploring behind the building would likely notice the state of the art satellite dish. Might recognize a radio mast. Morcant likes fog and snow. They render invisibility.

Dodger and the others live, eat and breathe the citadel. Everything provided that could actually keep them healthy. As though they are prized livestock. But no, the majority prefer Dodger's take-away and pilfering finesse. So, the place is also a dump.

Dodger had been recruited by an old hacker who died of kidney failure last summer's end. Skinny kid with a begging bowl, one arm tied behind his back in a pretense of amputation, the dangly sleeve of his layered garments attesting to some brutal event that vomited him out onto the streets of New Rathmore and who, when the street was empty because the cold hid whoever remained alive in whatever accommodation they could invent, snuck out his scavenged tablet to score up points. His only relief. An old game. Pirated pixels on a flatscreen.

The talent can be found anywhere but has to be sleuthed. No family. No friends. No lovers. No one to miss them and no one to notice they are gone. Pasts cease to exist once the chosen are condemned to the citadel and not one of them regrets anything. Never talk about where they've come from or the cruelty they experienced at home. No. Abandonment has led them here, and life is now one of privilege.

The basement elevator pings open, and two men carrying a new desk shuffle across the expanse of warehouse floor and place it close to one of the windows where tiny lines of natural light illuminate from between aluminum slats. Everyone takes notice as no one has been allowed that coveted space. The men stride back and forth bringing bed and bedding, computer console, paired monitors, 3D printers, speakers, headset, ergonomic chair and a stack of ten-terabyte external hard drives.

'I have a use for you.' Dodger hadn't heard Mad Dog, even when close, his breath eddying the soft hair at the nape of the boy's neck like soft grass at the edge of a lake.

Morcant isn't who he thinks he is. He's a remnant of someone who he thought was him. Roleplay can trap a person into a belief. Not always as far from reality as might be thought.

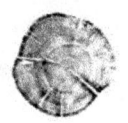

14

FOR LOVE OF A MORTAL

STREET WISDOM

Black Annis, accordion in its battered case over one shoulder, strides bent against the bluster of autumn wind that fractures the day like a squall of frozen blackbirds on a January afternoon. Come in from the sea with a mood as heavy as a threat. Her fine stubble of downy hair and faded tattoos cause people passing by to look the other way as though some possible crazy person could also be infectious. In some way they're right but the definition is so far removed from the truth of who and what magic is they would not recognize the wonder anywhere in life.

She comes to a standstill but Mercy doesn't look up. Engrossed in the *Complete Works of W. B. Yeats*. Revel, on the other hand, wags everything from head to tip of tail, tongue lolling, smiling from one floppy ear to the other. Annis squats down, plops into a cross legged sit and drags the big pup onto her lap for a thorough scratching of all the bits that matter.

'You in there?' she suggests to Mercy.

Mercy raises a middle finger and Annis understands. But she grins. Her joy. Her true wonder. Proud, she is, of how she managed

81

the education of this brat. Almost as much *shine* as anyone with the flood of rivers through their veins.

'You comin home soon, *mo chroí*?'

'Go back and tell the others to leave me to do what I need to do.'

When Annis gets to her feet she attempts, like pointlessness, to brush Revel's shed winter fur from her sweater and to act as though she is just a normal faerie. 'Just don't wait till spring, love,' she whispers. 'The slúagh, remember?'

'If Brighid sent you to spy, go tell her to back the fuck off. I've evil to kill and a ghost to banish. Nuns couldn't break me, remember?'

'Then stop being so good at what you're doing here on the street, *mo chroí*. It's like you're inviting trouble.'

Mercy grins. Then Annis laughs.

'The wind whispers my mother's name to me, Black Annis. Something terrible is living that shouldn't be. You of all faeries ought to recognize it. Can't you smell it?'

Black Annis' name, said with a distinct equality of inflection, is not lost for one second. She unshoulders her instrument and wanders towards Dimity's for a brew and to wait for the others. To wait for the bus, and Hunter, to take the lot of them to play tonight's gig at Mary Flannery's Tavern a couple of blocks away.

As she walks towards the comfort of the café, she calls back *Yep*. Mercy is no longer offended by Annis' back. She knows it well.

15

IT'S WITCHCRAFT

MAISIE RAITH

Why the nuns never sent a search or notified the authorities that Mercy had run away was a mystery never to be solved. But they did not. Even with the Travelers thronging Weary Bay awaiting the Rosie Rua to come to port Mercy Riley had been obtrusive. Brighid had done an intensive confusion spell but the shape of the girl, the magic that she wafted like woodsmoke, had not beaten the girl down enough. She was too young to journey with the Travelers, too difficult to explain when there were no other children with the troupe, so they were going to have to get her made normal somehow. For the moment.

Maisie was the village witch. Or druid. No one quite sure. Not the kind found in old fashioned children's books that made old women out to be ugly and cruel and also not like the ones that liked to dress up in long flowing robes with altars and multiple ceramic deity statues crowding the truth of the world. No. Maisie played the mandolin whenever there was a craic and she hunted near and far for healing worts and culinary wilds, in the last remaining stretch of woodland near this part of the coast. Acorns and hazelnuts and mushrooms, both for her dinner and for learning. Maisie used psilocybin once a year to be taught directly by wildness.

She was old and had been wed once, to another druid. He had died from bone cancer with her arms around him and a smile on his face at the inevitability of everything. Maisie shared her rambly old house and barns with many species that, oddly, got along. Foxes whose mother had been shot, the kits left to call her endlessly. Several barn owls in the overhead rafters so that Maisie did not keep mice for long. A python had been smuggled into the country once upon a time and been got rid of, in all likelihood when tipping twenty feet and swallowing a small dog. Goats and sheep for keeping the grass low, and for milk. Swans on the pond. An otter she had saved from that terrible oil spill up on the arctic coast a few years back when she had left her house and animals in the care of Janey Rumford because she could not sit and do nothing. She and the badger cubs played together. Her closest neighbors were nearly eight miles away. The human inhabitants of the region kept their distance unless they needed potions or curses, or to get their fortune told.

Her mother and her mother before her down the mist of days. Fathers came and went and were not on the agenda when sons or daughters were born but all the young went to the local school and learned the same as other children. There was no bigotry despite the catholicism of the villagers, because the Raiths had been residents of Weary Bay for as long as anyone.

So it was to Maisie that Annis brought Mercy. Aware of the irony. Their initials being the same and all. And Annis explained about Mercy and that she hoped Maisie would keep silent. 'Brighid's put a caul of spells around her, so she looks sorta ordinary,' she assured calmly.

Maisie drank in Mercy's appearance and cleared her throat, a confused smile lifting the corners of her mouth. Something achingly familiar in the features of this tormented child.

All three sat out in the pale autumn mist, hinting at the violet of evening but with the sun still lazy and low in a westering sky. Around the fire that Maisie liked to sit beside in the evenings while the world still held warmth. Had pulled out wood stumps from the big stack piled high under the eaves up against the barn. Drank fresh brewed Turkish coffee, a first for Mercy.

'You want to be my niece, Mercy?'

Mercy was brought back from her reverie, the otter curled like a mink-colored kitten in her lap. 'What?'

'My niece. From New Rathmore. Your father's been posted as ambassador to a war ravaged country and you're not allowed, on pain of death, to mention which one. Your mummy also works admin for the government and to save you from having to live the next five years of your life in the embassy of a country whose language you don't know.'

'That's funny.' Mercy was non-plussed, 'but I don't know what an embassy is, or an ambassador.'

'We can sort all that out before we enroll you in the school.'

Mercy's face fell. 'Why do I have to do that? If you can do all the things you said you can do then I'd rather just learn that, if that's okay.'

'What they teach you up in the prison, Mercy?' asked Black Annis. 'Did you learn to read?'

'Pretty much, I guess.'

'You know what I think.' Annis' chin jutted, cliff-like and intractable.

'I know what you think,' replied Maisie piling another couple of peat bricks onto the embers, 'but it's not about how useless school is to the most of them. It's the company. You've got to learn about how people on the outside of that place are. It's easier to get along and it'll hold her in good stead should she one day want to travel with these Folk. Annis?'

'Sorry, aren't I.' Annis grinned. 'You might as well be Brighid without the bitterness.'

Before Mercy took the bus to New Rathmore, many years later, she had Maisie shave off her distinctive ice-white hair. To the scalp

16

ROILING IN THE VOID

MONSTRUM

Morcant, back when he was till Madawg Morcant, had climbed the countless darkly glittering steps it took to abandon the unseelie court, the Monstrum, seemingly forever ago. He had not been acknowledged. The gall still burned the back of his throat. Where other bitter predecessors had walked the deserts of Mesopotamia whispering the idea of surplus into the minds of small indigenous grain gatherers and goatherds, Morcant had been learning the ways of another people. Red haired, pale skinned hunters. Black haired, amber skinned hunters. Black haired, black skinned hunters. Hunters who rode small shaggy horses across the vast tundra, a grassy relative of ice ages and other species. Hunters with sun-leathered skin and poison-tipped spears, silent as the jungle cats, bigger, by far, than any of them. Hunters that rode the ice on long skis and drilled holes within the frozen landscape. He was looking to make trouble but presumed he had an eternity to figure out the most effective way to do so. To claim his birthright in a mortal world. Absorbing their respective languages, with a plan forming like mold in moist darkness.

And that was how he thought it through and justified what he did. His work. His unerring quest.

All of them spoke with the tongue and song of landscape and otherkin. Of species revered, feared, hunted and entered into symbiosis with. These were not languages familiar to Morcant. In the halls of the Monstrum conversations were as whispered as prayer. Intrigue, disdain and hunger, but not of the food variety. Of that there was abundance. Hunger to be seen. To be important. The hunger of the usurper of brother; of prince. To be worshipped. Bowed down to. The right to rule and to be served. The authority to be lazy and condescending, the highest accolade. No one knew how it started. There was no legend. Stories faded in the unseelie court, an eternal now. Turned to dust in dungeons and penitentiaries, alongside those who sought poetry and art. And without the abject violence or the pushing of cruelty's boundaries, nothing stimulated that continuum. The only way, eventually, for the craven need to be requited was by taking that stairway into the unknown. All others, in the unseelie place, are either servile, vile, muted, despairing, or twisted into sometimes unrecognizable paradigms. Always calculating an advance move. Coerced into believing confession to some higher, but never seen entity, would negate perversity.

'There's a particular someone I want you to bring to me,' whispers Morcant, seducing the soft underbelly of the lobe of the Artful's uncovered ear.

'And?'

'Just to please me, Dodger. He's still in the Mater General but he'll be released soon.'

'You want me to go and convince him?'

'A cop's watching him.'

'So, no?'

'My god.'

'Sorry. How do I know who to look for?'

'Keep company with the muck down under MacLean Street Bridge. He hangs out with them. Sounds Irish. You won't be able to miss him. But if you're addled, just wait. Black hair, solid gold in his ears. Talks code. Unfriendly.'

'The desk?'

'Is there any other information you need or are you just being a little shit?'

'Sorry, Mad Dog.'

'He's a fairy.'

'Got it,' and Dodger frowns. Is that supposed to be funny?

Morcant can't read the kid but Dodger seems clueless, and the older man wants it to stay that way. Once he's sequestered the sídhe into the team, the draíocht will provide him with the capability of everything he dreams of becoming.

Everything he's been programmed to erase. Every chat room flooded with nonsense. Every conspiracy theorist, remaining within elfshot of a surviving system, to be enchanted and undone. Once he taps the beauty of the wild faerie's talent, once he's fed him enough junk, the poison will kill off even the language of that dirty great Mystery he's been indoctrinated to despise. Magic's music. The song of seasons and the memories of Forgotten Lake. Once that door is closed, no voice old enough will be able to keep the First Forest alive.

No culture, no seelie court, no further humiliation. No fucking music, and no more dreams of freedom and individuality. He can go home. Prince of the dirty night, monarch of the desolate. Lord of what remains of earth's *shine*. Into the embrace of the Monstrum.

Love is a curse. Raven knows it. He just can't help what happens. It strikes faster than anything even he can imagine. As old as the First Forest. Raven knows the stories. People have always been aware of his existence. Some call him coyote, some refer to him as crow. Loki. Joker. He's all over the place. That much he remembers as he wakes. That human people used to know him and not hurt him. Once upon a time he was thought of as the *luck*. Not anymore. Except for one.

Raven has made the mistake of coding the vastness of his awe for life into the music of that computer program. Anyone not sufficiently savvy would have missed it as it passed by their daily social media scrutiny like the crawler under the news feeds. Just a whisper. But, oh, what a whisper.

Tommy Ng watched the passage of bytes trickle down the right-hand side of the screen, where the continuous flow of newly input data was constantly surveyed by his algorithms for anything of interest. In these days of perpetual repetition, originality stood out. A person like Tommy registers anomalies in his gut. It takes a moment for his brain to catch up and he has to scramble to recall what data he can from the flow that has already passed into potential oblivion. What *is* that?

Translating the stream of ones and zeros into their intentional pattern raises the flesh on Ng's entire body. He does not know this music. He is used to the thinness of regurgitated *musak* that passes for white noise, to keep synapses alert during work. This anonymous code is as insane as it is broad. Almost as though it is life. Tommy is grief-stricken with something his modern body cannot name but that, perhaps, his violin can. He understands that it is somehow ancestral. Every nerve is alert to the desire to hear this, not just see it in terms of mathematics. Morcant happens to be passing Ng's console and feels the tension exuding from his prize boy.

'What?'

'Look.'

Morcant is momentarily unnerved. This should not be. He's worked forever, relentlessly, and ceaselessly it sometimes seems, to enable him to matter. To be the best. And now this. A language so clean, so environmental, he is numb. He is undone if this gets out. If anyone else notices, he will have lost his check upon the board. Who has done this? The violence in him is so desperate for an outlet that he has to relieve it before he acts. He pads back to the stairs and down into the basement, the elevator door pinging as it vaults. He takes his *old man* razor from its leather case and removes the blade. He unbelts his jeans and rolls them to below his knees. He cuts small, almost invisible cuts into his inner thigh, deeper and deeper to try to release the built up panic. When the blood flows without coagulating, he lets it. Onto the concrete floor. Where it joins other dark patterns that corrode the memory of living that lies dormant, aware, within the strangled aggregate of sand and gravel once languishing on the shore of a beach where seals migrated to bear young. Crushed stone who once lived in community with mother earth until men turned tranquility into the humiliation of a blast zone. If flooring could scream, able to register sensation, it would do so at this travesty. Because the concrete also heard that music. It fell in the blood. Like bees that have never known pollen. Like those poppy petals that leaked from Sparrow, only a night or two ago, or so it seems, in the frozen back streets of New Rathmore.

Tommy Ng is onto it immediately. He traces the source to the library on the west side, infiltrates the data files of the security cameras. Sees the face in the little square box on the far right of the console and feels sick. The man is beautiful. Face crisscrossed with the pale scars of many sharps, that do not diminish the honesty and fairness of the curve of the lips or the furrows, like railways tracks from having loved enough to worry, dissecting the flesh between his eyebrows.

What is his heritage? The thought comes from nowhere.

Ng is trapped by the face. Dark skin that he imagines tannin would be like. Eyes of an animal. *Horses*, he thinks. *Or dogs*. Ng does not like the allusion because he knows that Morcant will hurt him if he comprehends empathy, even for a split second. And Tommy can't deal with that. His conflict is overwhelming. He stands from his station and stretches like he used to do back when he trained in Aikido. It is all he remembers of before. He activates the screensaver, takes his violin case from under the bench, snicks the latches, opens the lid, rosins up the bow and moves across to the only window with the instrument tucked under his chin. He plays to the yellow sky and tries to remember his mother's face before she was destroyed because of propaganda to do with the color of her skin and the slant of her eyes.

17

ISLE OF SECRETS

THE MASKS OF KAIN

Merrin works the tables out back of Dimity's. Diminutive, dark-braided, goth, witch who loves deep red lipstick and freedom. She has a presence that Mercy acknowledged, with only a look, on the day they met. They share instances of the experience of living with their Travelers. Merrin loves Willie-the-Red. He's the fiddler in the band, a rocked up Irish mishmash called the Fianna. When they score gigs in the town pubs from the north of the country to the south, at the change of the seasons.

Before he disappeared, Raven had played bodhràn and sang in the old tongue, songs and music he created himself of the days on the road. Before the chaos. Willie is as old as the most ancient of the forests out of mist, as standing stones and tuaths and tors and winter geese and he has never aged more than a man of seeming forty. And because of him, but not him alone, Merrin lives her days and nights in a kind of peace that most people never experience. Willie comes and goes like the seasons, like snow and sunshine, but his love is utter. It's the way of the faerie to never do a thing in increments. Her poetry, her bewildering warehouse studio with its exotica of flowers, herbs, sculptures made from the ruins of other people's lives, all hidden from sight out back of the boarded-up and abandoned downtown sector of New Rathmore that had been zoned for development before the crash of '08 and has not been worth the trouble since. A haven for any of the folk traveling through. A bed to share with Willie when he's in the city. Merrin is almost immortal, never having been shot or hung or somesuch and she's taken to being Mercy's guardian as though the other woman is not made of the stuff of bad men's nightmares.

Merrin has drunk the Quicken brew, made from a child of the first legendary rowan tree—the one planted in honor of the truce between the Tuatha Dé Danann and the Milesians, the modern day Irish, two thousand years ago. Cut down out of sheer bastardy by Saxons who had no right to be there but who had been invited in by a jealous chieftain determined to be king. As so often happens. This offspring of the original peace-maker tree now lives and thrives on Inishrún, on the summit of the human-made hill called the Barrow, growing downwards through gnarled underground roots into a cavern of crypts: skulls, talismans, bronze-bound oak trunks of treasure, from the dawn of humanity, and lore, notched ogham, into walls of limestone.

This place is known only to the inhabitants of the island, just a few nautical miles off the coast of Weary Bay. Both she and Mercy know the harm that can be perpetrated by slúagh, sprung from the nightmare of the Monstrum, unseelie thing that it is. That its denizens are warned about by crows and cats, right here in the city. Because times change even though the sídhe do not.

'I'm to wander,' says Mercy, as Merrin joins her in the early autumn evening light, in the café's outside courtyard, bringing mugs of soup in one hand and carrying a bowl of leftover stew in the other, for Revel. The witch sits idly twisting the ring that pierces her septum and pushing one of the mugs across to Mercy.

'You okay to hang with me?' she asks the hound.

Revel seems to grin. It means that garden. Watching the koi in the bathtub. Pretending they are salmon and he, a mighty hunter. For Revel, Merrin's ramshackle but warm wilderness is preferable to the street, preferable to camping out at Dimity's. No matter his love for Mercy.

Until there is a fight he must occupy himself chasing gulls. There is nothing dignified in chasing gulls to a pup of Revels pedigree.

The women and the hound remain silent until the last of the patrons scrapes the chairs back and depart. Mercy downs the dregs of soup. Before she goes, she kisses Merrin's cheek and squats beside Revel, his head on her shoulder in solidarity and solemnity because nobody is ever sure of coming back. Fate can intervene. Luck can run dry. The city is a hard place since the food wars, and even though Mercy is an assassin, young as she is, a body never knows. She shoulders the pack that stores her life; walks away without looking back.

What's it about? This restlessness? During the days now the weather pretends to be milder Mercy sits on her blankets on the cobbles telling fortunes to the hopeful and the smiling desolate while watching for signs. She is calm in daylight. Come night she is an explorer. Driven. Trusting her gut. Searching the streets and riding the subway further and further from Copperhead Lane every time. There are threads and webs of mystery in this town. In the fog dark of every alley, hidden in the pockets of strangers who will never be allowed to forget what cruelty or naivety landed them here, amongst the skeletal trees and groves of St Brendon's Park where the sap rises unobserved, down by the wide man-made rimy fringed pond that reminds ghosts of Forgotten Lake, in the deep and confusing dusk betwixt day and night.

Mercy Riley catches the train into New Rathmore Central, alights to the smells peculiar to these places, from the sickly sweetness exuding from the fast food franchises to convict brick, soot, damp, something freshly dead giving up its fetor from deep within in an overflowing rubbish container. Coffee dregs in Styrofoam cups abandoned on the low walls of pretend-garden beds. She misses nothing as she tramps through the cathedral-like arches of nineteenth century architecture and out, into the unexpected mizzling bitter sleet that blurs the neon. She pulls up the hood of her jacket and braves the damp.

The heart of the business district has recently been ploughed of remaining snow, the sidewalk salted, enough to fool the tourists into thinking that New Rathmore is still a jewel in the crown of a bedraggled empire when it's really a mere façade, like a movie set romanticizing a bygone Victorian romance. Nowhere more so than Wallace Hope Plaza.

Exclusive restaurants, boutiques, art galleries and antique

outlets form a bespoke cul-de-sac, the gold and silver repository sharing the soft glow of buttery street lighting with the subdued glamor of jewelry and clock merchants. The capstone of it all, the three storey brownstone austerity of Straub's exclusive men-only club and a Masonic lodge.

Amidst shops and cafes that never close is a peculiar exception. A shadowed gallery.

The Masks of Kain in old typewriter font gilds the glass window. Not bars or any kind of theft-proofing. The owner either daft or brave. A green-patinaed copper or bronze mask, Mercy does not know which, the face of what could have been a man, could have been a boar, could have been some arcane mixture of many species, the only adornment to an otherwise gunmetal grey, plain locked door with a code-access entry key. Two storey place. The upper level exposing a wrought-iron balcony, the metal covered with a neurological skeleton of Virginia Creeper.

The name of the proprietor on the shopfront is Wolf Kain. The person living within is not Wolf Kain.

The door is opened just enough to show a hard, white-ochred, cinnamon brown face, and part of the body, of a woman holding a pre-second world war Japanese officer's katana, complete with prayer tags, threadbare and tattered, attached to the *tsuba*, the hilt, glinting in the light cast from the streetlight and held, seemingly nonchalantly, by her side. Déjàvu Delacroix. She wears well-worn khaki coveralls, streaked white with plaster, that are so old their color is vague. Her sweater, unraveling at the wrists, is stiff with paint and the grime of too much distraction. Dried blood from what?

Barefoot, despite the chill, her hair shaved clean off at the scalp when exposed from beneath her hood, Déjàvu and Mercy were unnervingly reminiscent of people in some cult. Her skin is the scarred and scarified ambiguity of an indigenous ancestry but her eyes are the ice green of the guovssahas that haunt the men on the North Sea oil rigs as though to warn them they are being judged for their transgression. And right now they pin Mercy like a butterfly to a board, her full, dark lips momentarily forming a savage line of suspicion. Mercy is stopped dead in her tracks. For once unnerved.

She is used to this feyness amongst the sídhe, but not in humans. Is this creature human? Is she some beast? Leave it, for now.

'Oops,' and se steps back, away.

'I know you,' Déjàvu whispers, her eyes curious, her battle-ready stance relaxing as she leans against the door jamb.

'No. You don't. I should go.'

Mercy pulls the hood of her jacket even deeper over her face, in an effort at invisibility as much as against the cold of the night.

'Come in for tea. I *do* know you. Twenty-something years ago. And I also know the company you have kept since. Please.' She pulls the door wider. Mercy looks past her, to the disorder and chaos of a studio, and not the neat shop that one would expect in this part of the city. Déjàvu just sighs.

Mercy brushes by her into the warmth of another world.

'You got your mother's jaw.' Déjàvu closes the door onto the frigid and apathetic outside.

The studio is crowded. A massive wooden bench, pitted and burned to a defined personality, is covered with tools, leather, paints and brushes, turpentine and glue, overstuffed packages of plaster of Paris, the floor covered in mattresses and mannequins, the heads of what at first seem like people, in various stages of transformation, each bearing a disturbance, like fish-bitten bodies floating in the Thames might have had in days gone by, or the empty maw of a fresh grave, desecrated by hungry men, when students at St Johns Hospital School of Medicine had been in short supply of fresh cadavers a hundred years ago. Or perhaps still.

Déjàvu leads the way through the perilous detritus, and up a narrow staircase to the top floor, the opposite, almost, of the studio. A space devoid of inner walls that once kept rooms apart. A bed, a kitchen bench and sink, a two burner gas cooker attached to a bottle of propane, shelves with a few pots and plates, a cupboard—door shut, presumably holding food—a small fridge beside a clothes rack, with everything from a floor-length dust jacket, thrown garments in seeming frenzy, lots of grey, and nondescript, utilitarian khaki, a pile of boots and shoes. A few fat and misshapen cushions puffed up about the floor.

One wall reminds Mercy of the old record section in back of the comics, in Dimity's place. Vinyl in original sleeves, looming like wizened scholars above a turntable probably worth a small fortune. Another is crammed with books: sci-fi, anthropology, nutrition, neuroscience, how-to's, astronomy, standing stones, caving.

'I only have plain tea,' Déjàvu explains, filling a glass kettle from the sink tap. 'Been busy on the streets for a while. People cold and lost. Haven't shopped.'

'You Wolf Kain?'

'Friend of hers.'

'What about my mother?'

Déjàvu lights the gas. 'I'm not out to give you grief but the thing is, there's a kind of protocol to my madness. Hospitality is a politeness I learned from living with gypsies, so please humor me. My name is Déjàvu Delacroix, and yes, it is a name made of what I do, not who I am. And no, I don't give out the real one to anybody anymore. And I will make us tea. You are?'

'Mercy Riley. I don't apologize, by the way.'

'Your real name, too. Mettlesome. Here—' She hands Mercy a pair of mismatched mugs, a jar of sugar, and a carton of milk from the fridge. 'We'll continue this on the veranda where I can listen to the foliage being born. Her name is lost but I remember her. She was never one to say much.'

'Her name?'

'You know what you've been taught. Not always from Black Annis, I'll hazard a guess. Your mother, yes.' Déjàvu does not intend inscrutability. She's always thinking in more than one place. 'Hurt by a couple slúagh been hunting her for ages because of you. Out for a killing they got caught up in a brawl with her, you already cooking inside her. Pieces of concrete and razor wire your mama couldn't fight, I assure you. I patched up the wounds, of course. No going to any hospital for her.' Déjàvu spoons loose leaf tea into some relic of a teapot and pours the boiling water over it before turning the pot three times to help it brew right. 'She was too strange to risk a stranger's questions, you understand. But someone got to her. She's been gone too long now.'

'How "strange". What does that mean?'

'That dark pink birthmark on her face. The scars. And old ink messages that even she could not explain. Or wouldn't. Her feralness. Society's idea of a wasted person. Like an addict. But also, just like a kid. Seeming to be one of the street people, the lost people. Like you, in a way that's also not like you, because you're still innocent. Her hunters. The police. The social workers that were something from a bad dream. We sorted out her injuries. They tried to destroy her, them slúagh. To stop you getting born. Legend has it they're little and mean but they're fucken huge and sharp and cut from the dark rot of dead oceans, more like. Your mother's the daughter of some queen-of-the-faeries-type enigma, you know.'

Mercy is uncomfortable listening to what well might be delusion, after all.

'That's why you are what you are.'

Mercy says nothing, just waits, her mind kaleidoscopic.

'When she realized she was pregnant she hid. Except they found her. My sweet little wild creature. Locked her behind walls with iron for bars. I know. She told me everything.'

Déjàvu moves the linseed oil and the wells of paint, the jars of gold leaf, the leather soaking in the old copper tubs. She accesses narrow French doors that open onto an intimate, iceless balcony.

'Then she was gone. Can you hear the music?'

Mercy is unmoving. She is back in the institution, her underpants around her ankles and a cane bearing down on her naked buttocks. 'She's dead?' She doesn't wait for another story, maintaining the suspicion, knowing how to read a voice, even one as believable as Déjàvu's. 'What music? You know how crazy this sounds, don't you?'

'Dead? I doubt that. Wherever you are from is where she ended up before she came to me. So, whenever you're ready.' Mercy can only stare. This woman, this stranger, likely mad.

'Go on, I won't be a minute.' Déjàvu pours them both tea as thick as glue. 'She was in my corner of the city, you know. Artist. Like some forensic something, so lifelike. Freaky l'il thing.' She smiles, her eyebrows arching, her head tilting, owl-like, a look that says admiration. 'With work to do, laid upon her like a curse. Or a gift, depending on how you deal with it. Oh, and I'm certainly not crazy. The traffic, the night. They have their own rhythm. If you listen, as they taught you, you'll hear it. If you stop being scared and bitter for a minute.'

'I should be beyond caring by now. That nobody gives me a true answer.'

'What's a name, Mercy, except a language to lay on a person? Sometimes it's necessary to reinvent ourselves. Probably a lot more than sometimes.'

18

A FAIR WIND TO STEER HER BY

CRYPT

'There's no such thing as faeries, and I'm not scared.'

There's a turn to Déjàvu's lips, a quirky smile that crinkles the skin around her eyes.

'Says you when you reek of 'em.'

'Why did you open the door?'

Déjàvu sits her enormous bulk down and spoons a small gift of honey into her tea. She leans her elbows and breasts on the table, her back unbent.

'Mercy, I'm a dreamer. I get so much information from mythworld that it's sometimes tricky living in a society where people try their hardest to dismiss the mysteries as figments of something subtly hinted at in books thought only suitable for children.' She barks a laugh. 'As though children should not be informed of the most profound things.'

'That's not an answer.'

'You were born in the asylum, weren't you?'

'I don't remember.'

'That's a lie. First and last, I hope.'

Mercy's mind is cloyed with the smell of stale porridge, corridors of mops and buckets, girls cutting the soft inside of their arms with whatever could gouge deeply enough for them to feel anything, the sadism of the beatings or the cold, knowing nothing about those older women in the courtyard that the young girls were banned from accessing, seen through chinks in the walls. Heads bowed with hopelessness, some almost as young as children, or the arrogance of the alpha female whose quest it was to claim some delusional position, in a culture of crushed affection.

'Was she there? I never understood. I knew nothing about her.'

'Would you like to?'

'You can tell me?'

'We can start tonight if you want. I sense you don't have long.'

Mercy downs the last of her tea, then looks into the depths of the cup, at the pattern of the leaves, as though into an oracle. She says nothing.

'I've met them you know.'

'Who?'

Déjàvu stands and spreads her legs for balance, arches her back to stretch out the kinks. Taking her time. She picks up the empty cups and Mercy follows her inside. Déjàvu rests them on the sink top before opening the cupboard Mercy had assumed held food. It does not.

Like the *Lion, the Witch and the Wardrobe* it leads onto the upper floor of the next door patisserie. A huge room, derelict with neglect. Deserted as though the inhabitants vanished into thin air at a christmas time. A table set for two, covered in yellowed newspaper, with mismatched floral plates, and the brittle-looking, mouse-bitten remnant of what once would have been dinner. Little glass tumblers, caked in dried wine dregs. The stump of a conifer, skeletal branches all that remain, the ruins of packages scattered, ravaged and in disarray amongst broken tinsel and the smashed fragments of baubles that had once adorned that pretend tree. An unmade bed, a dressing table sparsely decorated with perfume, a mother-of-pearl backed brush, a pot of face powder, the lid of a riot of hand-painted forget-me-nots and violets. The large mirror shards mottled with rot, the silver backing slowly peeling away like the skin of old sunburn.

As though this is not mystery enough shelves line the far wall, filled with faces. Row after row of mannequin heads covered with what looks to be taxidermized human skin, glass eyes hooded, some bright blue, or grey, or late summer hazel, black as crows, the features of each, unique. Old men, old women, the crepe and lines of delicate age untorn, unblemished. It is at once ethereal and terrifying. Amidst the representations, like some arcane funeral chapel, are the stubs of burned-down tallow and beeswax candles, opened envelopes in bundles and tied with ribbon, black, lavender, scarlet, like love letters. Tiny, whittled-wood beasts, delicate and clearly boar and weasel, horse and gull. None of it makes sense.

Mercy shivers but not with cold, although her breath frosts the arctic room with each shallow exhalation. Something like realization rushes along her spine and raises the hairs on her arms.

'Hers. Yes.' Déjàvu Delacroix crosses to the long, midnight-blue velvet curtains that obscure much of the light from the world of New Rathmore and parts them, slightly, letting in a thin blurry line of incandescence from outside. Some ordinary streetlamps in some ordinary city.

Mercy knows enough to realize the illusion of all that, but still she does not venture from the doorway.

'Your mother is a caretaker.'

'What?'

'A caretaker and a disbelieved prophet. Not all the sídhe make it back to Inishrún when the grief kills them. We all do the jobs we have been taught. Some might think this is macabre. But they'd be wrong. I'm looking after it until she comes back.'

'She'll come back?'

'In her season, Mercy Riley. She'll come. The despair of losing you. Knowing what would be done. How you might think. Aging her, so that when I found her years ago, half dead from an attack by the slúagh intent on her murder and the end of her work; intent on knowing your whereabouts, that she appeared, oh, maybe twenty years old.'

Mercy crosses the floor, her fingers tracing dust obscuring the once-polished exposed surfaces. To stand before the withered features of a woman, feline face, curved lips, the smile as real as though she is living.

'I have questions,' she says, eventually.

'Come away. We need to leave all this be.'

Mercy turns from examining the cadaver to face Déjàvu, her

features unreadable. 'I want to know. Here. In this room.'

Déjàvu pulls a chair from the table and sits, her head bowed, elbows on her spread knees. Solemn with what is to come.

'Suppose what you say is true.'

Déjàvu tilts her face sideways to observe the play of emotion.

'If what you say is true then where are these people's bodies? And how did she strip the skin from their skulls?'

'*That's* your first question?'

'It's two, actually.'

Déjàvu is put off her prepared script. She expected anything but this cold, analytical forensics. Who exactly is her visitor? 'She has her ways. I don't know all the details.'

'Really? A woman can flay the skin of a cadaver and do what with the left-overs? Where's the equipment she uses for the preserving?'

'The process would be respectful. Did you ever go to the island of Inishrún, off the coast of Weary Bay? Have you not met the queen? Seen what's in the Barrow?' Déjàvu is nauseous at the calculated emotionlessness of Mercy's interrogation. Refusing to be intimidated.

'For Samhain. When the Travelers come from all over. Just once. Last year. And yes, I met Holly. That queen. I was allowed to go for the summoning of the Mystery for her fire. I saw the skulls. Annis told me. The only thing to kill the sídhe is mindless human cruelty. I know. Why do you think I'm not freaking out seeing this? It makes perfect sense. If my mother is who and what you say she is.'

'Or the compound iron of a bullet or a blade.'

'What?'

'Kill the fáidh. Cold iron. The sheath of a bullet's drenched in that stuff.'

'No, it's not. I've read about it.'

'Wrong, little girl. But you believe me?'

'Little girl? Is that what I look like? And "believe"? Probably. Except for the tree shit. The very idea that a woman who is faerie-born would do christmas is absurd. I don't know why you are lying but I presume there is a purpose?'

'Sometimes all we need is an excuse to celebrate, Mercy. Midwinter, and no woodland for hours in any direction. Where's your imagination?'

Mercy's mind runs rampant. The years since escaping Our Ladys, her time spent with Black Annis and the other sídhe. Hunter, the First Forest that looked just like a big, dark man. Puck, his love. Brighid. Their occasional visits to Weary Bay. Learning the healing arts from Maisie and the killing arts from a woman whom Holly Tremenhere, while still in training with the pennies, summoned into the mortal world when the elder fáidh were threatened. A warrior named Scáthach. The Isle of Skye.

Every day away from the institution has been a celebration. Every skill of hunting and healing, learning of the land and the weather, the sea, especially, the conversations of squirrels and badgers, stoats and eagles. All liberation and wonder. The sídhe reading fortunes out of the backs of vans, helping the fishermen pack herring into ice on the shore, working with the locals at harvest, sharpening scissors and knives, all the while driving from field to field, trailer park to trailer park. Getting away when the ravens said *go, go*, because the cops would come by, think they were pikies and want to charge them with something. Keeping their distance from the prisons and the churches, and people who think these places serve a purpose.

Fifteen or sixteen years have passed since she killed that first person. A necessity. A bodyguard to men who would put Inishrún under development. A casino. Dispossess the inhabitants who could not withstand all that violation. Desecrate the stones that still stand, carved and brooding, raised in some dim and misted past, by tourists bringing their foreign crystals and singing neo-pagan chants. A man complicit in Holly's aunt's senseless, fear-driven murder, to the desolation of her faerie lover, Connor. That had aged him. That had sent him, once again, from the tribe of his own kind and back into the seedy bars and rum bottles on the dockside of New Rathmore. Into the future. Lost now.

She'd shot that man. An arrow through the lung. She'd never flinched. Never felt a qualm.

So who is my mother, Mercy wonders. And if she is alive, where is she now? Why, if she is so fey, so witchy, has she never looked for me? How is it she couldn't stop the priest who raped me or the nuns who beat me, and how did she, or Déjàvu who had known everything, allow me to be locked away from the world in that dreadful place? If she *has* done all this work with dead faces, is Mercy nothing to her? And if she is still alive, does she want to be found?

First execute the quarry, she thinks, *before you go looking for answers.*

'Is there a chance of more tea?' she asks Déjà, walking calmly back towards the balcony, the better to smell the wrack of the river. Déjàvu can read her guest's every thought and is afraid. She figures it's about time she stops being a hermit and gets back on the streets for long enough to forge familiarities, and alibies, in the company of strangers.

19

AND THERE HE KEPT HER VERY WELL

BASTARDS

Mother Superior. A title, not a name. Identity erased while not more than the age of a child. Trusting the seductive voices in her ear as her hair is shorn, her face crushed into the flagstones, her twice-violated body obscured within the rough cloth of the eternal penitent. A promise of security.

Mother Superior whose wordless mouth sucks the marrow from the souls of the young girls as though they are the cause of her ruin. Are they ruin? What is meant by that? Sin. No, don't think on it. The lie. The toxic song of an eternally suffering man who would never be her prince. Never to be allowed down from that cross just in case people regained their self-worth. Once the deception was revealed. The only man Mother Superior would ever be sanctioned to love. Not the one she dare not. Just because religion said there are no such things as faeries. No, a dead god. *His bride*, she'd been told, as the wedding ring slipped onto her finger. A sign she was taken. Owned.

She had brought herself here, years before her postulancy. Fifteen maybe, she didn't quite know. And pregnant, from love unrequited. The story she had spun was that she had been procured by a childless couple, another obliteration, and had lived with them in Brokeshire until all of them relocated to Weary Bay where there were still jobs in the herring factory. A lie, but it had seemed reasonable to protect what she had willingly done. She had known the cane. Had been used by the Brothers who haunted the children dressed as brides, or by men who had no faces, her head buried in a bag so they could not, or so she had once thought, see the eyes of a child they were breaking.

She understood the necessity of nundom. Her need to help those poor women driving her decision like a warrior on a reluctant horse riding into battle. The only option available besides that of the black lung from the fish stink and the cleaning jobs and the baby-bearing years, that she recognized as the fate of women gone to flab, eating burgers at Sizzlers for a night out, a reward to themselves, like vodka and Zoloft, for the pretense that everything was as it should be. The panacea handed out by the men.

She'd born a daughter. A new human being who had not cried. She was just gone. She'd been told she should not think of it again. *Mercy*, she remembered whispering. A plea? A statement? Informed that with the help of the chrism she would be cleansed of the sin of Eve. She never sought the child. And then the priest and another pregnancy, another stolen infant. *A boy* someone exclaimed although she wasn't able to see because of the board between her breasts and her belly. She wondered, only in the dark when she pleasured herself despite the shame, what it would have felt like to suckle. She touched her nipples over the muslin of her nightdress and stared at the ceiling thinking only of that god's son. So brutally betrayed. Fantasizing that he was alive and had found her. Said, I love you, and that what she was doing was allowed because she was made holy.

She has a *discipline* of knotted cords that have marked her back beyond healing. The only times she allows herself nakedness, the better to prevent the mess of blood-splatter. It became almost routine after many years of use. She has not forgotten the lie of assuagement, as perennial a wound as the mouths of vaginas of other girls sent here to Our Ladys, of her own fall from grace. Binding small breasts. Moans in the night. Eyes of confusion and uncertainty that eventually become pebbles like on the shore of Weary Bay.

The priest had told her she was special. God had lifted her above other women and some heaven or other would be her reward. Said she would remain virginal despite the stink and sting of his penis as it made her flesh raw. She remembered wondering why he bothered. She knew, just like the time before, what he was doing and that the beasts of the field did likewise. She took courage from the cows that seemed unfazed by the mounting. Dogs did this. To Mother Superior's by now warped mind dogs were dirty creatures so what was she? That the first time, by that gypsy man she'd never really met, who was simply passing through town and in need of revelry, would choose her? She didn't even remember him leaving. A relief of amnesia that is punctuated, now that she is old, by the sound of his dancing feet, bare as though he was summer.

The priest paid her pennies from the poor box and suggested unimaginable consequences if she spoke but the feeling of being polluted never left her.

She walks, in dreams, an old woman. Beyond the convent walls. Down cobbled lanes, bright with moonlight, on the arm of a modern man with light hair, a fine haircut, barber-shop trimmed, decked out in a well-cut suit over a spotlessly white T-shirt. She dreams he is her lover come to marry her and take her to her true home, a castle fortress where no one will hurt her ever again. Her knight. In the dream believing he will come for her. Then she wakes, knowing the night has fooled her again. In terror. Remembering who he really is. Knowing what she's done. No one in Our Ladys knows that beneath the wimple her hair is an inch long. Curly. Pale as clean snow. She is ashamed and proud simultaneously. A cocktail of conflict and secrecy she is determined to die without explaining.

She never dreams of a daughter. Did she give birth to a daughter? Does it matter?

She occasionally nightmares about a man with raven-dark hair and gold glinting at each earlobe.

It is she who orders the gates locked. She who sorts the beds and the medications. She who orders the food trucks up from Brokeshire. Like some regent. Oh, the power. She long ago forgot her true self. Or else hid it so deeply because it was as worthless as joy, convincing herself of the rightness of the work and her haughty position deserving of this place. She pretends she never called that unseen boy after the Welsh hero who voyaged the sea and whose father was the true king of all the Britons. Never read the books, as a girl, of legends and myths and stories of trouping ancestors atop tall white horses, with bells upon the saddles and pennants high in pristine skies. That these, after all, are her. A body of self, buried beneath the grave dirt of countless dead women and unlived babies who died the day they were supposed to be born, choosing the option that seemed most cunning.

The months following Mercy's escape the bishop came to Our Ladys. Hours behind the closed door of Mother Superior's office. Sisters passing in a severity of starched habits, their eyes downcast and their ears attuned to any loose accusation. Who would suffer? Who would taste the cilice upon their flaccid thigh for that girl's disappearance? Who would be confined to the isolation rooms?

Mother Superior had a massive stroke that day. She never said the words of love or spoke the name of the beloved that she had always hoped to say. Her anonymity was assured. The convenient fictions were buried amongst all the countless, burnable files that no one would ever examine. Or so it was always assumed. She was interred in the walled field behind the blackened brick. No marker. No memorial. Just another corpse taking her place in the peat, as though the dead have never been alone.

The night of her burial Hunter came. Robin, his son, came. Brighid, Black Annis, Puck, Willie-the-Red, the Rowan and Alan and as many who could move through time to pay homage, despite all she had been through, to who she really was and to weep for what had been done in this, most desolate of makings by the unseelie court. The ravens from the Weary Bay Memorial Park cabal came, carriers of news to other hunting grounds across the land; forest, fen, hamlet and ice-locked concrete city, so that Merrin, C'av'arn, Kathryn Shilton and Vincent Tanaka would mouth her name and remember who she really was. Whisper that name to the wind, all the way to Hy Brasil where the Mystery mourns the tattered remnant of innocence. Again. Still.

Laments are songs of loss. They are not played and sung for the old; those who lived life with the knowledge of love, those who held grandchildren in their arms and who wore silly hats at the kindergarten Easter fete. The ones allowed to forget and so to die and be remembered. No. Laments are set to roam amidst drowned ships. They are the black ice and the blizzard. The ice vortex. People always know, within the bones of them, that laments are the way humans keen. Upon summoned wind. Laments are sung for murdered men. Those in uniforms, promised tinsel medals, and those whose skin is black, or their eyes almond, or those who would not betray the truth of what they'd seen. Broken women. Blamed for their own inability to hit back. Those who take the beating to stop it including the children. Laments are reserved for the discarded who won't take the steps over the bodies and faith of the people who once loved them. For a buck. For power. For no explicable reason. Out of boredom. No. Those last ones get no song. Even when reality has been blurred into poison to get them by. They receive no summons by uillean pipes, or bodhràn, or flute, to join nightjars and wolverines and arctic-white barn owls. A moment came, for every one of them, to choose. A second to decide which fork in the road they would travel. And the consequences, while hardly ever understood, accepted sightlessly.

Mother Superior had no such choice. Her last whispered word was an accusation: *Morcant*. And not the name of the daughter she bore. And while the Good Folk everywhere heard this name, as did every hound and every horse and every walrus and every boar of the wildwoods, Mad Dog pretended he didn't. Pretended he'd imagined her. If he'd unstopped his ears? If he'd allowed that one voice to insinuate itself into him? No. Just no. He had shut himself in his cellar fortress and fucked Dodger until the lad bled and was shredded. And then he had ordered him to get out. And then he had shot up a hit that would take him to within a sigh of the evaporation that perhaps only a slúagh like him could experience without actually dying.

Of the two who should have heeded the call, one was Raven. He knew. And he hid in the bathroom with the flyblown windows and the unidentifiable stains on the ceramic tiles and he fell to his knees. And he wept, outraged, that he had not cared enough.

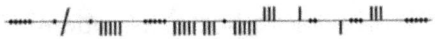

20

I AM AN INFANT: WHO BUT I

HENRY WAUBUN

Henry Waubun sleeps in his car. He wakes in terror, wiping drool from his cheek. Nothing. It is simply his beeper going off, the dream, that clusterfuck of crowds moving into his apartment bringing their families and all their junk with them, wilting sideways out of consciousness just like every other time.

His beeper means nothing. He has to report in is all. That kid. Or man. Or whatever he is. Birdie. Something haunting about him that hints at Henry's own childhood as though he has walked out of the pages of some brightly-colored kiddie book and shaped himself into a person. Waubun's childhood. So loved. So hilarious. His father had him on a horse when he was three. His mother taught him to read in English, he remembers remnants of his own native language and he is proficient at interpreting computer code. His mother's job was as a teacher at the local school where they'd lived a long way from most people, out below the snowline where the melt only happens every few years. He'd played the piano. He considers every now and then what life could have been if he'd been able to take that to some conclusion of achievement. He never did, though. He'd wanted a gun.

He had hate in his heart. He'd been amazed at himself; at his choice to become a cop. Especially later. Like now. He had begun as a mounted officer, his first horse, as a member of a kind of cavalry. A Warmblood Clydesdale mare named Petal who he loved more than he'd ever showed because cops and attachment are a bad mix. When the truck had slammed into her on the bridge, on the day of the terrorist attack, her legs broke. He'd sat with her until the vet came and gave her the shot. How does a man come back from that? From those silent eyes and that soft breath? Waubun likes to pretend to people like Birdie that he has a family but he doesn't. He's a *whisperer*. Of dogs and horses and magpies. People do his head in. He's tried to love women, hell, he even wondered if he was gay but he's just ambivalent unless they need him. Then it's the animal of them he will save. And protect.

Waubun is aware of his attraction towards Birdie. An almost incandescent musk that soothes him. Like Mount Avon with its spruce and fir. A hint of wonder that sometimes strikes the nose without reason. Split seconds of aching beauty that are gone as if they never existed. He is aware, but it means nothing to him. He has been assigned the task of questioning the man and then writing up a record. Then nothing. Next please. But Waubun is also aware of Birdie's record. Of the charges against him for killing that bastard hurting the little woman mare in France. Of him being sent to prison for it. What the seeming young criminal would have suffered, him being so beautiful and dangerous-looking.

There is something else going on here. Something of a rightness, not a wrongness, and so unique that he is not about to let it go.

'Morning.' He has two decent coffees from the cafeteria in the private sector of the hospital, so it's got some oomph to it and serves well as a peaceful approach to the damaged man in the bed.

'Henry. Been a while.' Raven carefully pulls himself up into a sitting position. His wounds are pale yellow and mauve, the swelling of his battered eye already gone, the splits on and around is lips pink with scar, but Waubun does not show surprise at the rapidity of healing. Aware as he is. 'What're we doing today?'

'There was a kid here earlier looking to speak to you. The nurses sent him away.'

'That supposed to make sense?'

'Who else knows you're here, Birdie?'

'As far as I know nobody even knows I'm alive, Waubun. I thought I'd pissed you off enough yesterday for you to go away.'

Waubun pulls out his phone and scrolls through his images until he finds a photo of Petal, her mane braided, her legs in pristine white polo wraps. Himself beside her, proud as he's ever been. He hands the phone to Raven who remains looking at the image for ages. His mind spinning silk from cobwebs. He returns the phone to Waubun and takes up the coffee.

'Yeah, okay,' he says, sipping.

'Someone's looking for you. The kid was off the street. Nurse at the desk said he was a right mess but with a swagger. So, what the fuck, Birdie?'

Raven swings his legs out of the bed and grunts with the pain that still haunts his ribcage. 'I'm leaving,' he says, pulling the sticking plaster from the back of his hand and removing the canula from the vein.

'They won't discharge you,' says Waubun but Raven smiles a slightness that suggests otherwise. 'I'm supposed to bring you in.'

'Not going to happen.'

Raven is oblivious to the hospital gown that is fully undone, exposing him. The entirety of his back, buttocks and legs, excepts for the support bandage around his torso, is mottled with tattoos of such intricate story Waubun stares, unembarrassed and reminded of his own grandfather, until the dark haired faerie pulls on jeans, dumps the *johnny* on the adjacent bathroom floor and washes what he can under a cold tap, mumbling under his breath.

'Where we going?' asks Waubun as though the two are already a team.

'Jaysus, Henry, are you still here?'

'What are you, Birdie?'

Raven pauses cleaning his teeth, taken aback, unusual for him, before continuing as though he hadn't heard. He opens drawers in the bedside chest and finds nothing. He pulls at the doors of the little metal wardrobe, wincing through a haze of vertigo. His sweater, boots, beanie and big old pea jacket are all neat on the dresser before the built-in mirror. 'Dumb fookin gabhdán,' he growls, noting the image that he refused to acknowledge in the bathroom.

'You see, Birdie, or whatever the fuck your name really is.'

'Can you spare a man a fag?'

'You can't smoke in here, Birdie, and besides, that shit'll kill you.'

Raven snorts a laugh, his black eyebrows lifting to a steepled arch of humor, and Waubun is convinced there is a much bigger story here than he previously imagined. 'Who wants you, Birdie?'

'No one.'

'That's not the way I see it. So I won't apologize.'

'For what? You haven't given me grief, copper.'

'I never do, Birdie, but I'm about to be your shadow whether you are okay with it or not. Till I work the fuck outa this bullshit you're telling me.

'Cunt.'

'Same to you, Birdie.'

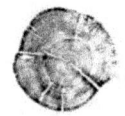

ııı ııı ıı ———ııı ıı ///// ——/ ııı •///// — /• ıı — —ıı ııı.ı ——ııı

SWEET DREAMS ARE MADE OF THIS

ARTFUL

Such a stupid mistake. How could someone as clever as him have thought going to the hospital would get him in? A weak man? A beaten man? Be a soft target. That was the flaw in his logic. It'd been easy enough. Just say you saw the attack. Just engage him. Simple. Then become his best friend. Be prepared to be vengeance.

Tell the quarry he'd seen the whole thing and that he knew the men who'd rolled him; that they'd thought he was holding contraband something. Seen him coming outa the library and into the march. Enough baton-wielding pepper-spraying, black armored Kevlar private security to arrest and maim every dissident from here to the southside. Tell him he's sorry. That he wasn't quick enough to prevent the bashing. Artful thought he had the plan down. And it could have worked if that cop hadn't been all over it like flies on roadkill.

But Morcant had hurt him instead. Bad. Busted his nuts and ripped him so hard it'd be a month before he could shit. So now he is also broken. Afraid to eat. Or of another reprimand. Unprepared, as he'd been, for the sheer strength of the Dog. Doesn't matter, he's in for more pain than he can handle if he doesn't get high. He's not brave enough to return to the citadel just yet so he's hanging out with the dispossessed that camp down the towpath under the bridge. Even Dodger has no idea how this big old crusty Chinaman managed to get this fat, because whenever he's stayed here before, and that's more often nowadays when he's too rooted to scavenge the required snackage the others demand from him; when his swagger pretense drops and the little boy gains control of his brain. The enormous feller has been off his face on ice, and food's not big with meth heads. He sells and barters the best oxy this side of Brackenridge, however, so it's all good.

It's pissing down rain when he finally wakes; full afternoon by the slant of the light so the goonies have gone but here's the birdman with who? Is this the cop? Artful's wits are in the river alongside every other dead thing rejected by the city, so he's not about to make the connection. Just utterly aware that he couldn't give a shit, laughing a little at his own joke, knowing that if he doesn't stuff up this time all will be well back at the fort.

He pulls out his bakkie pouch and rolls himself a smoke, handing the makings wordlessly to Raven who joins the little lad. Raven can sense the rasp of pain that leaks out of every pore of the kid's body, so he's stuck again, just like always, in the threads of somebody else's purpose.

'I seen you at the library a while back,' Artful explains, as guilelessly as he is capable of being. 'You a book person?'

'Computer time.'

Waubun tries invisibility, and also tries to not express the something that cops do that get them picked every time no matter how undercover they think they are.

'How?'

'How what?'

'How'd you happen to remember a thing like that with a fooken riot on?'

'Yiz pretty for a man.'

'Fook.'

'I'm nah hitting on you. I'm nah into that. Just sayin' I seen you. Felt sorry for how they just come on you like a pack like they done. Fuck me you given as good as you got. Never seen so much blood come outa one man.' He holds out a hand. 'I'm Artful.'

'Good for you.' Raven ignores the gesture, afraid of just how much more he can get sucked into the tragedy of the kid's life. What is he? Fifteen? Younger? Most of his teeth are gone so it's sometimes hard to pick. Humans rot easily.

Waubun leans across and shakes the hand. 'Henry Waubun. Not much of a name but I'm not what you're thinking.' Dodger shakes the hand, knowing the man's lying but not about to contest the fact of it. He knows the price of challenge. 'Why do I get the feeling you're not here by accident, Dodger?'

'You are.'

'What?'

'A cop.'

Raven passes back the tobacco, expertly rolls a thin cylinder of tobacco and lights it from a Zippo he pulls from a hidden inner pocket of his jacket. He takes a drag and exhales pale smoke into the paler frost of the early afternoon. He then lifts his undamaged arm and salutes the four directions in the way of *wakan* he learned in the long ago when the First People still held ceremony. 'Henry's a brother, Arty, so take a moment, love.'

Artful says nothing. He swims through his own brain like it's full of molasses and he can't swim. What is this all about and how come nobody warned him? Who are these men and why is he sitting here on the icy wet ground, pretending to be whatever *normal* is supposed to be—cool—when he's had enough torment in the past for twenty four hours to last a lifetime and this just looks like more.

'You on the run from something, Artful?'

Artful flips out and decides it's time to bolt but can't. He is unaware of the spellwork Raven's laid on him; spellwork, truthwork. Uncontrollable legs, foggy brain, and a trainwreck of intention.

Raven sighs. 'I smell something on you, man. You reek of fear. Who's got yer mummy tied up? Or yer old, lovely dog, eh? I can smell something putrid. So, what's the deal?'

Gulls swoop in syncopation over the sludge of river seeking its freedom in the wild sea.

There's nothing left to catch, but their instincts are still alert to fish and carrion so they dive as they have always done. Raven, as awed as ever, misses who? Homesick for what? There is a slither of memory firing along the synapses in his brain, off to the left, somewhere he doesn't go much anymore. Too colorful, too delightful. Too young and too oddly wise. That child. Woman. Mercy. Agnes? Pointless when all that remains is to wait out the slow death. If he allows this tatter of thought to surface he will cry again. Raven hates crying. It corrodes bits of his armor. But his eyes don't dry up. There's this voice. A haunting, languid lament for someone just dead. Who?

His inner sight flashes on empty ground. Straggles of blotchy grey snow over mounds and mounds of buried things. One fresh. No hint, yet, of young green. He senses the woman beneath the soil as though her eyes are wide open, like the recent blind, aching for light. Who is the other one? And how are they linked? Because he knows they are linked. Terribly and irrevocably.

Vertigo hits like a wave and Waubun catches him as Raven falls. Out. Gone. Shit. Mad scrambling as both he, and the circumstantially puny Artful, drag the faerie deeper into the blackness of the underpass, shifting the still-nodding lads—in their thermal blankets and eye-covering caps—with their booted feet, as they get the dead weight of Raven away from the sleet that is gaining momentum from seemingly out of nowhere, turning the day to a sheet of horizontal peril.

Waubun is conflicted. Should he bring his charge back to hospital? Will he die if they stay out here? Whose dumb idea was this? How can he have been so stupid as to follow this kid who calls himself nothing much at all, who's lying through his teeth about, oh, probably everything. What was he thinking? If he was a religious man he'd pray right about now, to whatever god could explain this profusion of complexity.

Reasonable, he thinks. *I am a reasonable man, and this is not reasonable.*

Artful is attentive only to Waubun. Afraid. He could go down for this. For the dope in his pockets. The Twinkies and chocolate chip cookies. His crack pipe. His guts are full of spiders. Each one fighting and eating the other. It's a warzone. And all he can do is play at being casual. He is sudden as he lunges for the embankment decline, vomiting up what's left of yesterday morning's pizza and Mountain Dew. All his swagger spewing up and out with the sick. He's just a little boy. And he has not one clever clue as to what to do now.

Every once in a millennium or so some faerie decides they love a specific species so profoundly that they are willing to take off the skin of magic and love amongst them, as one of them. Agnes did that. Humanity. Woman. Although she suffered what humans called disfigurement, during the transition, her face mottling with pigmentation where before there had been only millennia-old tattoo. So that when she walked as a mortal, she kept the hood of her jacket pulled low so no one would stare. It wasn't as though Raven was lacking but he vanished so often on whatever empathic quest he was into that she was left bereft and lonely.

Loneliness, to a faerie is impossible. Worse than death. Loneliness is the equivalent of one tree remaining where once a forest of profusion spoke oxygen to the wind and day. Agnes was never rejected by the Travelers, but she felt so exquisitely for the women and girls who were impregnated with human offspring they neither wanted nor intended, that they could not keep even if they'd wanted to, that she felt the need to pay whatever price was demanded of her to help them. To insinuate spells enough to dry up their milk once the infants were removed. To weave enchantments of forgetting and of shamelessness. They were almost non-existent when she became like a twelve year old mortal, taking stupid, illogical vows to some delusional character out of a Marvel comic, created by cunning old men once upon a time at a bucks' night historically renamed Council of Nicaea whose decisions and concocted rules had led to this travesty perpetuated on these girls and their babies.

She'd taken those vows, fully veiled and now invisible to the outside world, face-planting the stone floor of the lately-abandoned and derelict chapel in the heart of Brokeshire before being stationed at Our Lady of Perpetual Sorrow Mother and Baby Home intending to be the instrument for education and joy, rather than being cursed with remembering what happened. The dark draíocht of the church runs deep, like arsenic administered through a slow drip and becoming mortal, Agnes realizes way too late that all she can do is follow orders. Or else. She was informed, early into her tenure, what *or else* meant, and knew it was a way of explaining how little she, or any of them, mattered. That that nasty expression, rule of thumb, nowadays leaves scars. Nothing, ever, to do with religion. Nothing resembling compassion.

Even though her identity is interred in that deep ground along with what remains of a body, aged to at least fifty human years, she has never forgotten Raven. She lived to be a spiteful woman after the rapes by those men. After delivering the children, removed from her as though she was just like all the rejected women. The disappearances and sales, she presumed would be the result, just like all the others. Well, isn't that why did this? She hadn't really thought it through. Hadn't realized she'd be one of them. Experience what they did. That she'd be required to pretend and pretend and be quiet and ignore everything her flesh and blood body had yearned for. To cover herself from head to toe. The mouth, the holding, the rightness of woman and infant. Gone. Taken. Abandoned and forbidden to either challenge or charge this man scented breath of Guinness, or that man, the one *of the cloth*. One thing, though. The eyes of that small woman. The one people called Sparrow. They knew. As she'd walked as straight, and unaffected as she could, mere days after the delivery, on her way to the office, she'd been trapped in those eyes that could penetrate even the muslin underveil she is never without that said *I know what you are, and I know what's been done*. She knew Sparrow had seen something. Knew what had happened. There was something not quite right about the youngish woman with the ragged white hair and the white-hot anger. Something of kin. Agnes shut down after that. Dismayed. She'd recognized the scent as she'd passed the girl. Hy Brasil. All loamy and dripping with nectar. Basket of bloody and tear-stained bedding not diminishing the pungency of wild draíocht in the slightest.

She hides Raven in a cave within her imaginary abyss, the never-healing wound of his rejection as raw as the amphitheaters created from site blasts. It is only when she is deeply under the earth that she finally realises that the faerie in her has not quite achieved absolutely morbidity. And that Raven is never coming for her.

Agnes is semi-alive in that blackness, her eyes seeking an impossible sight, her condemnation to the transformation of flesh and organs by soil's microbial ecosystem, inevitable. Conned again by old stories of angels falling from heaven for love of a mortal.

Untruth.

She is potentially fated to an endlessness of unlife.

22

MOTHERS AND BABIES

INCONSEQUENTIAL LITTLE THING

Her thinking gets confused just before she has an attack. The nuns thought she was possessed by the devil but it was always just fear. Just. What kind of a word is that? *Just*? It seems to mean both righteous and mere. Just fear is immobilizing to a child whose night terrors are so severe she convulses. That deep hole in her gut where she sometimes imagines cockroaches make nests. Or snakes. Or any one of any number of creatures with teeth and barbs and noises that rumble like trains through tunnels. Her sanity is their nourishment. The only relief is when she draws. Terrible things. Prophesies of abomination. Mutilation. Sparrow does not want to think of these as anything other than art. The fáidh know this and don't much pull her up on it, understanding how damaged she has been. But she also fears that what she does is fated.

Sparrow was registered as having been born at Our Ladys. She knows the truth of this deception, however. She says nothing mostly. When she does, she will say she doesn't know what a parent is. She taps an index finger to the side of her nose and explains to any who ask, though, that she's as canny as any wee figment of myth. Sparrow stopped aging decades ago. She doesn't think about it. She's herself, is all. But she twigged about folk out of mythworld while still young.

She would have been twelve when she was first introduced to the nurseries. It was her job to push the trolleys to the laundry with the soiled linens and the abandoned clothing of dead children. She had seen, when the shadows had displayed something approaching form, what had walked the corridors at night rustling starched of cloth and the soft-chattering staccato of wooden beads. Slight, maggoty, insubstantial bundles in their arms.

She had been careless and curious simultaneously. Sparrow was proud of her ability to move throughout a day unnoticed. Intentionally obscure and uninteresting. Wispy pale blonde hair, waxen skin, eyes, usually downcast to obscure their deep bronze, like honey. Like sap. Stick thin but strong. Birthmark, deep rose colored, marking her face and almost expected to prevent invisibility. Often in the delivery rooms, using tongs to pick up the bloodied towels and the drenched bedding, keeping out of the way. Learning. Always learning. It could almost be that she had been behind the high, dark walls of the institution since it had been built. But that is not possible. Or is it?

People think they know everything and that everyone has an age to be born and a charted progression until death. That humans have always looked like themselves. Decrepitude is accepted as normal with the aging process and yet no one, to Sparrow's knowledge, knows everyone, so perhaps that's all optimism and agreed to propaganda to sell walking sticks and hip replacements.

Sparrow fell in love with newborns even as the nuns whisked

them away, still bloody, the umbilicus cut while still pulsing. That unacceptable child with the silence on her that came to define Sparrow herself. Sparrow was able to come and go from the children's wards and exercise yard because somebody had to clean up after infants and none of the other mothers were permitted. Sparrow had also always known when she was lied to, even though she did what was expected. She joined the nine nuns (always nine, other than Mother Superior) for lauds, and attended mass every morning at six. She learned never be in the chapel vestibule with the priest afterwards, as in hushed and whispered desperation she overheard the other girls and understood the danger.

The nuns were aging and cruel, unlike Mother Superior. Sparrow was aware that Agnes fought compassion in an attempt at assimilation. She was odd, though. Accepting Sparrow when everyone else feared or abhorred her unnerving canniness. Sparrow behaved as they did, prayed as they did and wordlessly assisted deliveries as they did. Most were oblivious to what she knew, which was everything. Every moan of desperate pleasure, every violence against both mothers and children, every pill used to sedate or, sometimes, kill.

The question remained unspoken amongst the revolving door of inmates sentenced to the institution: is Sparrow crazy? She speaks calmly of faeries; sees and communicates with them all the time. That they are everywhere—ravens, owls, bees in high summer. Voices in weather and wave. As perennial as the valleys and coastal cliffs and shoals, lochs, lakes, rivers, weather and chains of mountains, or daisies. People-seeming, sometimes. She speaks of them as though everyone should recognize them. Says a body could pass one in the street or listen to them playing Dirty Old Town with the last round of drinks at a local tavern. Think they are hippies or rough sleepers, or just plain peculiar, but that those assumptions would be wrong. And as likely get the smart-mouthed drunk and his whole town cursed with an outbreak of herpes as not. When the women who think they know better talk of fairy queens and princesses that they have read about, and that they're really just old stories like those of selkies and kelpies and bogles and goblins, Sparrow walks away.

When was your baby born? she is sometimes asked. Sparrow's eyes well up but she says nothing, so no one knows what happened. She never answers. When asked, occasionally if her infant is here in the children's section of Our Ladys the response is always the same. 'They all are.'

Oddities like Sparrow have always existed amongst people. Oddities who age every which way but otherwise make no sense. The women who are consigned to the Mother and Baby Home, and have nowhere to return to, so stay for the entirety of their lives. They note Sparrow coming and going about her duties and occasionally wonder. Some could say she is a chit of a thing worth no notice while others, that she had once been beautiful, as though the anorexic-looking woman who passed them carrying a basket of stinking nappies was old, when nothing about Sparrows physicality followed rules.

She'd been there the night Agnes' first child was pushed from the as-yet childlike body. When she was still Agnes. It was a dead giveaway that something about the newborn was not quite right. The eyes. They were not those of a baby and held something like forest green and woodland dark in their uneven depths. Sparrow knew what Agnes was. And Agnes knew she knew. Taken into confidence by the others she had met she had been warned that the faerie-turned-mortal was damaged. Brighid and Hunter had said to keep a lookout for signs of the *shine* and that if it ever came back from where she had sent it screaming into some bottomlessness on that night of crowns and laughter, fiddles and abandonment; that if Sparrow was to sing in the old tongue, a lullaby the faeries had pulled from the heart of summer for this purpose, they would come for them both.

Sparrow had snuck out of the delivery cell the night of the birth. With the tiny girl in an almost uselessly thin bunny rug. She never told a soul about that.

Agnes' eyes had begged, that night, as some other woman's dead newborn had been laid between her bloodied legs, that Sister Mary Dominic could write up in her ledger as an unsaleable item. Sparrow did that, sometimes, for the lifeless ones as though in some perverse penance. She had got that faerie-cross-human child onto the nursery, hidden in plain sight.

Agnes had been released into the care of the diocese at Brokeshire. Put to work in the kitchen of the rectory. When she'd been forced by the priest; when she'd become pregnant the second time her already disappearing *shine* vanished utterly. Mutilated beyond recognition and so, when she bore the second child, with hate in his newly-born eyes, she'd turned her back on him. That was the night Sparrow escaped.

Only then did Agnes realize she would never have whatever people said was an ordinary life. Would never know the love of a mortal. In a way she was dead. When the reason for taking human flesh, eventually decrepit, was understood to be pointless she abandoned herself. She took the vows to the very institution that would be the killing of her.

None of the nine remaining nuns were chosen to be the new Mother Superior. Times change, and less and less beds were in use. Church funding for Our Lady of Perpetual Sorrow Mother and Baby Home was drying up. No need to raise another woman to the post. Four nuns ministered to the pregnant women, two oversaw the work in the laundry and the grounds, one was tasked with teaching sewing and cooking and other duties that would perhaps, someday, provide employment to the otherwise damned. One did the ordering of supplies and the dispatch of laundry to and from the local towns and villages.

And one arranged the sale of the children. Kept the books as well as the vast sums of undeclared money in the wall safe behind the framed, bleeding heart print of an Anglo Saxon *Jesus*. This last nun, the backbone of the institution. Always was. Sister Mary Dominic ruled Mother Superior's every waking moment with as few words as possible, wielding sadism, the threat of exposure—of informing—a hammer over the younger woman's head: the slut of men whose *get* were disappeared as though they'd never been.

Twenty seven books, large ledgers going back at least a

hundred years, were in that safe. Meant never to be found. Only Sister Mary Dominic, now ninety-one but sprightly due to the sagacity of nourishment and a lifetime's physical endurance wielding a mattock and shovel knew the combination of the old wall safe; the code seared into her brain even as other faculties diminished. The nine remaining nuns would die rather than admit culpability for what they had witnessed and done. Each covering their crimes with silence: a warped venom of sanctity.

23

DON'T BE SO RECKLESS

DEARTHÁIR

Think. Artful is in overdrive. He knows he has to get the *Injun* or whatever he is, back to the factory before Mad Dog builds up to some punishment that makes no sense but that hurts intentionally to the point of disbelief. Raven is limp as a corpse but his breathing is like that of a sleeping child so both he and the cop wait.

Raven is out cold to New Rathmore but that does not mean he is unconscious. He has fled. To Forgotten Lake. He takes his boots off and rolls his jeans up to below his knees and wades into the pristine, unsullied water.

'You here?'

His deep voice spreads across the surface of the lake in silk and it seems like years before he hears the throat being cleared from behind him. Hunter is cross-legged on the ground beside the fallen log long ago hollowed by the teeth of beavers and now inhabited by a badger pair and their cubs.

'She's not coming, *deartháir*, so it's me. Sorry.' Calling Raven 'brother' even as the other man tries to forget what he can't.

'Hunter.'

'Not so blank now, are you, *a cara*?'

'I need to die, Hunter. Gimme a clue. I know I can do it, but nothing's worked so far.'

'It's because of your curse, Raven.'

'That's unfair. Just because I got one and you haven't.'

'What is this? Sibling rivalry? Cut it the feck out. Faerie in yer veins but not enough for the cold iron not to kill you. Never will, *deartháir*.'

'There's no point.'

'Never was.'

'Shut up, okay?'

'So you love? So don't be a fecken coward about it, is all.'

'Someone important died.'

'You didn't come. If I could feel ashamed for you, of you, it would be because of that.'

Raven is mortified by the truth of the words. He hadn't come. He had felt sorry for himself, instead. He knew someone important was gone but hadn't understood. What Hunter is just gleaning is that his brother is missing his *shine*. Now it is his turn to know surprise.

'You really don't remember?'

The shock of Raven's mutilation is overwhelming and Hunter fights with himself to stay. His instinct is to bolt as though from a chainsaw. 'What happened to you, man?'

'See, I remember the island. I remember the death of that woman and all the sídhe that followed her to the crypt. I recall the shrivelings and the bones and the niches in the halls of the Barrow.'

'But not Agnes? That you loved her as a man does? She was the healer from the First Forest who forgot on purpose, you know. Some other faerie. In that cottage the people wrote wrongly about. By all that's wilderness you think it's only you gets to wear a geis, that compels, despite what you know?'

Raven's face turns almost to stone as stories and defamations and profanities pass through the wire of his cage and into the full light of realization. He had taken shape for many years. His blue-black little cousins. Had seen her grow into such gentleness. Into empathy. Then, from the shadowed thickness of the yew behind the ice factory he saw what that man did to her. And so he forgot, because it was too late by then and the pain of her mortality destroyed him a bit more every day. He doesn't remember how long he was in that shape, not wanting to walk as a man ever again. But nature is what she is and he was back long enough to spend a summer and an autumn with the troupe camped outside Weary Bay, at *Úllcran Ciallmhar*: Woman, Apple Tree Wise. She had been his undoing.

'You ran away.'

'Did not.'

'Where's your light, *dearthái r*? Who stole your *shine*?'

'What?'

'You have to go back now. They're coming.'

Hunter shifts to standing, his great bulk blocking the twilight sun from his brother's face.

'Wake up, Raven.'

Wetness. The warmth of a tongue that is almost obscene in its insistent softness. Raven opens sleep-caked eyes to the huge head of the wolfhound only inches from his own, the tongue annoying, but healing him. Demanding. He groans. Then sits up. Then sees Waubun and that little woman with the shiv in both dirty boots who came here to claim him. Isn't that the way this is supposed to play out? The thin pale branch of a winter tree, scarred and inked and marked by a rosy birthmark, an art book under her arm, the hound at her side, but no Mercy.

'Jaysus, Mary and Joseph.' He whispers to the icy air, helpless to the astonishment of this moment. Is she close? Every spell, every invoked disregard for her existence blows away on the flinching, deceptively silvering the daylight with hope. Revel rolling onto his back as though imbolg is already written and he smells blossom, not a dying river and the relentless stink of a city without professional garbologists. Demanding a belly rub, his mouth floppy with smile. Waubun first to concede, strokes the soft underarms as though he knows exactly what dogs require. She's not here.

'You're to leave.' It's a statement to Artful, not a request. Sparrow ignores the others. Her legs are spread and her hands hidden within the folds of her mongrel coat. Artful goes to speak but she gives him a look. And he withers. Whoever this imperfect, winter-haired stranger is, she is not his friend, and he will not trick her with what he has learned. He comprehends without any coercion that she knows death. He is as in love as is humanly possible and fuck Mad Dog and whatever he wants because Dodger needs this more.

'Can I?' he asks. She looks him over, examining the deceits

written into every pore of his once broken, now offensively greasy face.

'Go home,' she says. And something in him wonders what that might be. Not the citadel. Or is home always a place of horror and satisfaction all curdled together to be undifferentiated? 'I have no idea what you mean, lady.'

'"Lady"? Insult me again and I'll break both your arms,' she says quietly, her eyes never leaving those of Raven.

'Where's home, then, arsehole?' He is fast regaining his mojo and refusing to allow the new love of his life to ride him like Mad Dog, no matter his awakening desire. Bluff, his best weapon.

Sparrow is amused at this.

'Artful, love,' she says. Gently this time. 'Time to undo you.'

She pulls a fifty dollar bill from the inside of her coat. 'There's a witch waiting for you in a place called Weary Bay. Ask anyone you meet how to find Maisie Raith. She'll remind you.'

'What?'

'What home is.'

Artful is perplexed but he takes the cash, confused because he didn't know there was any of this stuff still around since the food riots.

'There isn't a choice.'

He almost doesn't hear that, his mind alert to the gear he can score with this money. But something in the way she says it wakes up the fear, and the unrelenting monotony of his job at the factory and the absolute lack of choice. He is not going to affect this dark man, and Waubun is most certainly the law, so he's fucked any way he considers.

'Weary Bay?'

'Maisie Raith.'

'Got it.' And he blows kisses all around, before getting to his feet and climbing the embankment to the road. It's only a few blocks to the bus station. And the one he needs must be still running or she would have said otherwise. He knows instinctively she is honest. He also feels as if he's had some coercion spell laid over him. He doesn't mind, though.

Revel raises hackles and drops his ears back, listening. He walks, stiff-legged and pensive, in the direction of the docks along the southside answering a whisper of his name that only he and Sparrow and Raven hears. Mercy. Raven is as paralyzed with emotion as everyone but Henry dissolves into the white as unconsciousness takes him.

24

᠁ⅢⅡ᠁ ᐧᐧⅢ Ⅲ᠁ⅢⅠⅢⅡ᠁Ⅲ Ⅲ

INISHRÚN

MAISIE RAITH

The water is wide, I can't cross o'er and neither do I have wings to fly.

The old tune is hummed under the breath of Raurie Mór as he skippers the black-sailed Rosie Rua through the skin and roil of bottomless dark ocean; suicide to anyone else this time of year. As she tacks through the white water close towards the shore carrying his *wight* of passengers to the island from the relative winter safety of Weary Bay he thinks of the Caribbean and how sweet the shoals, how soft the sand. But he knows he is a creature of this wild wetness; ancestor to every mariner who drew a map and wondered at the stars for finding, and relative to every gummy shark and mackerel, every tern and albatross and the memory of the grand processional of whales up the coast into the arctic homeland in preparation for birth.

The Rosie Rua. An *bád mór* (big boat) is forty four feet long with main sail, foresail and jib, every inch of cloth made traditionally of calico, like the great grandchild of the Galway hookers, big enough to take faeries to and from the secret island.

Raurie is ungainly on land. His legs become rubber and his

bulk weighs more heavily than when it sways to the rhythm of swell and dip. But a promise is a promise and he heard Hunter. His allegiance is utter and when it comes to trouble he will turn towards shore without hesitation.

Holly is on the dock as the Rosie ties up to the bollards. With that man she loves, Charlie-somebody, and those hounds that never age, Oberon and Harry. Ridiculous that dogs can get this big and no one notices how strange that is. But then, not so many mortals come to the island nowadays. Not since the Trouble that had been wiped from human history as though it had never happened. Convenient, that. As though Holly's aunt had never been murdered, as though Mercy, not more than a child, had not killed one of the intruders.

This is the first time Maisie Raith has been asked to come. It isn't that Mercy is in trouble and needs the Weary Bay witch to worry. She was originally invited to take the blessing, because Maisie is getting old and her death would be a travesty. No wise woman to cure and curse in Weary Bay? No enchantress to save another little runaway? Because Our Ladys is not done yet. Not yet. But soon. And that is reason enough for the maladies of winter to be taken away by the *Quicken* medicine.

Maisie had complained, once or twice, to the ravens along the cove, of her aching bones and it was they who'd informed Brighid who told Hunter who summoned the fáidh, and the mortal lost (who had been found) from all over the country because this once there was not one enemy but two. And one of the two was as vast as the sky is wide so is unkillable, holistically, for now, but not its agents of despair. That, the faerie could ensorcel into kneeling. Would. The spotlight of delusion is bright now that Agnes, Mother Superior, has it pinned by her death.

But amidst all the drama Maisie told them all, *no thank you, maybe one day.'*

I'll come, she'd said, *but I won't do the forever medicine without Mercy.* And the faerie respected her but she had lived how she had lived without questioning and without thought for reward. For the love of a motherless girl. And this time of year when the Mystery is to be brought back to Inishrún in the flame of summer' brightness Maisie is to witness. She is granted this advantage while she lives. It is all Hunter and the faerie have to offer her that she does not already have. Is not already being.

Maisie is aboard the Rosie Rua, riding the prow like she watched that movie and figures there's a DiCaprio somewhere, even if simply her imagination. Kept in line, under the shelter of the bridge and curled like a kitten for warmth within the massive tow ropes, is Artful Dodger. Now he knows. And finally, he remembers how to sleep at night, so tired from training his weak and undernourished body that simply eating fish from the day's catch resulted in grumbles and hurt, as what remained of his teeth pained him so badly that he'd taken the compound the witch had made and slept, drugged into oblivion, through the extractions, keeping just enough unsullied teeth in his mouth to remember how to chew. He'd grow new ones soon enough.

Every possible car and tractor are up on the one street, walled from the roaring winter sea, as the troupe exit the turnstile on the wharf and load what luggage and instruments are necessary. The old priest, once the enemy of such misbelieved phenomena as magic, holds Artful's arm and mumbles kindness to him as the confused lad follows up the road on foot. All the way past the old and abandoned church with its standing stone and its weathered grave markers attesting that once upon a time humans also inhabited the island. All long dead.

Clans have come from everywhere. Maisie has no idea how they get here because they hadn't been on the boat. But she is so used to them all arriving around the time of Samhain, playing tunes at the pub and buying the local produce that she doesn't really question. Tents are erected and totemic pennants for wolf and boar, eagle and wren, bear, stag, raven, gull and stoat crack in the icy wind after the fires are lit, and hounds and horses gambol in search of offerings as is fitting their kind.

Inishrún is a seeming illusion. A little like the legend of Tír na nÓg, island of the ever-young where Oisin, the son of Finn McCool and the part-white doe, part-woman named Sadhbh went, a hint at shapeshifting that all faerie and all First Nation elders know about, for love of a faerie royal, and who thought he'd been gone just a few hours when time, outside of the madness of clocks and watches and computers, is as peculiar as the story of a virgin giving birth, which is odd enough without adding that it has to be believed to save a body from burning.

Inishrún is, at her foundation, granite. She is forty seven miles from tip to tail, and somewhere between sixteen and twenty miles at her widest girth. Inland is almost impossible to access as she is bordered by potentially unscaleable escarpments except for three miles on either side of the village that collapsed the absoluteness of the fortress in some distant cataclysm, the huge oddly rectangular rock dominos laying one upon the other. This is the most easterly aspect. A single cove that is the only sheltered anchorage. Three high, steep hills that the inhabitants called the Bens shelter pasture where black *bó chiarraí* cattle graze undisturbed, their women coming to the villagers for milking and, on occasion, for midwifing in the case of a difficult birthing.

Amidst the dense, untouched forest, doire-thick and holt, deer still graze, protected by tradition, and badgers, voles, small tan pigs and other creatures, root amongst the leafmeal and musgan left over from after Lamas, rustling unseen or else cackling, trilling and hooing in the thick overhead canopy.

The journey from the wharf to Holly Tremenhere's house, the caretaker of both the ogham tree covered mound called the Barrow and the eolithic henge at the base of the cliffs used, occasionally for ceremony before interment of the finally-dead sídhe, is five miles by narrow rutted road. A long unavoidable walk by those without horses, since the only car on the island died for lack of a mechanic not long after Holly took her place with the draíocht elders and ancestors. Holly is queen of Inishrún, the only human other than the old priest and Charlie, in the know about the fact of the place. Its impossible sanctity. The deep sadness and despair that brings faeries here to live out finally aged years until a form of demise. If they manage the journey after all. None are from New Rathmore, the city being too far. No. That work, of caretaking and responsibility is forsaken.

Maisie is sat atop one of the big horses, with Artful tied to her waist to stop him from falling. He has never known of horses and his anxiety would spook the most easy-going mount if not for Maisie's whispers. Almost a Clydesdale but not. No saddle, simply woven and embroidered blankets of linen and grasses one atop the other and a mane to hold for comfort. The day is coming on the pale grey of what constitutes twilight, just before four o'clock in the afternoon, as the group from the boat converge with the island inhabitants. They have shed the look of old people and shine in their haunting glory with eyes that can elfshot an intruder and clothing of brocade and bronze, riding high upon white horses that *do* have saddles, made from the finest hide of long-dead ancestors, that know exactly who they are, their front legs rising and falling almost in dance, the bells on their reins catching the coming night breeze in concert. The old priest amongst them on his dun Galloway, as proud, now that he knows, as any prince of any church anywhere.

The entrance to the Barrow is half a mile from the farm, out on the moor, hidden by rock and thistle, but the horses stop to graze closer to Holly's cottage so all dismount where light spills from the kitchen door into the gloaming. Holly, diminutive and gamine, is accompanied by a tall, gangly ginger haired man who has her wrapped in his arms as though he is her shawl, requiring no warmth other than his love. Two dogs: Oberon, a crossbreed wolfhound whose withers reach to Holly's chest and Harry, as pale and shorthaired as the mastiff mother who bore him, gamboling suicidally around the legs of the thirty-something horses, their tongues like limp sea creatures hanging from sloppy, smiling lips.

Hunter is the first to dismount and he proceeds to Holly and lightly bends the knee.

She ignores the gesture, pulls detritus from his dreadlocks but leaves the little feathers where they should be. She doesn't even try to look like some regent, preferring her tatty, functional overalls and the hip high waders she wore in the morning just gone where she realigned stones in the *hellier* on the edges of some wildness that this winter has dislodged. Spawning ground to salmon who make the dark Atlantic current crossing and who are in need of ancient respite.

She and Charlie are introduced to Maisie. Holly vaguely remembers her playing the mandolin, once, at a local craic, but whose fullness of purpose is discussed in a clipped sentence or two, words being almost meaningless chatter to Hunter. Of Artful he says nothing, merely directs the stunned and overawed lad to Charlie who never enters the Barrow out of guilt for how he was almost responsible for what had happened there once. Invaded and desecrated by unbelievers over a decade ago. The two enter the cottage with instructions from Hunter to explain what Artful thought only tales once told to dumb children. To wake him from the cruel dream of who he thinks he is.

Then the lad is to come.

The others troupe to the Barrow entrance like a pattern of clouds and in utter darkness move through the blindness and out into the wideness of a vast phosphorescent-lit chamber of such uncanniness that Maisie feels the spectral glisten of the once living, like hairs raising along her arms even from deep within her bulk of clothing. Niches nursing skulls hung with tannin'd faces so that their original skin color is in defiance of racism, the forever-ink faded into patterns she cannot hold in her mind's eye. Each niche is adorned with bones and berries, delicate crane skin bags, sgian-dubh that would have been worn by the faerie during their lifetime, whittled birds, bears, seals and many-tined deer. Talismans in bronze or gold, jet and amber. Twigs and tiny branches windblown from the ogham tress above, bundled together and bound in red thread. Stained with white ochre or the blue dye of woad. A dolmen stone lies like a sleeping giant at the center of the cavern, covered in the stubs of a million burned-down candles.

Quiet.

That's the thought that soothes Maisie's overstimulated brain as she is sits on the ground between Brighid and Black Annis, to what? Keep her still? To stop herself from falling when there's nowhere to fall? Somehow Maisie recognizes each sensation simultaneously, while both the other women leak humor and swift-mindedness, swallow-thoughts darting between them, needing no words.

And then Hunter comes in all his bigness. Swathed in a cloak made of the pelts of incalculable dead other-species cousins, that smells of old age and birth and straining against chains, of whales breaching the southern oceans and mammoths and kisses and petrichor. And he is the quietest of everything.

In New Rathmore, deep in the devastating blackness of the McLean Street Bridge underpass, Raven is held in the arms of a cop who, he doesn't fully understand yet, is hooked into this weave of complex tapestry. The dark faerie weeps and weeps because he should have followed Sparrow and Artful. Should be there, deep under the earth, with his bodhrán and his song and his savvy, and not be pretending to be a man with no real name because he is so afraid for the human race of creatures, even though he is aware that destiny is not in his hands. And Waubun cradles his perp knowing something, knowing something odd that seems like an answer to why he is still alive, and not being able to put his finger on it. On the southside Déjàvu assists the volunteers who run the delivery van dole out extra blankets and coffee and soup, sensing that the ice vortex could come again real soon and getting these folk as safe as possible. Before she disappears back behind the closed door of the Wallace Hope Plaza studio, now breached by one oddness named Mercy Riley, and another called Revel. Wondering, by all that's potentially sane, where the fuck Sparrow has gone this time.

Agnes rolls over in her grave, patient now.

Maisie is unsure of what to do and how to behave but Brighid picks at her cardigan with thin birdlike fingers and frowns a little, the knot between her brows scrunching as though she is serious when, like Annis, that would take a lot more than mere complexity to evoke in either woman. No, she frowns for the theatricality, and it works, because Maisie is calmed.

'Just witness, witch,' whispers Annis. 'Seems there are patterns in the Mystery's loom she wants disguised for now. It won't last. It never does. One cataclysm or another works out the kinks so just watch. And know. The stories are all true.'

All Maisie can do is try to suppress every folktale she has ever heard tell of, or read, wondering whether she has lived a lifetime missing the point of the Travelers, after all, as Artful sits and cradles her hand.

Hunter moves, eventually. He rests the palm of each wide hand on either side of Dodger's confused face.

'Time's up, *meaigín*.'

Hunter's cheek is beside that of his captive, his lips to the other's ear, and he whispers the name that no one else hears. The light comes back into Dodger's face and his *shine* is eyewatering.

'Oh,' he says to Hunter. Knowing that a magpie is exactly what he is.

25

UNSHRIVEN UNDEAD

SLÚAGH

There is no one alive, not human anyway, who knows everything. No one knows much at all. People learn what they are taught by other people because the retaliation paid onto a body who questions some unwritten status quo is always the threat of banishment. And for most other animals that is certain death. Or the rejected animal becomes forgetful of the manners and mannerisms of their own kind and change. Usually resulting in unfavorable outcomes.

Once upon a time Sparrow had thought that if she took her knowledge of the abductions and the beatings, the rapes and the blood and the unshriven buried to some authority or other she could actually do something to get Our Ladys spotlighted. Closed down. The prisoners freed. Thought it possible that some potential legal authority could enforce an enquiry into conditions, the practices of shame and brutality, the disappearances of both the women and the children. The foundlings (the nuns said that, of the babies as soon as they were torn or forceps from their mothers' bodies, never lost in the first place) and the illicit sale of whichever infant fits the criteria and bank accounts of those who wanted to own a person.

She went to the police station in the heart of New Rathmore

city and asked to speak to someone about murder and abduction. She had been assigned an office, several uniformed officers, two detectives, a photographer and a video operator.

The stirrings had given her courage. She had initially mentioned her concerns for the safety of women and children under threat, imprisoned without crime by some organization of which she was unsure. The sergeant of the desk had asked for her name, and she lied. Like Raven, no last name, never did have, so she used Déjà's. They asked for her residential address so she said she lived at Déjàvu's studio in the Wallace Hope Plaza, sending out telepathic messages, in hope filled thinking, that her mentor would get out. Just in case.

Déjàvu was not there when they had come. Sparrow, in all her wildness and mystery was unprepared for what happened. She had been asked for next of kin. Her date of birth. What day it was. Could she please provide identification? Everything, on that busted up broken Thursday several years ago, had been a setup. No one had considered the odd-looking, possibly drug-fucked, potentially iced off her head, skinny woman to be telling the truth. What did she want? She must have known that this crazy story would get her sectioned. It wasn't ten minutes into the interview when, as placid and pacific as she was behaving, the social workers in plain suits and saccharine smiles entered without knocking. They had two young men with them in the uniforms of paramedics and everyone had been gentle. Everyone tried to be calm. Tried to be calm. But it took the brute force of all of them to hold her down and administer the shot.

Slúagh, she realized as the sedation took away the day. She should have known they'd be watching for her and from far away. As she slid into the darkness she heard some odd sound. Something or someone in a state of satisfaction. And she comprehended that evil was everywhere and that it would never stop hunting and of course the nuns would be in league with the unseelie court. Our Lady of Perpetual Sorrow Mother and Baby Home was too potent an ugliness and lucrative an undertaking to not be in the employ of wicked forces.

Sparrow doesn't remember exactly her duration in that next institution, but she does remember doing the runner. She wasn't meant to get away from there, just as she was not supposed to be able to escape Our Ladys. In some weakly lit area, behind, or under, or in proximity to conscious thought, but dimly, came the image of Houdini who she'd read about in some old magazine. She was exhilarated. It was peculiar though. The doors hadn't been locked, there wasn't a guard, no razor wire, no alarm system. Surveillance cameras? Of course. When she had walked all the way to the docks on the southside and hidden in Dimity's, out back under the winter-barren tea roses that straddled the old brick wall, someone with dyed black hair and deeply seductive red lips had brought her a sweet tea without her asking. Hadn't said a word. Had a *shine* about her as strong as that of the faerie folk but wasn't one of them. The silence was a respite. Sparrow had realized what the consequences of invasive questioning could do to a creature like her and all thoughts of being a hero deserted her that day.

She didn't hear from Déjàvu from winter that year till winter this year. The big black woman's studio had been raided, a warrant produced, and her bogus ID scrutinized. It's a fine thing to know pirates, she understood. When the original owner of the premises, a woman called Wolf Kain, had met her, they had negotiated Wolf's disappearance and her contacts had produced forged papers and visual identity documents that had erased her. And built Déjàvu. For that knowledge to have been potentially scrutinized by a bureaucratic microscope was as close to a betrayal as Sparrow could imagine.

She was mortified at the possible consequences of her attempt at self-protection through using the name and details of the woman who saved her life as a cover. If Déjàvu had been a vengeful loa she would have destroyed Sparrow for incriminating her, but Sparrow is not of her people.

Déjàvu had repaired the broken front door to her studio, fixed the lock, cleaned up the overturned and disturbed search abuse and ascertained the cops had not broken through the spell of invisibility that hid the crypt next door. Her collection, not Sparrow's. Not ever. She had told Mercy what she did to give the kid a sense of significance. And also, to shut her up and get rid of her. Because of her impenetrable silences. Because she knows, in the gut of herself, that she is correct.

Isn't the truth sometimes the greater hurt? she thinks, burying the notion as ludicrous as soon as it has clawed to the surface.

Sparrow is allowed her drawing book and crayons. She is not permitted pencils, so her articulation is dulled by the inaccuracy of the tools at her disposal. But the images are recognizable. These are the slúagh. The face they are hunting is that of their intended next victim is no longer hers. From the prison of this white room, she draws a young man with gold in his earlobes, glossy black hair in two long, leather-bound braids, and a face that is, as is the brutal but honest truth of farseeing, as androgynous as some renaissance painting. She now has to work out how to get the pictures to Déjà. There is no one else she knows.

When she'd dared leave Dimity's for the streets in search of her mentor the slúagh had caught her after all. This time she's locked in an isolation unit and while she awaits her chance to give her captors the slip it takes all her concentration to remain herself as the Thorazine causes its havoc, making salivation impossible and a weakness to her resolve that she has never known in her life.

This prison of white is an oxymoron for an unseelie dungeon. It is almost nice.

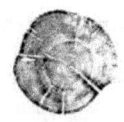

ACT 2

26

COME AWAY, O HUMAN CHILD!

RAVEN

Waubun unmoving. The smells of rain and ice and the river and the small dead creatures that float on the outgoing tide, eddying and expanding like some seemingly irrelevant banquet for the creatures of the wide sea. Intoxicating and repulsive. Food for mackerel and the whales that ride the oceanic laneways crisscrossed with the interference of shipping, crews of mainly men utterly unaware of the forests of mother kelp far beneath the huge, disruptive hulls, where the seeds and eggs of an unborn universe move in currents similar to those that transport spent plasma towards the heart of the sun to be recharged and then reborn; salt, phytoplankton, marine viruses and bacteria, krill and minute arctic cod all nourished by everyone and everything that seem, to the limited eyes of humans, dead and decaying. Some oddness of perspective that I will never understand.

I was born, I think, from the first cobbles that spewed from mother volcano as earth formed and groaned and broke and reformed and was rent and filled those tears with ocean. I love, with an immensity that is impossible to describe, the ways of gneiss and feldspar, red arctic lichen, the smells of autumn breaking down summer, the pull of North Atlantic Drift. I am the breath of the first snow to dust a moorland, noctilucent cloud that sometimes gets trapped in the colourwind of magnetic distribution of ionic particles, and kelpies, that gale-whipped-backward mane of white water from which legends spring, of wild wave spirits, white horses with magic in their eyes summoning the unwary from a battered shore, only to drown in breunloch, bog or léig-cruthaich, who are also me. And ancestors. Do I spring from ancestors? Funny, that. And a really dumb question but that's because she distracts me.

I am the microscopic valleys between the clickety clack of stacked, flat white rock, out on Inish Mór. I am both the protector and destroyer of worlds. Some no larger than Mercy's or Waubun's thumbs, some so enormous that I am mute in any attempt to explain a love affair with anyone. So why humans? And horses, and dog-people like Revel? Why do I bother? Why is love so obvious to me and yet so cruel when it is limited only to a shallow experience of a year or two or ten million, when I know love and love transcends the exquisite drift of continents?

'You in there?' Sparrow asks. She is not nice. I know why. Am I to say I'm sorry when I'm incapable of remorse? Should I say I honor you when I don't care to, even though I do? She is disinterested. A distractedness to her eyes. I know that look. It would ruin me if its intensity was the truth but that's not what I know this to be. This is heartache. Some people who have been broken heal so beautifully I swear the hoarfrost is giving, and that it has delicately bound her wounds with mallow and willow and the Silurian vividity of mosses so green that they are grace to the underside of cliff cave stone stories. So, I sigh, instead, knowing nothing I say can change where Mercy is right now. But assured that she knows me, and my relatives of sand and lime and brick and mortar, and she has offered them assurance of some kind of freedom that she doesn't even recognize. Such gentleness. Such fury. So much hope and such capacity for killing that my admiration overflows and I'm in flood. Fooken faerie shambles.

'Give me a hand, will you?' Waubun pleads, getting his arms under my shoulders. Sparrow creakingly picks me up by the ankles so my bum drags across the asphalt. They lift me into a sitting position and I resign myself to waking into the grayness of sleet-lit daylight. In the careless yet wanton demanding of these people.

'Fuck off the pair of yiz.' But they ignore me like I'm only thinking, not moving my mouth.

'You are my weapon.' Sparrow, her tone flat, is somehow threatening. And now it's a moment of confusion. Weapon? I have no such thing. I have canniness, and a capacity to realize things in advance because they're not quite ready to happen. Compassion, to a degree. But no weapon.

'I'm lost, *mo chroí*,' I say, bending what I'm really feeling just a bit.

'I am incapable of forgiveness, Raven. Or are you just another dumb fuck, after all?'

'I have no weapon.'

If Waubun's head could do the kind of twists owls can, it would. Looking from one to the other of what, to him, are really peculiar people is making him nauseous. 'Is this some kind of code? And what's your name, love?'

Both Sparrow and I ignore his police-issue question rulebook tone of voice but Sparrow rests a hand on his as though to reassure the cop that she is aware of him.

This entire conundrum, of whose making she has no idea, is a patchwork of briar and thistle and thorn, with under it all a trapped something that she needs to release. Mercy, an investment in justice. Years of learning from the Travelers and particularly Black Annis, from Maisie. Even the schooling spewed out at Our Ladys of what-not-to-do, and the art of exclusive and guileless cruelty, haven't provided her the skill necessary to kill an unnamed bogle of such immense vaguery. I feel her. Every thought. And each is as complex as the withering process of aging.

'I'm sorry,' I pretend. 'I don't remember much of anything.'

'Liar.' Sparrow's tone incites a warning growl from Revel. He doesn't arc up because he knowns what I am but his love for this woman, this friend to Mercy, is at least as strong and indestructible as mine. Even she is confused that he is not on his feet and preparing to bite my face off. 'You know who I am. You remember everything. At least treat me like I'm not some poor lost soul.'

'Aren't you?'

She shifts the black cordura bow case she has been getting to

Mercy, by way of Merrin, further onto her back. Now her hands are free. 'No. I might have been when you were around but that was a long time ago, Raven.'

'His name's Birdie,' says Waubun, hopelessly out of his depths.

'Sorry, Henry.' I drop my chin a bit so as to look as contrite and threatless as I can. He doesn't buy it.

'You been playing me, son?'

'Too old to be anyone's son, son,' I say. Hard for me to keep a straight face.

What's today? Wednesday? How long have I been out of action? I'm working hard to make any sense of what Sparrow means, and where Waubun fits into any of it. I'm a mess of fractured mirrors. Out of nowhere I remember Mercy. At the bus that first day. How much I wanted to hate her; the ache. The familiarity. That I knew her. No, I didn't. Did I know her mother? Her grandmother? Was I in love with one of them and that's why I reacted like I did? It's not incest. Is it? She is *not* human, not sídhe. What then? What if I'm wrong? Because where the feck, otherwise, does her *shine* come from? Never met a human with the *shine* so I wonder. I admit to the most confusion I have ever known and that's as ridiculous as saying this wet, killable slurry isn't snow. Then what?

'Okay,' I accede, 'so, say I am a weapon. Is that it?'

'No. Yes. Sort of.'

Waubun's knee ligaments make the sound of pain as he stands

and stretches his atrophied limbs, shoving mittened hands into his armpits in an attempt to prevent frostbite. 'Can we maybe find a diner? We can keep talking someplace warm. Please. I'm due to report in, and I have no idea what I am supposed to say about you, Raven, Birdie, Whatever. Or you, little miss whoever you are. So give a cop a break here. And please, also—' He helps Raven to his feet and tilts his head towards Sparrow's spindle-thin body, 'is that a rifle in the bag?'

'Bow,' says Sparrow. 'It's legal. A gift for a friend. Who are you, by the way? This is not police business.'

Henry Waubun has me. My arm is pulled tight over one shoulder so that my ribs feel like they're being butterflied like in the old Viking era. He drags me up the incline, away from those poor sad ended men out of it already with the light not even at day's zenith. Up the littered incline and over the guard rail. The road is eerie without traffic. Sirens in the distance attest to the city being wounded by the storm, but not terminally. Be a surprise to me if there is a café open anywhere but I'm wrong. We find a diner not two blocks away with its little neon *open* sign, flashing red and green like some parody of festivity, that allows the hound in because why not?

There's no other trade so the old man behind the counter is on his knees, giving Revel chin-scratches. His smile is beatific by the time he returns behind the counter, his eyes moist with memories. He's on his own, so he takes our order. I'm as ravenous as a man due for the gallows and even though he starts off pretending he's able to remember what we ask for he pulls out his little jotter when I get to the part of reciting a list of way too much food for a seeming weakling. And coffee. Lots of coffee.

'Why won't you trust me with your name?' Waubun has slid as far into the vinyl-covered booth seat as he can without actually touching the window, afraid that if he does, he'll stick to it. I have a momentary smile at images I've seen of people licking lamp posts when the weather is freezing but I don't say anything. 'What's your real name, Sparrow?'

'Who is he, to want to know my business?' She holds my gaze and it's unsettling. I'm unsure which eye I should be focusing on so I shift back and forth. She's indicating Waubun.

'Henry, no point asking her who she is. I don't even know why you're still here.'

'No way am I ever going to sleep again till I work you lot out.' Wabaun leans his elbows on the Formica benchtop and toys with the teaspoon. 'Besides, I got a feeling.'

I don't finish his sentence for him. Neither does Sparrow. Maybe he's right. There's a *something* about the man that is so stoic, so sheltering. 'Henry,' I begin, a bit distracted because I can smell the fry-up, aware I am using the coming pejorative intentionally, 'Do you believe in faeries?'

Merely discussing how we, as land and wind and river, valley, massif, shoal, hawk-hide and partridge-covey, dragon-lines of wolf trails and deer migrations, snow goose formation, and wrack upon a shingle beach from a drowner storm, have been lied about, in this current era of belittlement, and daunting. We have been alluded to as preposterous a phenomenon as any religion or misleading folktale. Waubun thinks quietly. I can hear every thread that exposes its authenticity from his ancestors' stories that he once considered trivial, or childish at best. I can't lie. Did I tell him that? He is getting his head around it, is all. The missionaries, Artful's minder, that thinks it's a slúagh and is after me, and doesn't know I know.

The Monstrum that invented it all so outstandingly uglily, Henry knows about them. He knows the pride of one whose family lived—made it—despite how perilous the forced marches and slaughters knowledge of the maelstrom of attempted genocide that has delineated the past few centuries.

'This weapon—' Waubun directs his attention to Sparrow, as unaffected by the deep warmth of her eyes as others are undone, 'don't fuck with me, okay?'

Sparrow is impressed at his grit, despite a universe of thought and calculation and consideration of consequence, but this has to come to an end. She has a destiny to ravel. Her target, the whole of it, has never deviated and this is a diversion. A big one, admittedly, but woven into some vaulted tapestry she will not comprehend until the threads are all woven.

'This is Hunter's fault,' she says. Flat. No answer required. Henry sucks on his second coffee as I deduce the math.

'That lad is performing. Something's peculiar.' I've pieced as much of this together as I can, so far.

'Artful?' She knows exactly who I mean.

'He was recruiting. That's his job.'

'Birdie, not fair.'

'Sorry, Henry, this is about language. I made a song. Music. I wrote the code into the computer at the New Rathmore Central Library. I reckon somebody like Artful hacked it and now they want me. I—' I stop before I say too much. 'And yeah, it's Raven, not Birdie.'

'Well fuck you Birdie, take me deeper. I'm getting a sense of this but so what? And 'I' what?'

'I can enchant stuff, Henry.' No point screwing with the man's mind. He's too important. I don't know why yet, but I sense it and I'm rarely wrong. 'I have to. It's my nature. Ensorcel and salvage. And Artful needs freedom just like I need to spellbind or release. The only way I know how to do that is with beauty, even when I get in the fooken way.' I see Sparrow in the periphery of all this. Some density of grief like the thorns of a Sleeping Beauty story distorting her for mere moments. I see the wound again, and I feel the dread like a wasp swarm.

'So, you did what?' Henry asks.

Revel's head is relaxed on his front paws but he lays his ears back. If I move a little too quickly, or probably if I move at all, he will be on me. And he is as much the spirit world as any of Scáthach's hounds, even Cú Chulain.

'Set a trap.'

'And we are to deal with what you found?' he asks, knowing the answer before I admit it.

'Deluded fuck, is what he is. Why the Mystery wants him on

the loom, I'll never understand. She knows when there's a warp in the pattern of consequence however. Even I can never see that deeply into the salmon pool.

'Is this supposed to make sense?' Waubun is a patient man. I've already got that. But I need to let Sparrow know she can trust me.

'There's a place gathering the words and wisdom of elder tribes,' I explain patiently. 'Replacing them with lack. Missionaries been traveling the world telling indigenous people their language is shit, or diabolical, or inferior, or whatever else they can think of to wreck the esteem people have for places, and wisdom that's been the minutiae of how they live with earth, forever. Was one of your people, Henry, said *You've got to know your language to understand your culture.* Some slúagh, it seems, although the intelligence on its true form is inconclusive, thought he got it all figured out. Wants some kind of power, like certain humans, that's as delusional and perverse as any dumbfuck ever. He's akin to one tree left standing in some old growth forest, and that's got to be a travesty. Gone bad. Like dead flesh in high summer. Hurt our little friend in the cruelest way I can think of. I've gotta be careful I don't meet him because then I'd be trapped. Because I'd care. You're in the thick of how this plays out, Henry. Mystery doesn't want him dead, he's a distraction. The real crime includes him as some kind of victim.'

'And despite none of what you just said meaning much of anything you're after him, anyway?'

'Yes.'

'What do you have to do with his game? What's Dodger got

to do with any of this? How is he relevant?'

I study those eyes. Dark as mine. Hold the wolf in 'em. Eagle. Caribou. Just about everybody. And I realize he knows, but he's learned to not ask so many questions he'd lose his badge over it. But he's lost more'n that, I know that. Some keenness. Some deep relentless grief, so I don't make him suffer. 'Artful is like me. That's what I have to do with this. Your other questions sit inside that first one.'

'He wants you because you're creating language on what's left of the internet? You shitting me?'

'Happens.'

'What?'

'People need other people to agree with them. Otherwise, who are they?'

'I could be considered way out of my depths here but—and this is just quoting you, Birdie—that he's not quite 'people'.'

'We can't live if we're alone. We'd shrivel and blow away. Become a face in a burial mound somewhere. Same with earth. She doesn't get her sweet words for gryke and cruach she's gonna rain and drown us. Or build up magma like a woman in labor and islands're gonna disappear. Someone describes greatness as gr8 and we've lost the ladder. Can't get out of the burning building, can't save the child fell down a well. Can't pick apples.'

'And so, you wrote a song.'

'In the old tongue. Yes. I hate it, Henry, but it's not for me.'

'And the music is to take someone down somehow?'

'That's not how this is to play out. Maybe. But there's more to it. This is not so simply put.'

Sparrow slides a delicate, blue veined hand across the expanse between her and the cop. With her eyes she indicates that she wants his leftovers. He slides the plate to the middle of the table beside the salt and the mustard squirt bottle. 'The music's a gift,' she says, shoving half the food into her mouth and sliding the rest across to Revel who has his chin on her knee. 'Raven's music'll relax the world, eh Revel?'

Revel is on his feet, his ears informing her that he is preparing for walkies. Or attack. Whatever. I'm ready to go. Everything broken inside me has knitted or filled with clean blood and bright life. 'You coming?'

'Hang on, Birdie. Where was Dodger was taking you? Do I need backup?'

I laugh. He's sincere. Slow, but sincere. 'Is the food on you?'

Waubun codes his quick response ID into the diner owner's transaction device, paying for everything on his work permit. I owe him, now.

'Where's Mercy?' I ask, as Sparrow stands to leave.

'That's not your business, Raven. You forswore that privilege years ago.'

I don't understand everything yet. That's all.

27

ⅢⅠ— ᵤ·ⅢI—ﬀﬀ ᵤ—ⅢⅡ— · ᵢᵢ—Ⅲ.ⅢⅠ Ⅲᵢ —·—ᵣᵢᵢⅢ

ᵣ—ﬀﬀᵢᵢᵢⅡ. ﬀⅢⅡ——ᵢᵢᵢ ·ᵢᵢᵢᵣᵢᵢ ᵣᵣ—— ·ᵢᵢᵢⅡ ᵢᵢᵢ¹—·Ⅱ—

THE WATER, LIKE A WITCH'S OILS,
BURNT GREEN, AND BLUE AND WHITE

MAISIE RAITH

'What's it done now?'

Barney Rumford has been up since just after four. He's on his second cup of coffee when the phone rings shrill and threatening from the wreck of a parlor that was set up to be a nice place to sit a day away when the actuality of a day away had seemed probable. It'll never happen now. Since his and Janey's son drowned, since Scáthach and Holly moved in their abandoned cottage across the brook, since the debacle with the murder on the island had upended the world, Barnie works until he drops.

He waits for Maisie Raith to ask him for help again. That fucken Defender. A sickening yellow. Old 1958 Series One job. Long wheelbase. It had been her project for over a year, way back when, because she didn't want a computerised vehicle. Suggested that if anything went awry she wouldn't know what to do. She'd acquired tools and insisted she'd be buggered if she had to rely on the mechanic in Brokeshire. That'd cost a tow truck that she could not afford as nobody paid her in actual cash. Maisie is single-minded in her determination to know most everything. He has to admit that the witch had done it, learned about the beast of a vehicle right down to the wiring. But she always does this. Turns on the ignition and walks away. Leaves it in idle *to warm up*. And there is a moment, just a mere few seconds, where that process outdistances its usefulness and cooks the coil.

'I've healed an albatross,' she begins. 'His wing was cut pretty deep with fishing line, but he's all healed up and he's in the crate. Got to get to the jetty before dawn. Sorry Barnie.'

'Bring the tractor?'

'Please.'

He replaces the handset in the cradle, downs the dregs of the coffee just as the toast pops. Janey is not in any mood to talk to him when she comes in. He hasn't lit the Aga. Thought she'd sleep for another hour so he figured there'd be time. Now she'll be pissed at him all day. He knows that things between them would someday come to a head. It's not that he wants to be a bastard, just that Barney still can't get himself to accept that the little woman is so much more. He wants them to be like the other old couples: work, eat a meal with the family, go to church on Sunday and take a little wreath to the funerals. Drink a Guinness and watch telly. *Bout time*, he thinks down in the darkness of his mental cellar, *that you wept, Barney*. But he can't. A man does not cry. Even when his only son dies. Even when he has to bury an empty coffin up on the headland where no fisherman was ever lowered into sod. Janey knew. She'd known. And he'd ridiculed her. Tealeaves can't predict a thing like that. He'd been so certain that he hadn't talked his son around.

He'd let him take the boat out even though the barometer was dropping at an alarming rate. *I know the sea*, Barney Rumford had assured himself.

'Maisie's got a bird needs wilding,' he says, by way of an excuse. Janey ignores him, builds up the starters, lays in the kindling and gets the old stove going. She still prefers the iron to the electric jug. Says the tea tastes completely different. He knows she's right but Barney is not, even after everything that's happened, a patient man.

Janey primes the pump and hefts the handle until the tap flows. She fills the battered kettle and lumps it on the hotplate closest to the chimney, the one that will taste the fire first.

'Am I to come?' She knows the answer but wants to break the tension.

'She's got some city lad to teach to be his true self and she's also got two more dogs to heal.' She's clutching the chook cup and spooning in the tiniest drizzle of honey, aware, somewhere, that any sugar is bad for her health and doing the best she can.

'Jaysus,' Barnie is seriously surprised. 'How many's that now?'

'Maybe fifty. Better to die with her than what they've gone through.' Matter of fact, that. Every dog or hound brought to her as a rescue could get her seriously hurt. Not by the dogs; by the men. They scout the left-over media and interstate newspaper notices for these good, kindly folk's ads to rehome their unwanted pets; people who can't keep the animals anymore because they got too big or the owner got too old or too something. They convince themselves this is better than a kill centre. Or the kids went away. *The cost of food is too much in this crisis and please take 'em for free*. It's that last bit. The pretence of the handlers.

The big yard, the floppy-lipped Great Dane that lollops through an expanse of wilderness cooch grass seemingly hanging out for another canine buddy. Sometimes when the disposer of the dog drives away, after the first few minutes of thinking they've done the right thing, the gnawing back-voice hints at what the truth is. What they've just done. The warnings issued on the internet. All too often that got in the way though. Better not to think about the fate of this once-friend. Ripped apart as bait-animals driving the fighting dogs to relinquish any semblance of sanity that might have possibly redeemed them before they tasted blood. In the pit. In the barn. Bad men who tried, once, to be good men; who had lost their families to the food wars and now had to get by with enough money to snort something that would stave off the hunger.

Scáthach's wolfhounds numbered seven. Some descendants, mongrel that they are, are still here, living in packs, like cove hound royalty. What they do, without recourse to pheasant or partridge, is to calm the desperate and the terrified. The ones that Maisie and Janey rescue that need caging first off because they're so scared they'll attack anyone and anything.

They don't remember how to play. Until the children of Cullyn and the others romp 'em into faith again. The perps also use the little dogs. And that's the worst because their wounds are often so deep and ugly there's nothing but to break their necks and wish their tiny souls goodbye with howls and rage and, for Maisie, more than a dram or ten of pirated Laphroag islay single malt whisky.

In the past decade Barney's come to understand that everything he was brought up to believe is untrue. And the most important piece of realization is that women run this town. The odd, the mystic, the warrior, the seer, the witch, the woman behind the bar at the pub, the postmistress, the creatures out of legend that he was once told aren't real. He had that foolishness disappeared out from under him like black ice takes a truck. Never saw it coming, that fateful day the big warrior woman came. The week of craziness when that lovely lass Mim, Holly's aunt, was murdered by those cocaine-fuelled lawyers from New Rathmore out to take the island. The one with the hunting rifle.

Stupid, stupid rich boys thinking they could do what they wanted, could acquire anything with enough kachinkachink, even before the bust. That bald woman out of myth, Scáthach, trained the local kids. With weapons.

Including Mercy Riley.

He remembers it like yesterday. The feralness of the faeries. That big dark man, Hunter. Even that old professor bloke who'd started the whole thing and who died protecting Holly. If he'd read about it in a book he would have laughed at how ridiculous the scenario had seemed. Except it had all been real.

And when the police came down from Brokeshire not a person in town had known a thing. No one had seen what happened. No one had any idea who shot that private security guard from the city. Everyone had been interviewed. No one went to the island though, because the winter storms were in cahoots with the Travelers and not even the Rosie Rua would attempt the mountains of water and ice-rain.

There was always the threat the investigation would start up again someday but because the head man. What was his name? Oh, it was all so long ago, and the coppers got more immediate strife to attend to. He had said that as far as he was concerned it had been some freak hunting accident. He had then gone all schtum because who, by all that's bent and broken, could ever get a straight word out of a lawyer? The case had been stranded and seemingly bottom-drawered.

Barney doesn't feel anything about what happened. What has happened since. Nothing. He is not unmanned. He gets on with the calving and the milking, shearing, butchering, gathering and packaging of eggs, tending the harvest, the bagging of manure for the locals' vegetable gardens and the deals with the independent grocers. It all seems to work like it used to before the crash and the money dried up, except now he knows. And he figured out a while back that he's just like one of those dogs getting rescued. He's had to learn all over again how to socialise. Him and his kin. And his friends down at the pub. All the men. They, also now know. And its settling in a way none of them ever thought it could be. The women do what they do best and neither the men nor the lads question it. They stopped even considering what the pastor said, or the prime minister, or whatever other expert on telly thought they could fix the world because they had a dick. Because they didn't fix a thing. The women did.

'Might need you,' he says, offhand.

'Did Maisie say?'

'She's rewilding the albatross.'

'Right. Five minutes.' Janey heads back into the hall and up the stairs. She returns in dungarees, a barrel-body of woollens and that cream beanie she traded for the extra rooster last autumn.

'You want a piece of this?' Barnie holds out one of the slices of toast and Janey kisses him on the lips, her fingers, as gentle as if she was stroking a robin's breast, running themselves down his cheek and he remembers. Every bit of her. Every year and all the times he disrespected this wife; this woman of such power. He is close to the edge and she knows it. Men don't live long when they don't feel important; when they're called out on the inappropriateness of bullying or apathy. Has he done that? Yes.

Their son's body was never found. That had originally punched a hole in Barney like nothing he'd have believed possible. And he'd seen Nam so the nightmares were already bad. Brutal. It was Scáthach and Janey and Holly, and the faeries, had saved him. Showed him what could be done. The desolation of Mim's sídhe companion, Connor, had shown him what a fine thing it is to howl. To keen. He'd heard the dogs. He'd learned from them about love. And when he cottoned onto how grief is as much a part of living as happiness, he broke. Might never be put back together again. Janey knows. She could be more dangerous than he comprehends but she loves him. She's also learned.

Together they load supplies and contraband medical supplies into the Massey Ferguson and chug on down the windy road into the silent, sleeping village and out along the isthmus to Maisie's place. The witch-woman has the enormous crate up on the pallet near the gate that only ever gets closed when the cows are grazed down from the high country. Not because Maisie's bothered they'll eat the vegetables in her patch but because of the geese. Best way to stampede a herd is threatened geese.

The dark spring dawn is cold but also as soft as a snuggle of ferrets and so the weather is their ally. The crate and a large canvas tote bag are both secured. The mist still far out to sea is rolling in, an ominous sign.

Barnie says nothing about the Defender. He doesn't need henbane slipped into his curry tonight, or even the mushrooms he took last summer when Maisie explained they'd keep him sane, and they did. If she wanted him to work on the motor she'd make an offer and she was going to owe him for this morning's diesel so he knows to shut up.

The three of them heft the covered crate onto the tractor's rear transport tray and Maisie sits with it, the tote bag on her lap. The witch hums a strange version of the *Water is Wide* that always seems the only thing to calm a spooked critter and that she learned from Mercy who'd learned it before her, from a pale women with a dark pink birthmark on her face like a map, back in Our Ladys. Some otherworldly sound deep in the throat that comes out more like purring or growling than song.

They drive down along the retreated tideline, the little dinghies and curraghs moored along the stranded shore with the sea way to ebb, barnacled and scurry-wizened by swarms of small brown crabs, held fast by galvanised pipes driven two foot into the muddy sand with gentle words of apology by the fishermen, and out to the furthest reach of the long finger of stone groyne that protects the little bay from the howl and roar of winter gales. Barnie turns off the ignition and pulls hard on the handbrake.

Up close, when Maisie lifts the cover from the crate, Barney's breath is taken away by the aesthetic ferocity. Every tawny feather is syncopated along the otherwise white body as though someone drew them on with digitally enhanced precision. There is no hint of lovability. If the great bird feels any emotion it is distrust. Distain perhaps. Obeisance. But not fear. There is no fear here. The albatross could take life easily. But one at a time. Not like Barney's lot. Not like his species.

'Get away,' warns Maisie, unclasping the wide door of the crate and joining Janey and Barney behind the mesh, distant from that beak and those talons. He might not be a raptor but he can damage, but he does not. He waddles. Out of the crate and along the narrow neck of the stone jetty to the farthest ledge where he hunkers down, the wind picking up and ruffling the fluff around his eyes. He does not move.

'Mollymawk,' Maisie offers. 'Lost his mate somewhere. He won't go off if the wind picks up or the fog turns to custard.'

'Thought you said it was an albatross,' says Barnie, looking first to Maisie, then to Janey as though for support on such a trivial subject. 'Fuck, it's enormous.'

'Experts thought they were extinct forty years ago.' Janey is flippant as though everyone ought to know this unspoken criticism of such people and she hasn't the time to discuss the lack with dumbasses like him. 'And he's a he, not an it.'

Maisie stomp foots back to the tractor, the cold affecting both her toes and her old knees. She grabs the canvas tote. On the stone she lays out a thermos off tea and thick chunks of pork pie. Mary Poppins-style, she delves deeply into the bag's seeming bottomlessness to extract the tin of fish bits that she carries to the wall's limit, to sit beside the bird.

She opens the tin and handfeeds her healed patient with an intimacy that brings a smile to Janey's otherwise deeply lined disquiet.

They stay for almost an hour. The wind drops. The albatross lifts off like some legend that should be a poem. He spirals higher and higher into the gloom of the stratosphere, gliding the momentarily compassionate thermal towards the island of Inishrún.

'That's odd,' says Maisie, her hand shading her eyes.

'Why?' asks Barnie as he packs away their mess while, understanding, watches without comment.

'Mollymawks're not usually concerned with the faerie island.'

'Maybe.'

'You take me home please Barney?'

'Not gonna elaborate on the Molly-bolly?'

She ignores him, indicating the tractor. 'You want me to back her up for you, Barnie?'

Barnie gives her the finger and she laughs.

He's right though, to ask. He's learned that nothing is necessarily as it seems, and some things are messengers that look like other species. They never are.

Maisie then wanders off alone along the waterline until the fog, now impenetrable, takes her.

'Where you off to?' Barnie asks, knowing the answer would rock him but that he would believe.

'The fog,' says Maisie. 'The boy's to go to the old people on the island.'

'Scare him,' adds Janey. 'It's what you do best. Gets results.'

Maisie, stubby and strong as a tugboat, glides through the density of fog like it is guiding her between worlds. Firstly to the cottage where Artful waits, confused and pretending indifference, his palms clasped between his knees as though in prayer, the cooked rabbit untouched because who eats something that once lived? The wort and fungi-gathering bag slung over her shoulder as she cocks her head to the messy lad in a gesture to follow, where they disappear from mortal sight within the *pogonip*.

Artful keeps hold of the belt at her jeans because he has never experienced this oddity of nature, even though he's seen it on the wilderness channels. His memory attempts to calculate if he's ever seen anyone like her and he has. But they're never clean. And lots of the times their ink is messy, the lines blurred. Borstals, they're called, and mostly tell of gangs or allegiances. Her's, however, are like jewelry. They cover every inch of skin, and she is never without her poisons. She'd been ready. Without her Mercy would not have become free. Without her Mercy would have remained clear of Our Lady of Perpetual Sorrow Mother and Baby Home but she would have remained vulnerable. It is not the way of the Travelers to teach the skills of an assassin but it was Scáthach's and she was still living at the old Rumford farm and even she, with all she has seen of legends and continents and kings and empires, was surprised at the silence and calculatedness of the small albinist child with eyebrows like rook wings and the saddest eyes the druí woman had ever seen.

And yet Scáthach had not asked. She was in synch with the witch and that was sufficient to explain one thing: she was enchanted.

But not the other.

The coldness, the ice in Mercy's never-smiling face, was a warning that Maisie had only ever seen on the faces of the dogs she'd earlier helped rescue. The deeper the wounds the more the hounds smiled, but behind that look they kept their tails between their legs because they knew what no wild canid ever would. Her scars are unhealable. She was born wounded. The pock marks on her otherwise exquisite face are part of her mystery. Scáthach and Maisie both knew those wounds. They are manifest courage. A child forced into becoming a nonentity by carelessness and apathy. Scáthach taught her what was her birthright. Revenge.

Now it's Maisie's work to teach the boy what Scáthach had taught Mercy about killing and self-defence but also what it takes to become himself. That full personal responsibility codec. To get him to understand that the games he's played are just that and that truth can never be had through war, only through agreement and understanding that conquest is just plain offensive. She must firstly, however, make him alive again through wonder. The cunning can come after she's cracked him to expose a germination of *shine*.

28

TUPPENNY HALFPENNY SNEEZE-BOX

ARTFUL DODGER

What the feck. What the almighty fecken feck am I doing here?

'We have a season for everything, Dodger me ol matey. And this is yours.' Annis licks the gummy rim of a thin cigarette and rolls it into itself. She lights it and blows pale smoke into the frigid air of the underground cavern. Me thinkin me balls is gone up into me guts, I'm so cold.

'Are you allowed to do that in here?' I asks, feeling stupid even as I says it. She's a freak, that's sure, and I've met lots of em, but nay like these people. She ignores me so I don't know what to think. I've sat in the dirt here for what? Hours? Days? This has got to be the wildest, craziest, but sorta the most beautiful thing I've ever experienced. Almost better'n DMT.

'What are you, *ten*?' Annis takes a drag through those grand red lips that don't for a second look like they've seen a filler needle.

'Why?'

She laughs rough and loud, more like a trucker than a whore. From the belly. The old fashioned word *guffaw* comes to me mind. 'I can read you, little boy.'

'Then what am I thinking, huh, smart cow?'

'You missing your mummy or something? Ooooh! I'm in the dark! It's been ages! I need a pee!'

'Yis a nasty bitch and I'm lost. Can you just not?'

Her face changes in the shifting light of a thousand or more candles and she is beautiful.

There is something of the coyote in her pointedness. In the way she sniffs the air as if seeking answers from the deep loamy fungal fecundity of this darkness of many thousands of years. Roots like stalactites frozen in their forest death of an aeon gone, unlike the young trees aboveland whose feather-and-taproots lace the ceiling, almost ghostly in the gloaming. I hates her. No, I don't. I dunno what this is.

And then I figure I'm lucid dreaming some Marvel movie. The big man with the black dreads and the quiet voice is back in the room like he's holographic or summat and there's this shadow person with him with the look of the old, old woman with the gingerbread house hook-nose-and-bonnet thing going on. She's got a basket of wet linen on one hip that's cocked out like a chippie on the High Street selling herself for a snort a snow while the other hand is held out in offering, an eerie eldritch flicker that looks, for real, like an actual flame dancing blue, green and purple on the unworried palm of a small child. Just a little thing but enough of a manifestation to blow me fucken mind.

'Who's the old biddie?' I whisper to Black Annis.

'She's doing the *ban-nighe* thing. You know, the Washer at

the Ford story. She always comes dressed up weird.'

'The what?'

'Women who die in childbirth. Or who get buried unwashed. Gives wishes to anyone who suckles from her. Fer fuck's sake, how young are you?'

I turn me head as far in Annis' direction as it'll go without all the ligaments popping from lack of mobility but she's nay laughing at the joke I thought she'd just made coz she's serious faced. And I also nay want to come across as a total dick by letting on how nowt of this makes sense.

'You'd'a have to have heard it from a proper bard. Hush yerself, now.'

Is this enigma? Am I in a mental institution and the drugs are so good I'm actually strapped to a chair in a padded white room in a medicated haze? Equal ingredients of terror, awe, seduction, ridiculousness and hunger for more? Am I going to have to shit meself before I wake out of this thing? Or did I fall in the river and die and this is some confusion of an afterlife?

The big woman with the muscles and the tattoos and the weapons and the shaved head and the herd of fucken huge dogs brings this pleasant straight man over and they both sit with us. Does she live on the island? Lord knows enuff been said about her. I thought she was dead or gone.

'You in there, Dodger?' Scáthach whispers, tapping the side of me head like it's a watermelon, listening for the hollowness. Like I'm supposed to take orders from a pirate. 'This here's the Rowan.'

Me somewhat premature adoration for Annis is shattered as the plain man in jeans and a grey puffer jacket sits beside her and snogs her face off. I want to cry. I am so lost.

'Not,' says Scáthach.

'What?'

'Lost.'

'Fuck.'

'Absolutely not.' She grins and there's gold instead of incisors. She's creepy but so, I should imagine, are pirates. She reminds me of a pirate. Not like me though. More like some har-har-me-harties-type pirate.

'Are you aware of anything that's happening, Artful? Or has all that screen time cooked your brain to porridge? Because if your brain is mush I am going to have to kill you for being a waste of my precious time if you don't buck the fuck up, son.'

I'm on full alert because she says this with totality and I'm under no illusion. She means it.

'Everything is out of whack,' she says, 'and you weren't supposed to get trapped for this long. It's like when the Rowan here, Annis' wee toyboy got dragged to a birthing because it's some kind of natural rule that there is a witness to these most awesome of magics that humans are too dimwitted and churchy to comprehend as anything except lollies for the kiddies, and that idiots call miracles when they don't know where the word comes from. So they make it about some *god* thing, when in truth it's the experience of smiling for no other reason than awe.'

'Okay.' I think this is the stupidest face I've ever worn but she doesn't flinch.

'But you're not one.'

'One *what*?'

'Jaysus,' moans Willie-the-Red from the edge of the giant stone, rolling his eyes and pulling his fiddle from its case.

'Shut up Willie,' yawns Scáthach.

'Or what? You gonna disrespect me like you're doing to this young fáidh, *mo chroí*?'

'I'm just explaining.'

'Arty, laddie, did you get the gist of what she just said?' He plucks at the *e* string but doesn't take his eyes from Scáthach. Is she me jailer? Me captor? I shakes me head. He grins. Scáthach rolls her eyes. Annis snuggles closer to the ordinary bloke and I wish I could just wake the fuck up.

Then it's as if me whole head explodes. About a hundred of the thus-far silent elf-people start on them drums. I must look green or summat because Rowan says, really kind like, 'They're bodhráns. We're on the move, love.' And just like that everybody what is been sitting rise in fluid motion as the old dear and that tree of a man named Hunter lead us back along the subterranean corridor towards the light of night.

I have so many questions, but I convince meself to wait for what happens next. And hope they're not into human sacrifice and I'm the piglet, oink, oink.

Now I'm told about Raven. And the copper. And Mercy Riley, the dog, Merrin, Willie-the-Red, Hunter. Mostly Raven. And why I has to go back. Seems like I can see forever now. Fucken spells of forgetten. Fucken faeries. Sorry. Me own kind, turns out. I can forgive that. Have to. Grudges feel like all I've felt on me back since I was a kid. But I wasn't a kid, was I? Never been other than who and what I am now.

So. It's not me job to mete out justice to Mad Dog after all. That's been set up. Poor bastard. Poor dumb gormless bastard.

This *shine* is better than any coke I've ever had.

29

WHO KILLED COCK ROBIN?

OUR LADY OF PERPETUAL SORROW

Sister Mary Dominic is small. Perhaps only a hundred and twenty centimeters high and weasel-thin of flesh and bone. Her skin is porcelain despite her advanced years, for Sister Mary Dominic is nearing ninety but moves like she's forty. Her face is unlined. Frozen into perpetual righteousness. That of a woman who is sexless and unapologetically so. A plain band of gold on the third finger of her right hand the only metal to touch her, and she habitually rubs her little finger against it in times of deep contemplation. A form of meditation, like casting spells of demand, by rosary, as is done by others.

Not for her that panacea. Sister Mary Dominique has a rat of a mind that she keeps caged and underfed so that its mewl for recognition is barely heard anymore. She is vain. She is proud that she is beautiful when all who surround her are somehow diminished because of her luster. A pearl. A calm sea.

Three small white-clad bundles are lined up on the desk blotter. She applied the wrapping herself, a precise discipline as she is not unlearned. Her father was a military man and her mother dead at her birth. As a girl she had traveled the world and gathered the skill and the terminology of many cultures, beauty alongside absurdities and cruelties. Very young she recognized the seeming dichotomy of the human dilemma. Some cultures seek to transform that which is cracked or shattered by enchantments of gold lacquer, an idea she vaguely admires. However, it means nothing.

The idea of imperfection being transformed through brokenness, as inherently transformative, too stupid to be but a passing reminiscence. These bundles represent the eventual breakage of everything, to her. She does not leave the wrapping to chance just as she does not leave out a single entry, in its traditional and historic detail and written in her exquisitely loopless cursive script, demanding addition to the ledgers. No. When each tiny figure is clean and dry Sister Mary Dominic performs the practice of preparation for disposal with a surgical yet artistic precision. The white cloth is brought in from the country of the linen's origin. She is well aware that it doesn't matter except that her work is that of a bride-in-perpetuity and, somewhat romantically, of an artist. The larger sheet is cut into ninety centimeter squares, her most trusted seamstress hemming each piece with an invisibility of white silk thread. The shroud is ironed and rolled by one of the nuns, never by the girls; never by the unclean. Each is stored in an ancient walnut armoire until the day purpose arrives. As it always does and always has.

Each infant is laid with their head and feet in the direction of corners. Straight and neat, their arms pinned to their sides so that no messy misalignment spoils the exquisite symmetry of the outcome. These corners are folded over the package. First one corner covers the face and torso, next the adjacent corner obscures the feet and genitalia. One corner is then folded over the form, the body tipped slightly to allow the leftover cloth bulk to be tucked neatly under the other side of the object. Then the package is rolled over and over until it is secure within the remaining linen, the final point turned back under itself to complete the process neatly. Bows are attached, bound several times around the core of the bundle to prevent accidental undoing.

Two blue cords, one pink. Clean. Tasteful. Sister Mary Dominic uses a fountain pen so that her calligraphy is not bastardized with anything immodest. Sister Mary Dominic abhors plastic-anything and none is allowed except for the utensils used by the girls when they eat. No need for murder. No need for revenge or self-harm. That's for her maker to decide and she is merely an instrument. She documents the date of demise, any known name of the breeder, whether true or made up being irrelevant, all medications that were of necessity administered to keep the breeder quiet. In case an audit ever happens.

Sister Mary Dominic always calls the diocese in Brokeshire as soon as it is understood that the package is lifeless, on the off chance a priest is available to perform a baptism and extreme unction before the cold sets into the flesh, but they never come. She has not managed to have one body shriven prior to its interment and, therefore, even within the white they are foul creatures that she has done the very best for. She understands. *Limbus infantium* Too young to have committed actual wrongs but not free of original sin. Most postmodern ecclesiastic terminology has changed its tune to say that no child can be condemned for transgressions committed by ancestors' ignorance, but she knows this is merely posturing to entice. To condone. Weakness and populism. Her own dear father would be disgusted. He was an upright and righteous man who had not suffered long when the dementia had sealed his fate. She had learned from their many trips to certain tribal peoples what was food and what was medicine. What was, therefore, available to her in order for her to assist his passing as gently as she could, as befits an only child so doted upon and loved.

She had documented the effect of slow buildup toxins with scientific accuracy. From minute amounts of the seed of the (she loves the title) chalice vine: the initial euphoria, the hallucinations, the endurable seizures and overheating, the urine retention, she had been prepared for all of it. She had nursed him through the paralysis with such compassion as she could glean, before the church had stopped the native practices. She had attended to his dryness. She had prepared his body for the necessity of medical attestation to heart failure, and after the burial she took care of the journals of his travel and exploration. Vaulted for posterity.

Then she had burned that house to the ground and took the vows.

She completes her entry and returns the register to the safe, removing the financial ledger and adding the unfortunate deficit. Three dead infants in two days. Impractical. However, it is what it is and there is no arguing doctrine. Once all is in order she lifts the bundles to within one armpit and carries them out to the field where Sister Mary Bernadette has dug the sod under the north wall, despite the freeze, and it is piled like some mucky discarded peat beside the maw of the winterish pit. Sister Mary Bernadette is mute and as placid as a cow. Usually assigned to the kitchen her brute physical strength is a blessing to a withering old woman such as Sister Mary Dominic. Digging the soil, along with the bucketing the coal for the furnace, is always assigned to Mary Bernadette.

Sister Mary Dominic drops the bundles into the hole casually and simultaneously aware that they are now nothing and sensing that momentary regret, of which she is occasionally perturbed even as she realises the silliness of the emotion, at the waste of good white linen. She slides her shoes over the damp soil, toeing it back into its arcane depths, the spectacle obscuring forever the waste of potential income, aware that the women who pushed the small corpses from those obscene orifices would not be informed.

'Oh look,' she exclaims aloud to no one, delightedly, as the snow comes gently for what is to be the final fall after winter. She often receives validation from on high for the virtue of her work.

And then the skies open with blackness and day turns to night and for the first time in her long life Sister Mary Dominic is truly afraid. *You'll catch yer death*, the women all said, and Sister Mary Dominic is frightened to die because of what will be waiting.

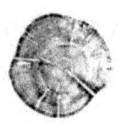

30

I CAN READ EVERY SOUL WHEN I SING IN THE DARK

DÉJÀVU

That's it. There is no escaping this final freeze for the people or the cats or the horses or the puppies that might not, yet, have learned of deep shelter, their dams desperate and confused at this blackness. Black ice, black sky, licorice density to the air. Snow no liberation of paleness or beauty.

What is this? I am seriously spooked by this darkness and I wonder, not for the first time, if there really is a one-god and this one-god is so pissed off at the carelessness of humanity towards mountain and once-thriving ocean, that a back, if a god could turn a back which, considering no form and considering continents and all those tiny, incalculable herds and coveys of limpets that seek shelter in tidal pools, despite any catastrophe, is turned. Of course not. This is earth communicating a need for the blood and tissue and flesh of the once-recognizable animal to awaken, through nourishment, future unborn life.

I ranged, last night, from that breath to that breath as, one after the other, breath ceases. Hidden, quiet, in the basements, in the hospital rooms powered by generators where the ice has taken down the lines and no repair crew possible.

I am called, like Marzanna, like yr Angau, Moddey Dhoo, like Death, and yet that could never be my name because the works of humankind have made me out, as a result of the fears caused by war and the uglification of transition, to be something unclean. I am not. I am a caretaker. Just that. Death is some other hustler's destiny.

Instead, I wander the landward environments and I collect. Yes, the sparkly bit left over from the being of a living animal, the remainder as nourishment for the yet-to-be-born, but I also hear the final exhalation of each terminated faerie who dissolves into unbeing and who had been too crippled or wretched to get to the island before the sadness and the loneliness extinguished their *shine*.

Did I lie to Mercy about Sparrow? Of course I did. We all have stories that we are certain happened. It's only in hindsight that someone else, who may have experienced the same event from another lens or from another way of seeing, gives up *rúin*, secrets, or a more aggressive insight.

I'm a big woman. I'm made up of so many lost and tormented spirits. They're in me. For safe keeping only, mind you, till the day comes they can begin again. Because they will, if the greed doesn't get too tricky and the ground too barren.

This malefic freeze is almost over. For the moment it is a comfort. When the thaw wakes the frozen from the graves of their beds the effect will be terrible, their bling faded to brass, so small mercies are soft. The dead are already dead, so there's no need to collect the corpses. Gone too far into the deep night, and the memory of people who once loved them or feared them or deserted them, I could not be bothered to think of anyone except Sparrow right now. And the last thing I saw her draw; her feet curled up under her for warmth and the bubble jacket almost giving her something like substance.

The sketchpad held at length; towards me. The pupils of her eyes were as big as the sky, but her lips were a warning, bloodless with the fate of this thing, as though she'd just solved the reason life exists and that everything anyone thinks they know is deeply flawed. I didn't want to look, I admit, but curiosity's a curse and she kept holding it up. For comment.

Through the veil of this ground cloud of ice and winter dread, with a face that asked for acceptance but didn't expect it.

I had to see.

Nuns. Kneeling in the stubble of a barren field. In a row. Barbs on a wire. I could see all their virginal, larval faces clear as day with the exception of one.

Seemed almost as though mouse claws had scratched hers right off. And a pale man's body immolated and blown to bits.

'Who you hate with a crosshatch this malicious?' It's one of the creepiest thing I've seen in forever. But she didn't answer me. Then I saw the victims. So many.

'I can help,' I'd said, giving nothing of myself away. She walked through the blizzard like she was a hot knife. Now I know.

And I wonder who should take down someone this appalling as my hands are tied in human affairs. Then I know that will be Mercy. Will be Raven. Someone will bear witness but it won't be me. It's my curse because of what I really am.

31

THE PEACE OF WILD THINGS

ARTFUL

I am to go back. Fucken faeries. No, wait. It's kinda like getting me tongue pierced. All that brightness. Positively nuclear. Then that calm. The intensity of what had been hidden. The beauty. The fucken beauty of us all. And now I has a quest. Mad Dog once said he had a use for me. He was correct. Just not like he thought. What was that? It crawled up me spine when that Mystery shifted to some other shape that swirled with night and colourwind, flitterings, rattling wings, white swans, hunting critters and dreams of things as real as me but said to be a bit of fluff for the kiddies. Excitement? Carelessness? Love? Revenge? All of it. Yes. This rapture is real? Does I truly know meself now? This changes everything. Because yes.

We load onto the Rosie Rua till she leans hard to starboard. Hunter boards last and his sheer bulk shifts the horizon to a line where sea and sky blur, white, glare, white, when he centers up and takes hold of the halyard like ten men should, and raises the mainsail even as Raurie sets coordinates at the helm and oversees the stability of the rigging, the ship sleek as a shark in the icy frothy swell.

I'm sitting with Annis and the Rowan, with Willie-the-Red.

It's a bit funny. Coming across to Inishrún I'm vomiting over the edge like a goose been fed foie gras for rich punters. I dunno what a mind does when the fog lifts so quick and so total but I'm strong for it. A thing I never knew I always knew. I hates the sea, mind, like most faeries, with Raurie being some freak of nature but me guts is comfy and not a skerrick of sugar in em either. And it's all been explained. Letting me think I was a fuckwit, silently shamed.

I been shown what's needed. And to be honest, when I finally got me brain around it all, it is the wickedest thing I ever did witness, and now I looks like I'm at least seventeen, so I'm soft. I learned that word from Brighid after she copped a mouthful of Annis' backtalk. Glad I never had a family even though it turns out this lot is. Me eyes well up with the grandeur, and I remember what I can of the lad I thought I was. I'm so full of hate I think I could break the world down if she was ever an enemy but she's not. She's love and woodlands and fjords and deserts and countless bug-people what lives beneath the asphalt. And we have an understanding. An entwining. And it's now like I always knew what that is. Better'n porn. No, porn's not even close. Even better'n ketamine.

That island. Not many of us there but other critters? I swear I have never seen a stoat. Or a badger. Or that many fucken horses all the colors of shingle and sky. I'm smitten by them big dogs. And that feral regent. And Charlie who she loves, and if I'm sick at all it's to be leaving. To understand what must come.

I'm not, however, that woman in the Scottish play what said, screw your courage to the sticking post and we'll not fail, because she did. I won't.

I understand the moves. It's like I'm Magnus Carlsen. It's also as weird as feck that I know who that is and that he was probably one of us out for the craic. The Mystery has it all sorted out, the pieces on the board being lost people, or scared women trying to protect themselves. Bullies in silent pretense. The clueless, like the crew at the citadel thinking they are chosen when they're sad and abandoned. And dumb. Like Mad Dog. I know what he is now. That's almost as sorrowful, somehow, except we all got choices. Even in a fog of fantasy that we're so sure is real. We all get to that moment.

The Rosie Rua maneuvers, a woman late for the ballet searching for her seat in the dark, bypassing buoys and little boats and outcrops of stacked stone, hundreds of years being lapped by lipless tides or raging winter hurricanes. I'm chucked a rope thicker'n me thigh and I watch what Raurie does and copies. He glances at me a bit like he's teaching, and I'm learning on the hoof so to speak. We ties off to the verdigris and mollusk-swarmed bollard fornicating deep into the strength of the ancient jetty.

Lighterman's hitch, comes into me head and all me lightbulbs go on when I come to understand we can talk without saying the words out loud. It's like code. This is what I had to realize and comprehend before they'd lift me shroud.

I understand, least I think I do. What Mad Dog wants with Raven. How it'll take him down and he's me brother and all. I know what I'm to do. And when. So this waiting is over.

When we climb aboard the bus, parked in the field where Woman, Apple Tree Wise branches her grace, I gets to sit in the passenger seat, up front next to Hunter, who's driving and saying nowt, with Puck up behind him like some piece of starlight and grit and the others as quiet as the freeze was. Even the hounds're not baying, just whuffling, playfighting, and releasing little disgusting dog farts every now and then. Up outa Weary Bay.

Heading back to New Rathmore. Getting colder as we chop across the skin of thawing tarmac and ear-splitting roar of full spring's birthing, cutting further north.

ACT 3

THE PEACE OF WILD THINGS

When despair for the world grows in me
and I wake in the night at the least sound
in fear of what my life and my children's lives may be,
I go and lie down where the wood drake
rests in his beauty on the water, and the great heron feeds.
I come into the peace of wild things
who do not tax their lives with forethought
of grief. I come into the presence of still water.
And I feel above me the day-blind stars
waiting with their light. For a time
I rest in the grace of the world, and am free.

Wendell Berry, *The Selected Poems of Wendell Berry*

···· ₥ ···· ···· · ₥·₥₥·₥₥ ₥·····₥ ··₥₥ ₥·₥···· ₥·₥₥····₥₥··₥₥

32

I SEE A DARK SAIL ON THE HORIZON
O'BENG

O'Beng navigates the streets of New Rathmore unrealized. Difficult to focus on. Smiling with shielded eyes. Wearing soft black leather boots, the soles also leather with arcane stitching unknown since the extinction of cobblers, under the black clothing of a minority, protected by the delusion they spun in the Depression Years. That presupposes a certain courage. A cool. There's only a particular kind of individual gets away with that display of affluence nowadays. If it is a display, which it is not. The very brave or the naïve dead. Shoes from before the crash will feed a family of four for months off the black market. If any of the trade is done in food and not opioids.

O'Beng is such a tease. Throughout history this conjure has worn a little body here, been a lithe champion who raises their arms high and wide as the ribbon is rent on the running track there. Milkman, a long time ago, fucking the young mother whose husband never comes home. The little boy in mummy's lipstick. It's always so easy. Propaganda. Spreading stories. Blaming one person so they kill another, the inevitability in both pairs of eyes when the bullet leaves the gun; when love is whispered through lying lips.

O'Beng knows. Has always known. Importances softly boasted about with deep conviction, over and over; whispered to a lover. Like a secret shared, becoming seemingly true. A stand is made and people take sides in a battle for that which they have never owned because no one owns the land. Or water. Or life. Napalm and spent nuclear warheads on some deserted foreign footbridge. Divide et imperium, once spoken never unspoken. O'Beng is big on keeping abreast of current human nature. The species wasn't always like this. Once people roamed savannahs, sailed catamarans across vast oceans assured by star patterns of the certainty of mythic islands. They rode the First Forests, and tagged *bob was here* on the walls of the vastness of underground chambers. They leaned into the ice of the tundra's endlessness of night. Ate what could be killed. Or were killed by what had been hunted. This primal intelligence is even now, after so much history shown to be the way of all life, denied. And the devil is told of, in stories meant to teach children to be frightened into obedience. Horns and a tail. And who is going to believe that once they have had their desires triggered by the smell of the sweat of sex? O'Beng is nice. Nice. A word dismissed by its very blandness. Meaning nothing. Hiding a real thought.

O'Beng changes form. Mercurial. O'Beng can be a best friend yesterday and an enemy today. Something of the person once known disappearing because of the touch; is it malefic? A caress that seduces with appropriate flattery; with the sigh of the damaged that brings out the heroic, or the strength of the hero when one seems to be needed. But this is O'Beng.

Corner after corner is cut, a chainsaw through an old growth forest, as O'Beng eradicates the obstacles of this body or that, touching passers-by with a thought that they are impervious to plunder and therefore do not notice the slow diminishment of their souls; their sense of themselves. Such a small sip. They won't miss it. They will merely wonder why they forgot what they ate last time they ate. Forget a name, the words to a song, a word, any word. Then that forgetting will pass, like winter, and no one will remember just how impossible it should have seemed.

O'Beng rounds the bend onto Copperhead Lane, from the direction of the docks, and strides the footpath looking for all the world like an old woman descended from Thailand, demure and slight. Smiling. Revel's hackles rise but he remains silent. Mercy misses nothing. She does not look in O'Beng's disguised direction, merely arranges her small stash of belongings into her backpack, rolls up the yoga mat and wanders slowly behind this unwanted, but necessary entity, until she can access Dimity's. She wanders out into the courtyard and sits up on the little wrought iron bench by the back door with Revel as an appendage. Until Merrin notices her and squashes between them.

Mercy's face is blanched of all color.

'I need you,' she says, her head bent over the ruff of the pup, his body tense, his ears almost meeting in the center of his head like an eroded dirt track, runnels where the rain has washed new directions into old soil.

'What's the deal?'

'You can't be killed, am I right?'

'Can.'

'Yeah, well.'

'Not easily though. Who's the quarry?'

'Not who, what.'

'Can you be more explicit?'

'Nup.'

'I'll get my pack.'

They reconnoiter at Merrin's studio. The lime tree overhanging the once-abandoned building is an eyewatering convergence of sap and bud that pronounces spring in neon. The parliament of ravens in the vaulted and untamed limbs numbering in the hundreds. Black rattle of juvenile wings. Purrs and murmurings, no louder than a presumption of sound. Ready. They are ready. Humans call them a murder for a reason.

Once explained about the smell, that certain emanation that Revel translates to Mercy, alerting her to the presence of a brightness, she understands her purpose. From the depths of hatred, despair, hopelessness and violation this *something* lives in increments. In love, or loves, but not love. Is it the child or the father? Is it a ghost? A *mulo* that the gypsies parked under the Woman, Apple Tree Wise talk of when a death happens? Banished when the vardo is torched? Yes. But all small, personal acknowledgments for that which is vast. Mercy comprehends that she can't kill that which has never lived but is also aware that it is not death, clean death, but the absence of mourning and the traditions around the remains of the burned or buried that moves through the world seeking purchase on the living. Parasitic. Pretending to flesh, like the wafer, that perversely represents some man who supposedly died centuries ago. His blood. Obscenity.

'Where's it going? Do you know?' Back at her warehouse studio Merrin stokes the fire and adds seasoned branches of scavenged wood, more precious to her than property.

Mercy says nothing but Merrin scries the truth of the intimation. This is big. Bigger than she thought. Bigger than anything Willie has told her of. Bigger than the winter just gone. How Mercy will kill this, assist it or maim it, or even mess with its purpose, she can't begin to guess. What she does know is that this is why Mercy is here. Why she was born. Because O'Beng has come. None of this was ever about a single human being. The unquiet despaired dead. Our Ladys dead. Unremembered dead. Lied about as though they were never born. The *dead*. Silenced carelessly. Deviously. It's as though a storm of wild bees passes through Merrin's awareness in search of a new hive, following the would-be queen. Not the dead beneath the snow. That is clean. Always happens, season after season, volcano, flood, wildfires, re-greening. Food for other life, the Great Mystery, who sings their names on wind, in cloud, in mist. Frees them from flesh and bone. Consigns them to both be, and give, nourishment and regrowth within forever forests, whether they are already themselves or yet to be deeply into becoming.

The big old double decker bus maneuvers clogged backstreets, then along the maze of asphalt still treacherous with slick, that leads to Shannon's 24/7 Parking down on the southside, opposite the abandoned club called Lucy's where Hunter and the warrior Travelers took out a cohort of slúagh several years ago. The streets are empty except for the homeless pushing loaded supermarket trolleys, mobile homes of green wire birdcages holding loot and water damaged family photographs of an era that no longer matters, except in memory and grief. Black garbage bags and battered guitar cases. All hope long fled of fronting some rock band.

Most of the inhabitants stay in the bus, organizing instruments, exotic outfits and paraphernalia befitting the paid gig at Mary Flannery's Tavern every night this week. The money earned will keep them in supplies and gasoline for a month, maybe longer. Willie-the-Red had raised his hand, volunteering to be Artful's companion on phase one of his mission, to meet Mercy at Merrin's place; to act as a decoy if her *shine* should be recognized by any entity in violation of the code by which faeries abide, to virtually never meddle in human affairs. Almost never. Like the one that their old friend Hippocrates learned of, and wrote about, as an oath of care, that eventually became known as *first do no harm* back in what is called the seventeenth century, that human doctors are quite abysmal at keeping up with.

Willie collapses into Merrin's arms, a soldier from a doomed warzone, the epic Dark Knight.

The taint of winter's doom heavy on him. The cries of loneliness aging him, alarming Merrin despite what she knows. Artful waits by the outside bathtub, aware of the koi beneath the green fluorescence and microscopic flowers of surfaced duckweed, exuberant with unrealized sensory stimulation, now he's away from the fumes and decomposition of the city arterials that led them here.

He is a piece on the board. This does not faze Artful in the slightest. New moons, slivers of silver in the early evening, do not question their seeming slightness because of awe. Humans do that when they encounter beauty. All this new knowledge about people he thought were like him but are not. Not at all. He was born from the pages of a story that was conceived in the imagination of an author who had pulled it from some future or some past, when neither are the truth. He'd always thought he must have had a mother. A father. Funny thoughts. He never had any such consideration. He is not human. It was no wonder, however, that he'd been the provider to the others at the citadel because once, up along the arctic nor'west passage, he'd been nestled in a meadow, along the mycelium line of fungi that gave the dreamer sight. So he understands the need for color. At this exact moment the realization that he has been most likely poisoning his companions with the fakery of food brings pink to his throat and cheeks, embarrassed at his undereducated view of necessity.

'You feeling the cold, *mo chroí*?' Merrin holds out a cup of soup that smells of summer. Artful takes it with what he presumes is a smile even though he doesn't ever remember having used his mouth in the shape of happiness before. Even as a faerie. All he remembers is pain and attitude. Pretending toughness or naivety. The effect of years he thought of, a mere week ago, as all he'd ever known. 'Willie tells me you're to be bait.'

'What about Raven and that copper?'

'Dunno more'n you. Much. Except Raven has to remember his skilling and the *shine*, and Mercy gonna fix that problem before she kills who she's destined to kill.'

'She knows him?'

'He loves her. It's a curse sometimes because the reason for it is sometimes awry.'

'Oh.' He shuffles the hint of left-over snow under the frame that supports the tub, sips the soup and looks with guileless, confused intensity at Merrin.

'What, Arty? You're leaking questions.'

'What's love?'

O'Beng is sated. The souls of angry and abandoned dead fill the chimera with a nourishing stillness and the steps are lighter, the soft leather boots becoming too tight for what passes for feet in an otherwise shapeless mélange of people-looking attributes.

O'Beng is neither he nor she. An exogeny of emotion and self-sense that people claim is internal when nothing is internal except organs, blood, bone, connective tissue, excrement and several trillion creatures small enough to inhabit the pointy end of a very sharp blade. O'Beng closes the distance from the city edges to Wallace Hope Plaza and stands unremarkably out front of The Masks of Kain. Pissed off.

Déjàvu is not there but is aware of what walks the streets of this city from where she tends the wounded men coming down from the inaccessibility of heroin.

She is as aware of it as iron is to the magnetic poles of earth. Aware that these spasming, puking men call to it with the despair of need. *Hmm*, she muses as she lays the last man down on the pallet of hessian. And walks away, becoming night.

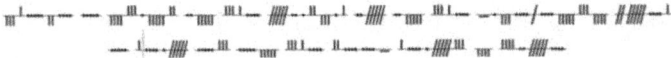

33

WHILE I STAND ON THE ROADWAY
OR ON THE PAVEMENTS GREY
I HEAR IT IN THE DEEP HEART'S CORE

THE GREAT MYSTERY

No name. Not anything real. She makes them up for the hopeful. A poet. A chef. A chieftain. A hunter of seeds who recognises what ancestors have taught will become food in the season of plenty. She wades to the shore of Forgotten Lake, removing the pelt of a seal as she navigates the susurration of tide-to-shingle, to sit cross-legged beside Hunter, on the stump of giant ancient elm lying as sanctuary, lightning-hollowed and inviting, the badger cubs having grown and moved on.

'What have you done?' He doesn't admonish or accuse. Not her. Not the heart of love. But the question is necessary if he is to bend the knee to life's bidding and therefore cause tomorrow to even be.

'O'Beng has come. We are in balance. But don't you fret, *anam cara*. You keep soft this time and let the pieces fall where they are destined. This is the gathering, don't you realize? We can set a tack free of wrack and detritus. A passage through the ice is access-ible for a few short wild days.

'Are you worried?'

'I'm always worried, Hunter. I'd never be a hurricane if I didn't worry. Never be tide at ebb and flow.'

'Can you bring my brother back?'

'There's a reason I never look the same twice, Hunter.'

The twilight silence muffles curlew and dove; the movement of wolves amongst the ferns. The flow of eagle wing and the slice of pale owl through the gloaming. While the human-looking body of Hunter, the First Forest made manifest, considers strategy before realising she has already made all the moves.

'You just changed the subject.'

'Don't try me, Hunter.'

'I'm not sorry.'

The Great Mystery chortles like a child and dissolves, now, into the autumnal shimmer of insects above the bottomless blood-amber water that can never be other than the calm sister to the wild free oceanic brother.

'Hold your course,' she whispers, with the skyward order of a V of snow geese sighting land after this, most recent, ancestral migration.

‖⋯‖⋯‖⋯⋯‖‖ ‖‖‖⋯ ‖‖⋯‖‖‖ ‖‖⋯‖‖‖ ‖‖⋯⋯‖‖‖ ⋯‖‖‖ ‖‖‖⋯ ‖‖⋯⋯ ‖‖‖‖‖‖‖⋯‖‖‖

34

BETWEEN THE SALT WATER AND THE SEA STRANDS

MORCANT

What is this? What the almighty fuck is going on? I am incapable of regret but the absence of the Dodger is disturbing. He has a mission. It has not been fulfilled. Now what? I am incapable of regret. I am incapable of regret. I am incapable of regret. So what are these fingers doing shredding my nervous system? Rapunzel's fucking hair hanging like branching synapses down my spine. Or tower. Or fortress. Turret. Whatever approximation of *a high dungeon* and *a wicked witch* that's been rewritten so many times, and incorrectly at that. No wonder I have this quest within me to rid the world of inconsistencies like chatter. What the fuck is this hole, then?

I'm not going upstairs. They'll smell me. I know they'll get a fix on this gaping thing that makes no sense. It's not in me. I don't have an in. That's the gift bestowed on an unseelie lord such as I. No gut, no grief. If I don't show myself, however, there'll be something go wrong. There is something wrong. What is it? This wrong? I feel as though I am the page, sixty, that's just been turned but pages sixty two onwards have been ripped out. Where's the fucking plot? What is this? Fear? I am incapable of fear. How can I think fear when I am incapable of fear? Am I repeating myself? For fuck's sake why the almighty fucking fuck am I repeating myself? Am I? There're burn marks at the edges of the hole. A cigarette dropped onto the preface. Pick it up, the coming cause of a conflagration. Can no one see? Who dropped it? This wounding. Who? Who or what? How can an idea be simply abandoned? A sliver of imagination be cremated? An image invented to give vividity to something I don't understand. How can I not understand? I have lived forever to see this day. This week. This winter. An end. A homecoming. Not a fucking cigarette burning a hole on the first pages. Dear Monstrum, I'm at the fucking epilogue and this makes no sense.

Go upstairs. Get dressed. Don't let it show. Do not allow one motherfucking human midget slattern of a species an excuse to recognize that this hole has happened. Pomade. Give orders, say *my dear* to the bent ear of your subjects and wait. He'll come back. He'll bring the song-maker. And Cheetos. And all that sugary shit that keeps the illusion of fresh food vibrant. Hologramic. Unrealized illusion. The plan. It's all in the plan and when a move this unexpected is released on the world and I have checkmated that fucking Mystery on its island, by its lake, on its shoreline down somewhere, on that ship; the train, on the other side of winter? When I have slayed that bus, those frilled and fancy faeries, and, and, and?

I have a destiny. I follow the depths of wisdom. I pray to their idea of a deity and I take what I need. I will be crowned as is fitting for what I have achieved and how it will be, then, and that I will be known forever. The work is almost done. Just erase the song. When that is done, what is left? Of hope? Of deep language. Nothing. No more will be written. I have suffered for so long without a single ally to turn to. Haven't I?

Haven't I?

Then what is this hole? I can see through it now. A finger of stone. What is that? What's the word I'm looking for? Isthmus. Yes. The words are in me and I should be fat with others' consumed language and be healthy because of what I do. Of who I am. Aren't I? Why the fuck am I asking questions? No one is listening. No one ever has. They won't start now.

O'Beng hears and is untouched. O'Beng only cares to affect the living. Not a thing created to look like the living. O'Beng knows its creator. Is that what women are? If O'Beng could blink O'Beng would not. To blink is to expose a weakness; a chink. Anything could move— pounce—if an animal closes their eyes, let alone an enigma as wide and incomprehensible as the Monstrum.

The problem is that life in this tiny region of earth is waking from the deep dark and that will put O'Beng to sleep for another season. Anything could happen in the waking of the world. Attention could be grabbed by a living myth: some faerie, some flight of snowy owls with their three-hundred-and-sixty-degree-turning rat-heads. The land and chalk cliffs, the walrus and oceanic bears off Weary Bay. They could all be told stories of. Someone could remember wonder. O'Beng does not care. Not really and not ever. Particularly for a thing such as Madawg Morcant.

O'Beng is known to the Travelers. To gypsies of every allegiance and ethnicity. They would know O'Beng. Other people, clinging to the Monstrum even whilst believing they don't; while maintaining doctrinal tenets by default do not know of O'Beng; the so-called devil. Way too sophisticated to adhere to childish obfuscations and fictions, like ghouls and entities and little spirit beings living in hollow hills or the back of an overgrown patch of woodland resembling a mad garden or a forest of lumber not yet razed: clanless, tribeless, their ancestors lost to irrelevance within the parish records and registers, proclaiming them saved from something anonymous but threatening, eventually; that provides no juice, no clarity. They will not see O'Beng. They will be trained to think that the fáidh are evil, as is winter in darkness. Or any of the many trivialized accomplices of some parable, or other lie. Yes. And that First Forest will be forgotten. Forgotten Lake erased from the minds of humans, replaced with ideas of torment, burning, punishment, cut-and-paste, chatroom and MP3. Those small ailments that happen when a captor becomes the victor and subsequently imposes new rules that really turn out to be the same as always.

The Great Mystery will become old. Placed in some delusional fluffy place, some white cloudiness. Go away. O'Beng does not plan this. O'Beng is the thing that the Monstrum pretends to despise but needs. Not the Monstrum's. If the Monstrum is dismantled over the course of millennia O'Beng will continue, oblivious to the erasure of its mimic. Like, but not like, the Pied Piper, it will take the children. It will kill the unborn while they are restless in the womb. Remove the new life from mother? That's the Monstrum, not O'Beng. The Monstrum will sell it. The Monstrum that disposes of life as it deems appropriate for invented crimes. Burn the woman, castrate the warlock, cut the genitals and cover the hair. Whereby the Monstrum amasses fortunes for the few, O'Beng merely drowns the fishermen in wild seas, burns the forest with lightning from a black and wounded sky, inundates a village simply because tectonic plates are what they are.

Morcant decides to do nothing. To him this is preferable to reacting prematurely and being exposed as ineffectual. He perches, tentative and angry, on the edge of an apparition resembling, to his mind, an opulent bed, the hidden shame of a ragged mattress—beneath a synthetic protector—obscuring territorial crowds of cimices deep within both the core and ticking, unseen to the naked eye, down in the basement of the citadel.

Morcant waits, fruitlessly and pointlessly, for his Artful Dodger, but O'Beng is abroad.

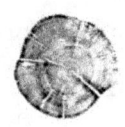

35

TO SEE A FINE LADY UPON A WHITE HORSE

C'AV'ARN

Sky black and turbulent. Snow? Can't be. But it can, that's the point. A seeming battle between light and dark, winter and spring. Funny that. Thought of as a fight when it is love. Mating between wildnesses for the evocation of birth, like the atomic explosion as sperm unites with egg, quickening disparate and separate concepts into life, where there was once none.

That's how wildness works. It only seems to emanate violence because humanity is such a small and misguided species that it is entertained by such.

In the most common type of cloud-to-ground lightning a riverbed of negative charge—a stepped leader—zigzags to earth in roughly forty five meter segments. An artistic forked dragon-tongue. The ground is struck in less time than it would take to blink, if anyone was desperate enough to be out tonight. On the journey from cloud to earth the negatively charged stepped leader causes streamer channels of its positive counterpoint to yearn skyward, from the tallest points available: tree, house, satellite dish atop the razor of hotel towers, along the light-electrical-wifi powerlines to junction poles where we know not to perch. When the opposition leader and streamer connect, electrical current, like a rip at sea, manifests. This return stroke wave of strobe travels at sixty thousand miles a second back towards the roil of skyborne blackness. Like black mold and bruising that preens like a fat old cat above the city of New Rathmore as though to prevent escape. We knew the gig would be cancelled. That our kindred would seek cover, at least for tonight. We also know that this will be their last night in New Rathmore until the season calls them back. That a table is set for a reckoning. And so most of them stay on the bus and Hunter hands the wheel to Rowan for the drive to Copperhead Lane. He takes a seat beside Puck, rests his head in her lap and sighs as she traces the line of his lips and kisses both his kohl-dark closed eyes. We watch from the powerlines, wings unrattled, opinions kept to purrs. And we see what comes.

Rowan is capable of managing what is set to be a tricky drive to the docks. First to warn Dimity to take the perilous trip out to Kathryn and Vincent's little farm where the faeries often winter now, the territorial cabal of us all fluffed, by the hundreds, in the leafless, season-hardened walnut tree. Critters will be ushered to safety under cover and Dimity will put the soup on the hob for when the other clans are sure to come. As they will, because Kathryn is soon to deliver a baby in the safety of the Mystery's critters.

Then Merrin, who has packed what she knows she will need for a very long time away. Mercy sits on the stoop out front of the shop while Revel leaps, biting fat drops of rain before they become a blizzard of thunder, then sleet, then ice, bored to be sitting too long, as pups of his caliber always are. They are to cross to the westside, telepathic vibrations like filings on an iron board, to the invisible men beneath the MacLean Street Bridge where Raven stretches the imagination-trapped wire cage door wide, releasing the *shine* he has kept en-dungeoned and enchanted through the trauma and the grief of necessity. He hums, in near-silence, the music he created in a code so desired by the feckless Morcant.

Morcant, so deluded a poor thing that the hearts of the fáidh could almost feel for him, *would* feel for him, if he had ever been more than a cruel almost-man. Him thinking like he does, always the pawn, never meant to persist this long, tricked into considering himself a king—a small boy indoctrinated by the Monstrum into believing in this purported absolute. That he is what he will never be; that he stole the voices of trees and rivers, maps and music, from the language of a beaten people. The vanity of initiation. The desire for being more. Certain that tomorrow will manifest deliverance when he interprets Raven's code into music. And deletes it.

Henry Waubun is quiet beside Raven. Hearing that hum and experiencing the ache of summoned majesty. Not for the first time he wishes he was more in touch with his heritage. That he could smoke sacred ground, the abandoned men, his companion. Raven is a faerie. Henry knows that now. Understands the cruelty of kiddie stories with an agenda that forms caricature from wonder; the invention of diminutive and harmless little winged things when Henry now knows that for the lie of an agreed-to conquerage, the extermination and carnage of land and water that must, for expedience, come to be considered as nothing important. For the taking. With turkey feathers gathered in a clutch and bound in soft buckskin to be held by one who knows the spiritworld, the smoke of a cedar fire; dancing in moccasins as soft as barefoot, made by mothers and decorated with little bells of shell and turquois, the quills of consumed porcupine and the beads drilled and sewn from the bones of ancestor kin.

Almost nobody is out on the roads tonight. The druids and seers, called nowadays meteorologists, were wrong when they suggested spring has finally come. Assurances from blondes in red dresses directing their hands to a greenscreen and hoping they don't point to the isotope of a day yet to be. Each layer of cumulonimbus is more abundant than that of five minutes gone. Flickers at the edges. Not lightning yet but coming.

The city is long locked down as Déjàvu struggles the final distance of her pilgrimage with her load. The jerry cans are lowered to the concrete. Déjàvu extracts the key to the opulent and intricate solid brass padlock, an indulgence not her own; a choice by the former tenant as a final quixotic touch to such a creative enterprise as The Masks of Kain. We are silent, so often, about human affairs, and what we know and who is disappeared and how devious each invisibility is, how easily forgotten that no one even asked after Wolf Kain. Where she went, if she went. Did she go anywhere? Why would she, when this place is her love? Is she still here then? Is hers a face among the many, one storey from ground level? Kept on a shelf? With offerings?

Lies—deceptions—are all around us tonight. Adamancies that never knew substance. I am veryvery alert. Keeping account and relaying what I see to Hunter who seems to sleep but does not, who sits beside my *Brighid*-body down at the water's edge of Forgotten Lake as the Great Mystery swims in otter-circles wider and wider. And in that movement alone, I am unnerved.

We watch from the power lines. The Bentley Forst High School cabal in black lines of ruffle and rattle and telepathy. Anybody outdoors on a night like this, looking up (which people don't do anymore) would wonder at our numbers. Would perhaps conclude that the rains were not coming because birds would know, wouldn't they? They may have forgotten that the Mystery demands there be witness to this bitterness as well as spring's eventual reveal. To the most mostess, the mostess of mostesses and I, C'av'arn, oldest of the high school raven parliament and therefore an elder, gloss of black and health? Will watch. Nobility of corvidness. The poise and grandeur of the free, all of us here, by the thousand, sentinels upon the wire, the gables, the gutters, the edge of dumpsters, the perimeter of pallets left to first freeze then thaw into rottenness, are thus committed to see the light returning.

Déjàvu bums the heavy door open, lifting the cans in calloused, scarred strong fists and depositing them just inside. A thin light goes on just as the sky is rent with messages. O'Beng has come, and that creates a problem: this keeping of trickery and betrayal a seeming reality. O'Beng should not come for her. She simply plays her part in the ruse. Mercy must not know or the world will come back. The glamour of neon and silliness will fail, like Rome. And terror will overcome the minds of those who think themselves superior. The effect could last a thousand years. Two. Three. Ten thousand. And that could get yawningly dull.

Déjàvu is aware of *en passant* and the arrogant foolishness of taking a name she should not have done as she sprays gasoline onto the downstairs, then the upstairs, the door and the passage to the room of faces, collected without permission and without need. Their torsos, feet and skinless skulls at the bottom of the river, bloated, consumed, dissipated, hung about with concrete and steel, caught before the realization of murder changed their mouths to outrage or howly-looking, worthless discards wrapped in plastic at the bottom of a dumpster, their scents hidden by the stink of mortal decay.

Déjàvu is a thing of the Monstrum. The making of her, a bloated poppet, *golem*, some might call her, through adoration of the tortured, a necessary ingredient of a pious spell, a believable apparition of relief to the frightened and the addled. Sent, like a sniffer dog at a festival, to hunt down Sparrow and to take her sketchbooks if she comes too close to the truth of what is being done to all those women, their fathers, their children. The taken.

Déjàvu has been so loved that there is a moment before she sits at the abandoned table and strikes the match, when she wishes her reality had been honestly soft. That she really was who she was thought to be. The scratch of red phosphorous against the abrasion on the edge of the little box is consumed, instantly, in a flame meant to annihilate the evidence of the aberration; the lie she told Mercy to insinuate her mother. Her fucking mother. Who knew she could vanish like that? The drawings of incrimination gone with her to heavens knows where.

The gas bottles out back in the alley behind the illusion of affluence that is the Wallace Hope Plaza ignite the inferno, engulfing several buildings including Straub's, the exclusive men's club whispered to also be a Middle Ages masonic lodge in some parody of gold, within the blackness of an ineffable darkness punctuated by Taranis' rage and the shattering of human security in the face of an unprecedented electrical storm.

By the time the fire trucks make it to the scene several buildings are engulfed and even as the firefighters unfurl the hoses and raise the ladders they are aware that something about the conflagration should not be. Some of it the smell of flesh cooking.

From the top floor of the long-deserted patisserie, the eldritch, salt-laden taint that flame should not flaunt reaches far into the twilight dark. Ethereal pennants as the languages of the dead fáidh seek release from the travesty of their mannequins. Blue as summer. Mauve, it is, and green. So green it reminds all who have braved the ice of the night, evacuate, help or to, out of the necessity of curiosity, to simply watch and try to understand, this *something* that the taught senses cannot name. But that we can. That the Great Mystery can.

Each separate flicker is the scavenged face of something once filled with grace. Sister Mary Dominic turns in her sleep, sweating with dread, her eyes tricking her into thinking dawn is near.

Realization that she is in the heart of night tearing her away again, to somewhere her body does not know.

Agnes, Mother Superior, tragics the corner of her mouth, the outer cleft down-turning in understanding. She gave birth to such a tiny boy. Never knew if he lived or died. Her pregnancy should have been such a lovely thing. Not this. She understands, in the cold black sod, just how dreadfully she has been used.

36

III.. III.I.... III.•III.—IIII.IIII .•IIIII.II III.I.... III.•••••IIII.II

TO THE WATERS AND THE WILD

LOVE

Mercy laughs when she trips over Revel's legs in his bounding rumble-tumble onto the Traveler's ratty old double decker. The concertina door is levered closed behind her and she tips into a vacant seat close behind the Rowan as the engine revs, the bus pulling out into the shadows of night maneuvering, like the Rosie Rua at port, through alleys of abandoned vehicles, the bacteria in the waterlogged fuel tanks corroding any chance of resuscitation come full spring.

The Rowan is bent over the steering wheel in solitude and concentration as they pass boarded up shops that once were supermarkets or fast food joints their produce and usefulness—their excuse for nutrition—long since raided, shelves and service bays empty and broken. Everyone she knows is aboard, and some she has not been introduced to yet, muffled in the pelts of long dead rabbit, fox, deer, sheep and seal. Other than Willie-the-Red and Merrin, Hunter and Puck, Brighid, Matt, Trevor, Alan and Gypsy. Black Annis is grim, like she could bite the head off a live chicken should such a thing pass her by and Artful, twitchy with anticipation. He doesn't want to come this way. He is mightily pissed off that he has not been included in the plan. Do his companions actually have a plan? They don't behave as though they are on a mission. He thinks he's learning way too slowly and he is suspicious that he is yet to be completely trusted. He is also mighty scared.

Driving away from the arterial that will lead them south towards Weary Bay the bus navigates the central city, still aglow with neon and lit office building windows, when shouldn't they have turned those useless lights off by this time of night? When no one is there and nothing to do that can ever amend a problem caused a hundred years ago and yet to realize the error?

Mercy is silent. The atmosphere in the bus is charged, an electric flickering of ionic particles like an arctic colorwind. Faeries' most influential weather.

Everyone in the company knows to leave her be when she is on high alert. When she doesn't recognize the terrain and when she is deep in readiness for trouble. What Mercy does not yet understand is that every one of them is also on edge. What if Raven hasn't remembered himself yet? How will they respond if he hasn't and how can they win his favor, or ensorcel one of their own, if he is aggressive or acting dumb? Knowing from Artful's intel that he has a cop with him, has been smashed and broken, that Dodger's boss at the citadel wants the dark fáidh badly, something like a sickness or a comedown, and that if they have any reason to go there he wants out; away. Anywhere else. He is not ready to face his tormentor because his longevity doesn't yet compute.

Then the smell, and the rent sky that ribbons with refracted mist like strings of eerie festival lights. The silence amongst the Travelers raises the hairs on Mercy's arms. They know what this is but none say a word. How had their disappeared city clan died? Why? Who did this? What is this keening. Howling; screeching like a cat-trapped mouse that is warning and afraid simultaneously. Smoke at first filters through the seals of the windows and doors. The burning stink of rubber and asbestos, old wood and chemicals. Then the barbecue reek of cooking flesh.

The remnant of the wild reel; clan Ulchabhán, named for the owl, who'd taken camp down by the lake in St Brendan's Park almost ten years ago, after the troubles in New Rathmore when the lights had gone out back in the day that all those fey folk were murdered and then on Inishrún when she'd almost succumbed to developers. Made up their minds that perimeters were problematic and spooked them enough to try making a go of living in the very core of the city. That was before the crash, of course, but none had come to the gatherings for most of those ten years and no one had thought to check in on them. Not one clan realized their relatives had died, let alone what violation they would have witnessed, or experienced, for it to happen so quickly and completely that the flesh they wore was sundered.

Names fill the air. Counties and beinn, standing stones, lochs, burns, glens, fjords and spruce forests. Rock above the snowline of clegr, too high for a bothy because a human couldn't breathe at this altitude and so the wildness remains safe. Too many names whispered far too quickly but recognized because the memory of the places they have been are still fresh in the language of Hy Brasil. Still Rowan drives. Firetrucks and high wide spray from their unfrozen hoses fill the air as the big old red bus rounds Bank Street from Napier Lane and from there out onto the M32 arterial that bypasses Wallace Hope Plaza, guiding the Travelers to the west side of the city.

Mercy's face and hands are glued to the window as she comprehends where they are and that this somehow has to do with her mother's work. Or so she has been told. That the buildings on fire in the distance include the Masks of Kain. She knows. She taught herself to map by walking the streets of the city and she never gets lost. She understands then, so precisely, that it can't be anywhere else. That it is those spectral, seemingly sleeping faces of flesh and ink and distinction she had encountered just a week ago now being destroyed, their remnant inhabitants seeking some verdancy not yet awake within its season.

Raven groans with exertion, the pain in his ribs still taking the breath from him, smelling the distant seelie smoke and sensing calamity in his waters. Waubun helps him stand and pulls his charge's jacket tighter around him, Raven laughing a little at the ministrations of the detective. He indicates the incandescence of the high yellow light at the junction of bridge and road without saying anything except *Ow*, placing one heavy-booted foot in front of the other and then running the steep incline towards the bridge because it seems cleverer than doing it slowly. Henry Waubun keeps pace. Over the low metal retaining railing, onto the slick asphalt just as the sleet, silent when it should sound like a swarm of midges, strikes the water of the river with some unspoken vengeance. Raven mumbles.

'You say something?' asks Waubun.

'O'Beng.'

'That supposed to mean something, Birdie?

'Henry, there's always a time for everything. Why does this one thing need explaining?'

'Jesus, Birdie, I have no idea what the fuck you're on but man, if I was off duty—'

'Copper, you better figure yourself off duty.' Raven stops beneath the tower of a streetlight, pulls out his tobacco pouch and papers and, as though he's under some invisible awning, rolls himself a dry cigarette and lights it with a little brass Zippo with a faded engraved crown on its shiny side. 'You want this?'

'That shit'll kill you, Birdie.' He checks the time, tries his cell phone but gets no signal.

Raven is impervious to the joke as he returns the makings to an inside pocket, the ferret-voice of ancestral caves and a low whistle taking purchase in him, wisdom dawning, his instinctive actions ahead of his movements. Knowing they are coming; whoever *they* are. With wildflowers and the softness of summer grass among them. Or is it the scent of that druí woman—not Mercy—who has haunted his every waking moment with no identity behind the exquisite perfume except the blossoms of the Woman, Apple Tree Wise, and kelp, and open sea?

'I'm gonna have to get back to the station, Birdie. Sorry. But that means whatever is on your mind will have to wait. I'm overdue to call in and assumptions'll be made.'

'No.'

'Raven—'

'No.'

The bus lights strobe the white and grey open as it looms down on the pair, Rowan pulling up clever inches from running the two men down. The door pleats open and thumps into its fixture. The interior is almost dark with a hint of lamplight and the echo of a low whistle but no movement or welcome voice.

'Fook me,' Raven sighs in hushed whispers. 'It's on, *mo chrói.* After you.'

'What is this, Birdie?'

Raven plants his wide hand on Henry's back and, as though compelled by the warmth of bodies exuding like the memory of his grandmother's village, he is spellbound into momentary uselessness. The sugaring season. Smells of fish from the lake. Manoomin, dried and parched, danced and winnowed, he wants it to stop. He's just a cop. Out of his depths but nothing other than. Is he? Isn't he? Inside are just people. And dogs. Not junkies, not something he can name or box easily. Every hair on his head and arms, however, stands on end as though he touches a live wire, as though his grandfather's ghost walks through him. 'Sorry,' he says, but no one replies. He moves aside and Raven pushes past him lightly heading between the bits of bed and furniture and seating to stand, astonished but internal, before Mercy Riley. He bends his head so she can't see how undone he is.

Revel scabbles over the back of the seat in front of Mercy and makes a leap for Raven that is as joyful and welcoming as no one around them. And Hunter grunts from further down the bus.

'Yes?' calls the Rowan.

'Yes,' replies Hunter, getting to his feet and moving like a man half his size to his brother. Taking him in his huge arms, enfolding him in homecoming. Raven's *shine* fractures the dark; a relief he hasn't wanted to feel for years, a relaxation washing through him, evoking a kaleidoscopic cirrus of ice crystal brightness from the depths of his brokenness. Fixing him. Drawing the pus of human depravity from him to clean him. Hunter does not let go even as the bus lumbers into a deep U turn and drives out towards the freeway, towards Weary Bay and the reckoning.

Mercy is aware of Raven. She is unmoved by his potent self-control. But she knows. Is not who he thinks she is, because he is still clueless; blind to the big picture. What Raven has not understood, but will, eventually, is what she is to him. That she is also incapable of love. It was presented to her too late. From Maisie. It had died years ago in the ice of bleakness that drowned her plea for the comforting breast of her mother. For a real name. The two men, who are not men, pass her, note that she stares into the night like a witch at tarot whose lips have been sewn shut by invisible thread, seeing and thinking, blending into stone that grabs at her lower abdomen causing her to remember she is just about to bleed, and that hers is not a body to bear children into a world this flawed with grief and callous denial of simple compassion. Hunter's grip on his brother's arm is soft compared to what it could be and the growl down deep in some cavern-cold night of him brings Raven back to himself. There is a travesty to be undone and his sibling needs to concentrate and not do this lose-yourself-to-the-moment thing that's got his *shine* doing its best to evoke even a speck of anything familiar from Mercy that he can fill with summer. He lost that right when Agnes became invisible to him all those years ago.

Henry Waubun might seem like just another mortal, clueless and guileless, except his ancestors are strong in him. He is the first of his father's line to acknowledge a responsibility to a culture, and to a cause, that has come perilously close to decimating all his relatives.

Poverty, booze, crack, smack, tenements, prison, songs silenced, braids of sweetgrass sold in trashy little new age shops along with eagle feathers and ochre, moccasins made in some far away third world country, from the hides of caged and uneaten kin. He is aware. These people might not be manitou but what's a word? His badge and his gun. They want him for these. He wonders, and not for the first time, if Raven, Birdie's, injuries were a lure. So he sits on the edge of the little chair beside the potbelly at the back of the bus and pulls off, firstly, his thick boots, then his damp socks, and holds them to the warmth to dry. It can all wait. No one needs to explain. He's got it. Their language of silence. He doesn't need a lecture. He just knows he's in. He simply wonders what that will entail and what he will do if the plan is against what he now-questioningly thinks of as legal.

The bus finally trails the city stink behind it. Rowan takes an off ramp with a sign that indicates a byway west. Towards the coast. The sea.

Waubun has never been to the sea. He seems oblivious to the company he is in, the moods, the tension, the pretense of laughter. This is big, and he knows he's passed some invisible marker of respectability.

Whatever is required of him, he understands, is beyond laws made by men.

37

COME AWAY OH HUMAN CHILD

HY BRASIL—FORGOTTEN LAKE

It is said, in modern day parlance, that I don't exist. That I am some atlantis of the imagination of nineteenth century scholars who are supposed to know about such things. It is those same men who think of myth as untruth. Something invented for children to be erased when commerce takes center stage and I am consumed by producers of syrupy muck, appearing on screens as a gaudy blonde princess with a castle and spindles and slippers and small people overwhelmed by men with kisses.

Whenever I raise my song to object, I become a hurricane assaulting a coastline, pulling multiple species into my own gravity to be churned into food for sharks and kraken, seaweed left in rock pools at ocean's ebb, that will be gathered and eventually suckle eroded soils to back to health with oceanic nourishment.

It needs mentioning that I am here and I am there and I am the brightness of memory unsullied by the cane or some bully-wielding but unnatural silence, since silence has never existed other than in the depths of fear, or contentment, and that I am also a great mystery because what is living if there are no questions remaining?

I am the destroyer of worlds, depending on the face of those who see me either as they have been advised by monkish academics with pretense their garment, or through the eyes and mind of the brandisher of a magic wand, by a free child, that is a stick tipped with stardust that will free the dragon from the prison, the citadel, wherever it is intended that light is never night, and sleep, and dreams and flight.

The bus shudders and tilts, like an old drunk, along rutted byroads once smothered in asphalt that now, after the fall, have cracked open like dinosaur eggs, revealing grass and briar, an awoken tundra yet to know the full extent of sunlight within the fissures. Open wounds emitting unforeseen life. Springtime on the backroads. Ice dissolved during the milder night, in puddles that, right now, catch a pewter young sun making driving the backroads less perilous, and while most of the other occupants of the bus—faeries, forest and reclaimed lost— seem to sleep, Black Annis sits in the blue and faded yellow velour seat, its springs a continuous avoidance of bum and hip, up front beside the Rowan. Deep in her own private thoughts.

A long drive. Almost, she thinks, too long. As though there is no more time and this journey is a fraud and all they are doing is going around and around the seeming same maze of illusion that replaced standing stones with cathedral spires, leading deeper and fatally into Brocéliande where some story, as yet unknown, awaits a victim, like a clapped out old double decker bus containing creatures deliberately obliterated from humanity, sister-species though she is.

'Okay?' she asks. The Rowan grunts, his shoulders slumped

over the wheel as though he navigates through gravy when the night is eerily clear of fog out here and contains no threat except for the hares that do dodgems the moment he loses concentration.

He slides an arm across the back of her seat and she leans into him. This love of hers. This wordless man who once worked the bar in a dockland pub with no seeming future and all the surprises still in brown paper, gummy with something distasteful. She takes the hand that rests on her shoulder and looks, through the gloaming of backlash from headlights, at the pale fingertips, once so human, now near-immortal with his solemn consummation of the Quicken brew.

'We'll be there before dawn,' he whispers, not sure of anything except the unpredictable tarmac beneath the wheels and the quiet quest for the deliverance of an innocence from evil that has been laid on him like a geis. Accepted, but not easily. Never easily. Never without a million questions about repercussions and who will suffer and whether that is just and whether there is a way other than violence and seeming-revenge. Accepted because he has agreed, when informed, because none of these creatures know how to lie. Black Annis never does, no matter who she offends. He loves her so. Driving this bus is, to him, no different than chauffeuring a queen in a gilded coach to her night of self-claimed beauty at the annual ugliness ball except for the annoying grind of a clutch when the gears change.

Hunter wades through hip high bracken, the peewit of eagles, family, the clan of iolair perhaps, piping high overhead in the perpetual autumn amber twilight. He moves as a man; a tall wide quiet man with dreadlocks to his waist, captured in skeins of ragged linen at the crown of him, waterfalling with blackbird feathers, his skin rough and tannin as oak bark, his eyes a bottomless, drowning black. He has not been to the far side of the lake for an aeon but too much is abroad these human nights for him to sit in complacence and agreement on the easily accessed fallen log. Here, in the shadow of the wild hills is the other entrance to the Barrow. Clustered standing stones that dwarf him, carved in runic chatter, ogham counting and celestial patterning looking for all the world like broken things strung together and seemingly meaningless, show him that passage in. And down. To the hoard of elder treasure collected over millennia in bone and gold and fur with neither mite or mold to lessen their viridian brightness, or the black that is purple and blue and gold depending on the light or absence of.

Within the very night of the underland barrow, vast as Lascaux, a menhir lies flat against the deep loam. Some sleeping majesty. And upon her, legs spread in defiance and readiness, sits the apparition of Sparrow, hair pieces of ice and scars like an initiation or a punishment, eyes unseeable from his vantage point but shoulders square upon the small unforgiving body, shocking Hunter into some semblance of confusion.

'And you are here, why?' he asks, mirroring her as he sits, eyes forward on the gem-scattered but otherwise stony ground.

'What do you think this is?' She scuffs the ground with a booted foot, moving detritus, releasing the scent of peat from beneath.

'You think I want to look this way?'

'Sparrow?'

'Don't ask, Hunter.'

His composure is shattered for an atomic second as he realises this is the Mystery and wondering at the garment she wears.

'You're never to know who does what, Hunter. It is best.'

'O'Beng?'

'We have a date.'

'Oh.'

'Give Mercy her head.'

'None of her doing has ever been in my hands and she is not a horse.'

'Are we in some B-grade move that I need your exposition, *mo chrói*?'

But his head rests on Puck's shoulder and he wonders if he imagined what just happened as the bus takes the S bend and noses down the steep decline. Weary Bay, dark of town but light of wild water beyond, depicting the shape of cloud far out to sea resembling an island. Is an island. Too many of her would-be inhabitants pennanting towards it in a borealis of blues and greens, unrecognized to the observers, thought just some oddly burning something caught, momentarily in the ice of winter's end, coming here, eventually, with the thaw, to Inishrún. Every faerie is awake on the bus this dawn though not that an observer would know, and each of them is aware that complacency is the cloak that covers the truth of anything.

And Sparrow has come and gone. Tea with Maisie Raith. They discussed Mercy and waited. And Sparrow told the truth of everything before she went away. Of the mother, buried deep beneath the sod alongside hundreds and hundreds of skeletal remains of children who never suckled. An abandonment of young women, teeth shredded of lips, bellies long gone, feeding the grass that will bear seeds for robin and wren, along with their real names if such a thing as *real* can ever describe this travesty of faux-marriage for the betrayal of the hope of love or a night of wild enchantment. And all the while O'Beng corners alley after alley, hidden amidst the ghosts of fogs of the forgotten dead, seeking the quarry that dams the river of change as surely as the refuse of a catastrophic flood, work of his sister-wild as clear as battle lines drawn upon some ancient territorial map.

Hunting the essence of Déjàvu, her body burned to ash, her soul a razorblade that has, to so many, taken on the semblance of a good person for all of winter, hearing his sister-world's voice clacking in sap not yet risen to the rattle of branches in St Brendan's Park's botanical future forest saying: *there is always more than one enemy.*

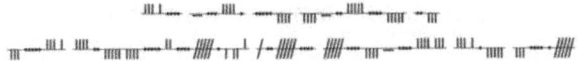

38

THE PÚCA IS SPOKEN OF WITH CONSIDERABLY MORE RESPECT THAN FEAR

SPARROW'S BAIN

'The fucking book.'

She hears the swift bite of the crop slice air before it lands on her exposed buttocks. Her head is all muffly with some bag and she is tied face down on pallets. Her nose is between the slats otherwise breathing would be a problem. Sparrow almost smiles at the perversity of her situation, unsure as she is as to where her body lies. Cold. Like deep beneath the North Sea. She imagines the enormous cables of oil rigs, baffled or ballast-tanked, driven deep into some substrata to hold that mass of violation above the black of offended ocean. She knows they are *sunk*. And she is sure that is her own destiny after today. Air, always a friend to a wild sídhe like Sparrow, now offers apology to her lower body that is also being rendered impotent against assault, and she is as outraged as she is curious as to the nature of the slúagh that trapped her as she kissed Maisie goodbye, going out into the white but sightless fog.

Everything is chained. With cold iron. Wrists, neck,

ankles. She remembers this trick but she's been around humans for so many millennia that the impact is annoying rather than deadly.

The ravens had warned her. Deep in the night, along the pier with its little shuttered kiosk. The old hazel trees withered and skeletal. The 3 AM birdliness rule that they should have been sleeping but had waited for her. That big one with the white eyes. C'av'arn, she remembers. *Run,* had been the rustle of blue-black hackle feathers. *Someone with the sight has spaed what you have rendered in grey.* She had time to secret the drawing book but not her pencils. She had slid it through the final bluster of winter to the heart of the Barrow on Inishrún where only the Travelers, or Holly, or the Mystery would find it. She knew they would, sooner or later.

And when they do, she grimaces, *there will be a reckoning.* Whether she is alive or rotting at the bottom of some pit or bog, or under some random rock, is irrelevant. She has been hurt so many times that once more will not matter. She has drawn the spell of murder and complicity. She has rendered killer and victim in graphite. But every sending she has tried since waking to this cage just seems to create more determined a frenzy from her tormentor. One? Is there one or are there several? Do they take turns? Is it day or night? Does it matter? The wish for numbness is a waste of thought so she abandons it and keeps faith that her muteness will protect her.

'Where is the fucking book?' An utterance breathed like a bead on a rosary.

A man's voice. Deep and velvety. Cherried with vitality. Sparrow says nothing.

The agony behind her left knee as a sharpened graphite pencil is pounded into the muscle. Then another. The other leg, the tendon split, blood pooling in hematomas unable to escape the quick healing of her dermis. So she knows her death is immanent because now she can't run. The shattered nerves gather at the base of her spine, mycelium-vast, lacerating her ability to think. She doesn't have a plan. Never did. But then her hearing, as acute as any hound, recognizes the echo of voices calling in the evening: Deus, in adiutorium meum intende. Domine, ad adiuvandum me festina. Gloria Patri, et Filio, et Spiritui Sancto. Sicut erat in principio, et nunc et semper.

She is somewhere within the depths of the soot-blackened brick of Our Lady of Perpetual Sorrows Mother and Baby Home. She is being hurt. Déjàvu, sent to seduce her into trust, is burned to death amongst the ruin of ancient faces. A horse whip. *Giddyup, ma wee pony.* Her insides raw with the semen of old men who were here when? Yesterday? A year ago? Always? Sparrow can smell it. Her own shit. The sweat beneath her arms metallic with the hormones of adrenalin. Her own voice a thousand miles beneath the surface of life; so far into the crevasses that not even the slúagh can catch her talking to herself. At first berating. But there is no logic explaining how this happened. Pleading is pointless, she realises. Is this it? All the witnessing worthless?

Every runaway's name is etched, Maeshowe-like, into her subarctic memory. An impenetrable fortress. This is how the land is. Holding the stories of those cobbles and gravel and lime trapped in city architecture. The reasoning being that only a clever species can draw a straight line and therefore create buildings that are upright coffins. Such a catastrophic consequence to the meandering nature of freedom. The nuns hire such men that would have become priests if their lusts were not sadistic and rapacious. They serve this purpose and Sparrow is nothing to them. An Our Father on a future deathbed, despite what they believe to be a destination afterlife too horrific to turn a mind to.

Slash. The back of her head stings with the horse whip. Slash again. There are words she can't understand. Quiet words, gentle words, sentences of encouragement. Meaningless as treaties. The simplicity even more ironic. That her persecutors don't realize not who she is but *what*. Blood pools around her nose, finding exits. Seeping from wounds she cannot touch, it drips through the hessian sack onto a floor she cannot see.

'I am here.' She speaks to the dead, a mother from some folk tale who has torn herself but cares little for the agony of briars and thorns when she is in sight of the blasted tower; when focus and finality become weapons. When her living daughter is at her greatest peril and she, the real-life liberator of that wicked curse.

The graphite pencils are knives. They rip from popliteal fossa to ischial tuberosity with the inaccuracy of a careless surgical intern off his face on nitrous oxide. Now she screams.

'Fookin scrappy wee cuntie,' he whispers seductively in her ear. Then, *Nowt* he yells, defeated, and a key turns in a lock. A small key in a small lock. The soft shush of long clothing, no sound to the movement of feet. Sparrow smells myrrh and porridge, and something like lavender scented chemical toilet cleaner.

'For the love of god.' A youngish woman's voice upbraids. Hints of compassion.

''Um—' The man's voice. His reluctance to do this. The knowledge that he could be in the position of his captive at the whim of a nun's discretion.

'Her tongue and her eyes. Her hands.'

The swish of cloth returns the way it came and Sparrow knows panic for the first time since she became this human-shape. If they can do this to an animal akin to them it is no wonder she has been unable to alter anything. She could not prevent the razing of herself, as a seemingly immutable hill of limestone and gneiss that had overlooked the bay for forever. She could not prevent the cement or the iron bars and metallic grilles, or the straps for holding the girls down. Or the shovels. Once she was a wayshower: between the island and the mainland where kestrels, like sentries, kept vigil against the unwelcome; a veined and cave-pocked sliabh. A mountain that has seen the close of day on so many evenings, from the vantage of the cairns erected by ancestral two-leggeds to initiate the young in the druid lore of orality, that to think of counting them would be to ridicule the seasons. She was blown apart and gouged. Almost two hundred years around the sun ago. And she became, through decimation, her own valley, with a confession of sad, dank browns formed into a warren of freezing boxes, built by bent men who were paid in clemency for sins they didn't even know existed and whose families died of the hunger or cultural genocide despite this brazen ruse of deified forgiveness.

What remains of a mountain's bright strength? It became the smallness of Sparrow as she appears to the eyes of others, and she is here again, as she has almost always been. Gone feral within the city of New Rathmore for a bit of variety, always hunted but never found. Taken in by that huge, scarified woman, who she was sincerely and stupidly fooled into thinking was a friend, because loneliness can sometimes be too overwhelming.

But home is home and self is self and all this buried shame is hers, also, and so she must bear witness to a species that makes no sense but that prides itself on whatever it considers rational. Oxymoronic, really, she knows now. Has done for one hundred and ninety nine years.

The sounds that come from her when her eyes are cut out are shushed by that soft man's voice. That problem is resolved when he removes her tongue. He saws her hands from her body while they remain strapped to the pallet just in case she somehow has sufficient will to defy him, despite everything.

Sparrow withers where she lies, disturbing her torturer who will now never recover from what he sees. What he assumed was merely another woman. Not understanding that he has dealt death, when simply ordered to cause harm, to something that he did not know was wonderful. When he leaves the basement dungeon of Our Ladys all that remains is desiccated skin over bone, the color of softly-tanned bark, the rose-colored birthmark a blur. The ink mere whisps of remembered blue.

Tonight the rooms of pregnant girls, the stirrup'd alcoves, the hallways of ghosts, reverberates with the sound of keening, as though every dog in and around the village of Weary Bay awakens from a nightmare to find their person had deserted them, has trapped them behind a door from which they cannot escape. With a small lock.

The eighth of the nine nuns, Sister Mary Bernadette, taps with hushed deference upon the door of the office and waits. For minutes.

'Mother?' she whispers.

And finally, 'Enter'.

Mary Bernadette pulls at the heavy oak doors and steps into the stark reality of Mary Dominic's (*lair*, is the word that comes to Bernadette's mind) apartment and says, *It is done.*

'Where's the book?'

'She wouldn't tell. Mother, she was never going to tell.'

'I beg your pardon?'

'She's gone.'

'Where?'

'I mean, mea culpa mea culpa mea maxima culpa, she died even as our man did not kill her,' and she punches her own chest in penance for the mistake.

Silence is sometimes like the axe about to fall on the neck of a traitor, or the excuse, or the innocent whose righteousness cannot be condoned. The room is filled with it. Suffocatingly so. Sister Mary Bernadette has done merely as she has always done. With tongs and scalpel, sutures, hammer and shovel. Her duty. The treacle of threat is punctuated with the question marks of uncertainty. Hasn't she acted with holiness? Isn't this just another dirty girl like all the others?

Obviously not. Sister Mary Dominique's jaw twitches but her lips remain an unforgiving thin line. She offers no order and no succor. But Bernadette knows not to stay.

For the only time in her life Mary Dominic has doubt, thinking again and again, seeking an overgrown track through some vast unmapped forest.

Where, if I was a fucking faerie, that had witnessed the fucking way of my world, would I hide that fucking book?

39

I WISH I WISH, I WISH IN VAIN

ARTFUL DODGER

'Where have you been?' Morcant demands so softly that no one, other than Artful with the recently-acquired the heightened sense of a dog, hears.

Artful shrugs, says nothing and dumps the plastic bin liner full of faux-chocolate skittles, iced donuts, potato crisps, soda pop, gum and microwavable pizza onto his workstation. All the heads lift at the familiar sound of habitual nourishment, some seeking the baggies of LSD micro-caps that should be with the stash. To help them think straight.

'And this has taken you days because?'

Morcant's breath stinks. Like he's been eating fish out of a can. Cat food. Rotting from the inside. Something definitely unclean about the man who is never grubby. A pallor like wax sheened in perspiration. Artful has never smelled anything so rank but he carefully conceals his revulsion.

'Where is he? I sent you out for the music man, not this shit.'

'Lost him. He was took in a patrol car amongst coppers.'

'And?'

'And what?'

'He was down by the bridge. He was out. You're lying.'

'Can I go now?'

Morcant tilts his chin up. Who is this runt of a boy that he should do the dismissing? There is no logic to his rage but it is a white, acidic magma. Burning from his gut, up his esophagus to form bile at the back of his throat. A wire wounding his brain with nonsense. He has a feeling he knows this anger from some other time in space but cannot for the life of him recall the source. He has wandered with the generations of Monstrum men and women for so long that recall becomes a blur. Tonight though, like last night, the severe taste of wrongness coats his lips like exhaust fumes. He might just have snorted some oopsie white powder and done something gruesome to his sinuses. He doesn't know. He can't remember. Is addled and does not recognize the sensation.

For days he has been assaulted by a cacophony, bedlam and river-abuse of whitewater tinnitus, and is disoriented. This is new. He is certain it began the night he last cut himself. As though it was not an outpouring of blood that escaped onto the basement floor but an invasion of imps, squeezing through the clefts of wounded flesh and up, through the cells and neurons of his nervous system into his brain, frying synapsed memory and replacing it all with intrusion and discord. He hasn't been able to switch off thought. Words. How he hates words. His work away from the court of his regality feels so close to completion that Mary Shelley should roll over in her fictitious Frankenstein grave in envy. So why? And what has Dodger got to do with any of it? Because Morcant knows he is in the heart of this interruption.

Artful sits at his station, his head on his outflung arm, and seems to sleep. He is waiting. He is listening. Everything. He hears the passage of events unfold and he shows nothing of the tragedy. He has been given one task only. Be quiet. Like Hunter. Like Raven has been through necessity.

Not long now.

Morcant does not realize the deception or the deceit. He goes to the window of the newly decorated cubicle and rests silently on the ergonomic chair, weightless and abstract. He runs both index fingers across the edge of the desk, in opposite directions, as though smoothing out a funereal shroud. He opens the cover of the laptop, enters his passcode and is immediately admitted to the home screen, the curser enticing *come, come, come*. He accesses the cluster of networks allocated to the citadel and interfaces with each of his crew, checking on data disruption and code, strings of whaling targets, the insertion of his ghostware into phished sites of encyclopedic accumulation. So many gone.

Chatrooms, replete with an amalgam of fractured letters and numbers as invasive as hemlock: GR8, LOL, E123, 10-7B, the police radio codes 10/22, 11/80 or simply 203 for mayhem, spreading from what are still unbroken sites and politically strategic institutions, what remain of universities and emergency call centers and from radio comm to radio comm, ceaselessly.

He hacks effortlessly into Tommy Ng's system to once again

view the byte-and-integer music theory embedded in the library's cloud storage and wishes he could actually hear it live, just once, before he corrupts it forever. The memory of how to translate the ones and zeros, and intervals, is distant. From before the crash. He has to stretch his mind to recall what keywords are necessary to understand what he used to all day, any day. Rusty as a corroded door in a drowned submarine, he reads: *scales are Ionian, Dorian, Phrygian, Lydian, Mixolydian, Aeolian and Locrian. The modes of the other scales will vary in both shape and intervallic formulae—*

Morcant is so angry at his own ineptitude that he takes several minutes to slow his heartbeat and prevent his sense of himself from further fracturing. Composed, he rolls the chair, on its silicon coasters, away from the port allowing him to rise elegantly and with the threat becoming a creature such as he. He pads unheard, in delightful, contraband, lime green Converse, to the stainless steel doors. He keys in his code. The doors ping open. He descends into a demure lamplit near-darkness, his only thought cocaine, his old-man razor and some endless masturbation. Not once does he deign to look in Dodger's direction as he leaves the aboveland.

Without being told by anyone or anything, hearing only the distant rattle of the fledgling wings of incalculable numbers of rooftop and cable-balancing corvids, Artful is comforted by the realization that his captor, his owner, his tormentor, is not special. Is certainly neither seelie nor unseelie. Is not some suave Joker from the Marvel series. Is not even able to 13375p34k. He now has the experience of this wildest of wild webs, one he'd never have recognized before the night of the Barrow, and knows he cannot be harmed again. Morcant beguiled him and all his colleagues in this war against words, so effortlessly, with his seemingly endless supply of funds, bespoke hardware and treats befitting the banquet hall of a prince that no one has even thought to question his wisdom or his sources of acquisition.

Who has this gentrified pale man really been all this time? Artful is now aware. Nothing; he is nothing. The newly awoken fáidh intuitively knows to pace himself. He smells Morcant for what it is, but he now has the patience of a hunter. The eventuality of what comes next can wait. He can wait. Aware that there is no such delusion as time he is excited in his own quirky way. The Rowan, once upon a time, had been picked out of the mass of humanity to be privileged; invited to experience wonder. Now he, the Artful Dodger, is to bear witness to the undoing of a misspell, and a mousetrap of such persuasion, that this travesty of a denizen, an *unenchanted* who believes himself unseelie but who has never been, truly thinks that everything he has been programmed to be convinced of as real *is* real.

While Dodger waits for events in Weary Bay to set the winds of eventuality a'sail he reroutes Raven's code from the mainframe of the citadel to his private SQL independent database, a virtual LAN that he hadn't realized, even in his moments of unsugared clarity, is as unbreachable as some gold standard. He stifles a grin; wonderfully aware of how much fun being a faerie really is.

Who woulda thought? he realizes, completing the transfer and deleting the evidence from the cache as surely as if it had never existed.

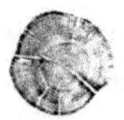

40

ALBAN EILER
(EQUINOX)

LEATHER

O'Beng takes the train. It's almost funny to see him sitting on the tattered faux leather seat, the carriage smelling of urine, old wine and vomit. O'Beng doesn't care. Has a phone. It causes others in the cheap seats to look sideways. Does he have reception or is he reading a book on that little screen? O'Beng is smiling, so the other rail-riders frown a little, queasy at the seeming-dark man's familiarity. There is, however, nothing approachable about O'Beng, handsome as he is in an ominous way, attractive to fertile women. The bad boy look that deep within the limbic brain shouts *good breeder* as though tamer men carry a debased DNA.

O'Beng could as easily have moved through air. Been night. Changed shape. Too easy. There is little in the world made manifest that attracts O'Beng as succulently as surprise, however, and the train is full of it. The phone is just for show. A dull throb of memory in the oldest people. They remember when every face turned down, always. Trapped within the sorcery of those small devices. Cobras used to do that, as did human zoos and sideshow freaks. O'Beng has always been overjoyed at the curiosities. Like artificial flavor and color in ice cream and coca cola in glass bottles and stock exchanges, and such antiquities as capability with hands.

O'Beng sighs. Bored now. Sitting back in the seat, spreading long legs encased in unforgiving black jeans with only small slitted rips as though the wearer has spent days on bended knees doing what no one could imagine so they automatically, unconsciously, think praying. Funny.

The journey from New Rathmore to Brokeshire takes just over three hours and O'Beng arrives somewhere between twilight and day in the hours that paramedics call the *dead zone* even though it's also when most babies are born. O'Beng exits the turnstile without paying as the attendant, busy rolling a joint behind the guardhouse, didn't see anyone get off the train. O'Beng walks the dirty blocks of the old steel town like royalty. Cap on straight. No insignia. People remember insignia. They are either for or against. The problem with noticing is that the memory, no matter how small, will affect who they are for the remainder of their lives. They don't know it but that's how a personality gets built. One tiny detail of attraction or repulsion mixed in with another. From the cradleboard to the grave, or the crematorium, people are made of gristle and accumulated observations ruminated on without even awareness. Hence bigotry. Hence what caused the food wars. Of no consequence to O'Beng. O'Beng realizes this is all display in a kaleidoscope of five pieces that never repeat the same pattern twice but contain, in their very essence, the exactitude of each other.

O'Beng has acquired a heavy wool coat as black as Africa.

The collar is, or once was, velvet, now nothing more than the felting that supported elegance. Turned up against the metaphor of coldness. The hem is down around his calves because yes, O'Beng looks like a man, and the fabric flaps nicely in the crack of dawn wind as he walks. His boots silent on the slick of thin ice as long as he does not insult grass. Grass is still crunchy with the rime of a new day's testament to playing seasons both ways. A veiled dove grey sun, still horizontal, reminding him of walking through flood water, just below the surface and he whistles the tune of an elder song, The Highwayman, because it's both fitting and appropriately cool, knowing that whistling is a superstition that one should not do, considered it is said to attract evil.

O'Beng comes at last to the hill overlooking Weary Bat and glides wetly through the sweet young grass that pushes against the remnant snow. He hears the Traveler's bus, still hours away. Woman, Apple Tree Wise summons him, a queen to her consort, on this pale rarified sea air. O'Beng would come anyway as his love is in her roots, the druid with spells and vast memory that spans five thousand years, with her tales of tragedy and elation. He ties a small ribbon, yellow, around a low and barren silver branch.

'Still here,' he whispers.

No answer. None expected. The irony of the clootie noted.

O'Beng walks the final stretch to Weary Bay just as Henry Poe unlocks the doors of the pub on the off chance anyone local needs one of Alice's breakfasts, the severity and austerity of the recession not felt this far south. Just as the trawlers chug from port in hope of lobster or mackerel. Just as Barney Rumford drives the Massey Ferguson along the street keeping as far to the side as he can out of habit, in case of vehicles coming the other way.

Barney notices O'Beng but minds his business. Maisie Raith has taken the long walk this early for when the produce store lifts the metal garage doors. She needs hay for the donkey. Someone abandoned a donkey and the poor sad half frozen woman of a thing, when found, was brought to Maisie last night, an udder painful with mastitis, foal nowhere. She had been abandoned in the park opposite Sizzlers, beside the preposterous war memorial with its three names carved in polished granite. Tied to a hazel tree on a short thick piece of pink packing twine.

Maisie notices O'Beng and grunts in his direction. He lifts his cap in a greeting that could be a hundred years old. Maisie knows what he is. She twitches from a sensation in her chest, a squeezing, and he smiles. A smile like summer. Maisie understands, then, that he has not come for her, so she smiles back as O'Beng turns to enter the pub.

He orders the Big Breakfast and a pot of loose leaf tea and pays in actual cash. He has the look about him that settles Henry Poe into believing his guest is merely a nice man.

In the bay, out beyond the moorings of small craft, buoys, bells on punts that can warn of dangerous submerged secrets to incoming hookers when the season allows traffic, seals by the hundreds lift wizened, smooth, bald and speckled heads above the slate grey sea skin's mercurial pelt, awareness of draíocht thick in the day, a scent uncanny and vital, skimming the lightness of the dawn breeze in swallow-darting loveliness and intensity. Vengeance has come. Justice. A form of death. Waiting only because he can, not because he has to. And not for them. The work of their culling is that of men.

'Tonight is for fun,' confides Sister Mary Dominic to the gathering of nuns over their eggs and coffee. A sense of foreboding always attends words such as these within the bodies of the women gathered together in such short gaps of time between duties. There are infants to be pulled from women's bodies today, like any other day. There are perinea to cut, pull wide then suture, like christmas packages unwrapped before being discarded. There is shit to clean up. Duty rosters to fill for the women behind the mothers' wall, broken arms and bloody knees to sanitize and wrap and forget, on the children's side. Babies to weigh, bottles and teats to boil. Afterbirth to burn in the downstairs incinerator. They wait.

'Today is Alban Eiler and you, Sister Therese, are to build a little pyre in the field. We shall roast potatoes and celebrate our lord getting us through such a harsh and unnatural winter. The devil is banished, you see. I have been outside and seen green poking through the sod of the garden.

This oddity has occurred at the end of winter for as long as each woman has lived at Our Ladys. Without questioning it, the *diabolism* of the act is wondered at. No fire is lit at Christmas or All Souls Night. Not during Lent or at any of the feast days. Not even at the celebration of the Resurrection, or the Assumption of Mary. No one asks why though. All understand that Sister Mary Dominic punishes challenges to her authority as an act of extreme penitence.

Whether rain or snow, consumption or stroke, whether in a wheelchair or suffering burns from feeding the monster of a boiler in the basement, the equinox at winter's end is celebrated in the garden of buried children. It's a *thing*, although none know why and would not say if they did. And today is turning out quite fine, so Sister Mary Therese is composed about taking on the woodshed, despite her dread of spiders.

No one inside the bus speaks. Faeries and their once-mortal companions are aware that something momentous is afoot. Mercy Riley, the only mortal amongst them all, has her array of weapons laid out on Black Annis bed bunk and checks each broadhead for signs of rust, each fletch for winter molt or parasites. Her bow is compound. A small Hoyt RX-5 with personally redesigned limb dampener and shock pods. No peep sights necessary as she's never been able to miss a target. She checks the riser and ascertains no wobble to the bolts as the weapon has been stored for many years, brought out in midsummer, when she lived with Maisie, to take down a deer to share meat with local folk to give them strength for their preparations in the weeks before the first gypsies come.

The Rowan steers the precious cargo of eldritch allies down the perilous and inconsistent road that leads to the final stretch of tarmac before the field of that one apple tree. The beck is still frozen black although her moss and lichen are in early bloom, livid and vivid in green and pale pink. The moment has come for all the threads to interweave, this transition of day and night and the ferz no longer required. Nor the pawns.

Alban Eiler is the Mystery's move now. It all comes down to this. Rooks to their queen. C'av'arn and the murder from the Bently Fort High School cabal have sent ahead and crowd the roof of the pub much to the quizzicality of Alice and Henry Poe. C'av'arn, her once-apprentice Beatha and the hundred other corvid alliances that usually hang around in the old walnut tree out back of Katherine and Vincent's house, the winter holt of this clan of fáidh. They already line the rhombic slate roof above dormitories within which breathe ache, loss and abandonment that the human triscele: the west wing of Our Lady of Perpetual Sorrows Mother and Baby Home. And as the nuns go about what remains of their duties, with so few pregnant in the age of contraception but enough, nonetheless, to require midwives. If nuns, who never knew penetration except by their own hand, can be called such.

Maisie also whistles on her way back to her cottage by the estuary.

Sister Mary Dominic is not stupid. She is aware of the air; of the presences that she has hoped would never come while she remained alive. Of the moaning tiny creatures in her bowel. That the waiting will likely end with the spring tide overtaking the oak king's reign before his allotted season. Doesn't matter. She has done what she was ordered. Fulfilled destiny. She enters the office in a hush of black serge, pulls the Zero Halliburton case from the closet beside the cold, stale fireplace, opens it and moves efficiently to the wall. She keys in the code to the safe, extracts the contents, stacks the journals, register, thin digital notebook and banded stacks of cash in the case, closes it and sets the lock. She telephones the rectory in Brokeshire informing the suffragan bishop's lesser man that the package will be available for courier that afternoon and would they please come as early as is fortuitous, unaware, as a final touch of magic, that outside of this sheltered coastal locality all transportation will ground to collapse as the springtime blizzard of '28. Eventually to be recorded as historic, dumps three foot of snow under fifty five mile an hour winds creating zero visibility, knocking out power from Brokeshire and Orm Bay, through New Rathmore and as far to the north as the magnetic pole. A nun can't be a seer, after all. Do the others know? That the hiding is finished?

Legend remembers such events as a reckoning, even when people forget.

Hunter returns to his physical form. On the bus, beside his love, Puck's hands dug into the back of his jeans under the dark blue Aran sweater. He has Sparrow's book. The final pages of silvery-grey crosshatched graphic drawing, of murderer and victims, depicts the artist and seer's final accusation. They all look. Now nothing is open to questioning and Raven grunts acknowledgment into the warmth of a comfort of companions. Not at the injustice but of what is yet to be done; at the ramifications and tragedy. He lies the little art journal open at the final accusatory page, in Henry Waubun's lap.

'Why not leave it to the law?'

Raven's look is filled with sparkles that could be humor but are not. 'You know that saying love in blind?'

Waubun's eyes are on Mercy, contemplating all he has been informed of her, knowing the unhuman fact of his companions. So ancient. So young. He doesn't reply.

'You know that image of the lady with the scales?'

This time Henry turns, tries, but extracts no more relevant information from the eyes of his new friend, so like those of a horse or a bear, maybe. His stillness requires the last piece of a winding tangled and unchartered map.

'The law permits this place. Precedent and shite, man. Justice is what?'

The detective studies the drawing before handing the book back. He enters a deep state of contemplation. Sees it all played out in a mind made malleable and complex through countless generations of cunning and violation. Considers how the questions will be asked, how he will counter them, what moves he must make before others make theirs, what jurisdiction he can call on, who he knows in forensics, and even which suits or uniforms owe him a favor. How he is to circumvent official denial and whether to involve the media. Because now he knows his reason. The elders had scolded him before he'd gone away, at seventeen, that he'd regret leaving ancestral lands.

But he hadn't understood.

॥⌐·⋯ ꠥ⋯·⋯ꠥ⋯ ⋯//// ·—=ꠥ·⋯ꠥ ·ꠥ ॥⌐·⋯ /·⋯ꠥ

41

THE SILVER APPLES OF THE MOON

NINE GREEN BOTTLES HANGIN ON THE WALL

Like the old christmas poem not a creature was stirring, not even a mouse. I doubt the women and children are sleeping. Some nights are ominous and, so, silent. Humans are animals after all and the pretense of abandonment is enacted—usually by the parent critter—when predators threaten the burrow or the den, the lair or the nest. In this case, the prison or the fortress depending on one's point of view. Me? I don't give a tuppenny fuck.

Like a bunch of tramps. Like carnies but quiet. Even Revel. I catch up with them halfway up the hill. Hunter, he just tips his head sending a flurry of black feathers into the white night but the others ignore little old me. I'm just O'Beng. Nothing to see here folks. Except for two of them. Mercy Riley smiles at me and I'd swear, if I was capable of it and there was someone to swear to, that she is flirting. But no. She is fey as any of the few human animals that allow such. She is simply familiar in the soul of her, of me. Acknowledgment. Pleasant, that. And Henry Waubun. The eyes and mind of a cop, with a surround of ancestral ghosts that pay homage to my process and always have done, ever since ever. He stares straight at me as if trying to see my eyes. Not gonna happen, man. And I watch the cobbles and bend my knees as the hill inclines annoyingly when I am wearing this fucken flesh with these fucken knees.

I can smell the smoke from their fire. Bitches took boughs from Woman, Apple Tree Wise, in some meanness I will remember, when I do what is to be done. The plovers call. Owls. It's late into night but curlew. Susseration of the incoming tide miles down the hill. Smells of life waking, blood sap rising in elder and rowan. Grass. Dear me, I love grass. Just not lawns. Tear those things up and meadow the ground. Grass is for sheep and sheep don't belong in faerielands. No. Yes. Cock's-foot, mat-grass, sweet vernal, meadow fox-tail. And dock and mallow. Dandelion. Nettle, sorrel, plaintain. Nipplewort. I love nipplewort just for the name. And snowbells. Buttercups. I smell like a dog does. Well, not like a dog so much as *as* a dog, and Revel takes to my side as though we are wolves and have done this since winter's near-starvation became a thing.

And what's that? A mandolin. Someone's tuning up a mandolin. Then the fiddle. The accordion. A craic down in the village. Shoulda known Maisie would want to celebrate. The roll of two bodhrans in synchopation are like massive bull mastiffs whuffling at kittens, as Mercy pulls the string behind the guard, settles the quiver at her back and takes the grip in her left hand, humble, almost invisible, by her side.

What a procession. Legend calls this a trouping. Ravens call it a murder. I have a penchant for collecting collective nouns but I just call it *the fuckening*. Brighid is not here and that means she's with the corvids. Is C'av'arn. And they have work to do before the next dawn. This won't be pretty.

Wow. I'm impressed. Ugliness exuding from the vast bog-brown walls, the window ledges covered in pigeon guano, chimneys that suck no smoke into the waning sky, stalagmites of pointlessness and desperation. This was once a family home. The wealthy. The privileged. Gone. Sold to the Monstrum for this harvest of humanity's shame. No telling the lack of empathy some people are born into, eh?

Hunter does this small dip of one knee, an enticing gesture, and Puck, royalty, magic's young, pale mother of a forest, takes the handles of the massive carved oak doors and pulls them wide, the stink of old cloth and damp assaulting noses used to forest. Nothing is lit. In that nothing is sweat. Desolation. It seeps through the ceiling from the dormitories upstairs. From the nurseries, attended by sterilized women who light their fags despite the babies. Snuck contraband while the nuns, only hours before, crowded the furnace in an otherwise dank, shudderingly cold basement. The miasma of baby poo and cheap talcum powder mixed with the fugue of brightly colored magazine ink and cigarette carcinogens dusting the air of newborns.

Through the kitchen, cockroaches scudding for cover in darkness in swarms of little black and brown bodies and cellar spiders spinning like distaffs from thread as though as high tensile cable, the faeries and their companions take the final strides across hand-scrubbed linoleum to a back door, pull open onto an expanse of light and shadow kitchen garden swathed in mist. And beyond the low drystone to the high-walled umbra and disorienting meadow. Filled with sin. To an end. I turn my cap backwards, unbutton this silly jacket and shake it off, tattooed arms psychedelic in the half-light, corded with muscle and gristle and incalculable strength, steel toed boots the only sound beyond the birds and crack of apple wood as it spits sap into a heartless blaze, wishing that Brighid was here because she's the only fáidh I'd love to lie with. Sighing because I never have and I never will because, well, just because.

Then the wall, topped with glued-on broken bottles, jagged end up. The bricks have also taken to the silence. What they know, poor innocent creatures of lines and mortar that they are. I hear Mercy send out a shush and a calm to them. Woman's full of love for people that don't seem like people to people. They listen because a long time is not a permanancy and so she's not lying, just recognizing and attesting to their witness. The high, wide, metal gate with the cross on top. Chained shut. I almost laugh at the irony. Oh, sorry, excuse the pun. Hunter gives a little tug at the chain and she succumbs, a lover to a giant's gentle persuasion. Smoke is everywhere. And fog as thick as clotted cream. Nice night, maybe. The smell of my lady's limbs, still green, smouldering to no purpose except the vanity of an old woman who is no woman at all, attended by acolytes who believe the motherfucken farce they've been indoctrinated to believe: that there is someplace for them when they die that is other than earth when what do they think feeds the waking of the world that is happening right before their eyes? Bound with rags, is sight. Bloodied with the living.

The cutting and the hacking and the mounds in the meadow that are richer, than horse shit by far, with cowslip and red clover. More high fashion models than furrows. Obvious thing, is the burial of meat.

Mercy pulls her bow from the cordura case as Revel begins to dig at a mound without foliage. Fresh turned, wet; soft.

It's as though time stops and everyone is frozen between seconds because he is a strong and virile hound, his claws and muscled forelegs dragging wet soil away. And away and deeper down. Until he is deep enough. Three tiny, damp bundles in cloth stained as though from tea are exhumed and stinking with corpulence. The air is filled with ugliness. Revel sits back on his haunches, nose dark with mud, ears browner. Big lug is pleased with himself. Everbody looking. Henry taking out his phone and photographing. The nuns unmoving, backs straight, watching us, not what we find.

Eight nuns supposed to be having fun. The ninth, a slúagh in a habit. On concertina camp chairs the eight human of them have their arms wrapped around numb and fruitless torsos in some useless parody of self-embrace, while the Sister-Mary-What's-Her-Real-Name-Dominic slúagh glares past the eerie, uninvited company with slitted eyes believing, truly believing, that *she* has summoned *me*. So busy, also, with the feeding of boughs into the oddly-flamed pyre that she is oblivious to the fact that the courier never came. She actually smiles but, as always, does so through closed lips with no pretense of wit reaching her eyes. She explores my apparition: the image of fantasies, year after pointless year, of masturbation or the further ruin of any girl she chose, deemed clean enough. I have finally come in the flesh. I who would chortle at the fun of it, if such had been appropriate.

One shot after the other, each bolt enters heart after heart until eight bodies die. No blood seepage. Eight women falling back into the damp loam, everything about them except their flesh now gone. Sister Mary Dominic unable to shift her gaze from me, unconscious to the trap. That I am a tooth for a tooth, violence, death yes, but not lust. Never that. She thinks I have come for her. Romantically, oh, I can't breathe, this is hilarious, when the reality is so far removed it's as though her religion is real; as though her pretense is actual and as though her work here is an act of grace instead of a grotesquerie.

Mercy, with Black Annis, move to the corpses. Mercy cracks each arrow in two, extracting both ends and bags them for spare parts later. Annis closes each entry and exit point with the agility of perennial spellcasting, so that no one, medical, constabulary or media, will understand the reason they died tonight, writing heart failure on each official certificate, the end of them, forever and ever, amen, as though they'd never been. Except for the mess the ravens leave after doing what is in their nature to do, because they will not be found for days, until the Alban Eiler fire has turned to ash. Softer white than snow to dust the countless graves. Until Henry conceives his moves.

An odd memory of Déjàvu Delacroix's birthmark map comes to Mercy's mind and she realizes, in an ice of insight, that it was of this landscape. Hidden in plain sight, isn't that the saying? She comprehends that some things are beyond her current capacity to understand. The Great Mystery plants clues to living but the answers are not always obvious until retrospectively.

Sister Mary Dominic has eyes for none of it. What's the problem? She sees me, that's all. I extract a bright shiny rosy-red apple from inside the pocket of my jacket and hold it, palm out, towards her. I don't think she cottons-on to the joke, the irony, though. 'Here,' I smile, 'I brought you a present, little girl.'

Raven stays with Waubun, witnessing. This is what I have come for because I am no ordinary death. I am the death summoned by gypsies. Revenge, resolution. I can never be light. I therefore get to work.

RECKONING

And all is quiet, for a split second of splashed, undeniable blackness, like a dead star that could not possibly retain even a mote of light.

'Fucken slúagh,' Henry hears, from the dissolving shadow of O'Beng, before plovers resume their warnings and the faint shooshing of sea on shingle murmurs from the tideline, reaching through the oddity of sound amplification that fog makes, that thins even as night occults the slaughter. As the stars before dawn appear. Then clusters. The Plough, clearly delineated against an indelible indigo. Darker green against lighter. Mound after mound after mound, as though life had lifted beds of soil with the weight of buried nutriment, the music from the village fading to nothing. Maisie stepping down from the front steps of the community center and beginning the arduous climb up the hill to Our Ladys, knowing her life turns bright with extended purpose.

Where Sister Dominic had raised her arms in rapture towards O'Beng is nothing. No one. Checkmate. Bog. While the last of the flames of the spring equinox blaze wrap air in pale blues, vivid greens, violet and daffodil yellow, somewhat like a very quiet tornado, the life-force of the murdered elder fáidh that Déjàvu had hunted and vandalized, playing the nice big woman while setting trophies on shelves like putrescent parodies of those in the Barrow of Inishrún, another slúagh, in a pretense of something clean and warm-blooded, inventing a father and a history that never were true, bites the dust.

An upstairs light goes on. Faces crowd window after window. Nothing is clearly visible. A collective nightmare dissolving. One after another psychic lightbulbs light up in the mind of each girl and woman. That they are released. Animals knowing the circus cage lock has been sprung. They move, in baggy nightdresses and bare feet, down corridors that have never experiences the tread by any of them except for the sound of the bell clanging them to lauds. Some access the nursery, nipples leaking and hearts pounding, genitals stinging with new thread, to find babies who turn their heads at the scent of mother. Others run to the children's quarters in hope that maybe the faces are recognizable, of those that were not taken.

As dawn pinks a sky with a blush not seen in a year the faeries return, unseen or unrecognized, through the empty downstairs foyer, pulling the great oak doors shut and crunching the gravel, tread to those wide open metal gates, and then to the bus, where the Rowan, and the companions not invited to the shit-show, wait in contented amiability. The Rowan kicks over the engine, determined to wait for Raven.

Henry stands with Hunter until Raven catches up, lagging behind the trouping faeries, his mind a whirl of necessary escape plans. He takes the detective in an embrace of solidarity before ceasing to even register the cop's existence.

'What about me, Birdie? You can't just walk, man.' Henry feigns a kind of officialdom that is so obviously a ruse; in truth just despair. The dark-haired fáidh does not reply. He takes Mercy by the hand and they return to the scene of the atrocity in the meadow. Things still left undone.

Raven, head down, leads Mercy Riley to the one grave that bears no green. He says nothing and neither does she. A million years are lived in seconds.

'Will you be with me?' he asks.

'No. I know who you are, see?' She does not look at him; fiddles. 'I was born here, and we waited for you, and you never came. To rescue us. Me, my mother, Sparrow. You never came, so no. This place, and Maisie's house. This is home. I was born to heal, Raven, not to hurt people. I also won't say sorry.'

Mercy hands Raven the bow and quiver. As she walks from the grave of her mother towards the inside of what had been her prison, she waits for Maisie, knowing these women will need help today. In giving birth. Healing. To escape the walls.

Raven is still a moment longer, then continues past the high, dark brick wall, towards his own fate.

The bus takes off without them, Brighid, now herself, tipping her head sideways, crow-like, to the Rowan indicating the pointlessness of hope.

Hunter did not tell Raven that Mercy is his child.

Henry Waubun walks back the way he came, knowing why he has been chosen and determined to see his destiny to fruition. He stands at the kitchen door in the dawn, seeing the garden and the meadow beyond. The dead. The graves. He scans the scene, almost mindless in astonishment at what has been done. The witness, as there always must be, to any event of momentous change.

The detective lacks all capacity to call this in yet. To consider the moves he must willingly make. To think of how to explain his presence here. To head the investigation. So he takes his time, mesmerized by the feasting of ravens on the flesh of what were once human animals in clothes but are now just meat, and he purposely strides to the exhumed grave, covering the shapes of decomposing babies, pulling the sod over them so they remain safe from this predation, in this form at least, before reentering the vulgar fortress and accessing its main office. He finds the light switch, igniting fluorescence and sees the locked metal case on the desk.

Outside, in the fluidity of a bright spring morning, Agnes moves the soil from where the coffin lid has broken.

Yeah Birdie, thinks Henry Waubun, contemplating events and nuances about his companion he has learned. *I'm soft, orrite?*

42

IIII ..... III . II ....
                     II

CITADEL

CHANGELING

In the citadel Artful hears the crackle. He strides, confident and resolute, to the forbidden cellar and hacks the lock. The door huffs open and a blast of heat rushes past. Embers. Fire. In the shape of a man. Artful returns to the main floor of the warehouse and suggests, quite quietly, that everyone leave before the place becomes an inferno. Consoles are abandoned. What Morcant thought was his life's work now yesterday's news. Irrelevant.

At the fortress of dead dreams, called erroneously Our Lady of Perpetual Sorrow Mother and Baby Home, O'Beng absorbs the worst of the pain of Morcant's destruction. A man who never was. The changeling born of a nun who also never really was either. A caricature created by alchemists amongst the Monstrum. For profit.

The Dodger walks all day through fine, not-so-cold misty rain, ignoring a drenching. To Dimity's Bookshop. He sits in the courtyard out back, under the shelter of the only awning and Merrin brings two coffees.

'Mind if I join you while you wait?'

'How'd you know I'm waiting?'

Revel lollops into the yard, tiny stars of wet shaken over the two people, condescending for a biscuit.

'For him?'

'Me mate, yes.'

He ruffles the huge pup behind his filthy, mud-crusted ears. 'Me punkin carriage coming, is it, me old chum?'

If Revel's ears were in better shape he would prick them.

'Your drivers'll be faeries, not mice though. You cool with that?' Merrin blows on the coffee, still difficult stuff to get even on the black market, too hot to sip just yet.'

'Fair enough.' Always Artful, always with the last word.

Nobody in the human world has yet to hear Raven's music. The Great Mystery will know when to use it.

EPILOGUE

COME AWAY, O HUMAN CHILD
TO THE WATERS AND THE WILD
WITH A FAERY, HAND IN HAND
FOR THE WORLD'S MORE FULL OF WEEPING THAN YOU
CAN UNDERSTAND.

HY BRASIL

Hunter, high up on the escarpment overlooking Forgotten Lake. In the shape of a massive silver wolf. The Great Mystery, all spongy moss, glittering rime with little darty fish in a cloak of lakelight, climbs the final rocky path and squats, her hands in his ruff.

'It doesn't matter how they die, Hunter.'

'I know.'

'What do you know?'

'That none of this should have happened; should have been allowed to happen.'

'But don't you realize the beauty in it all?'

'Is it ever going to stop?'

'Pup?'

'You know what I mean.'

'Beauty shows itself from the ugliest of things, Hunter.'

'Yeah, I know.'

'Then enough with the questions.'

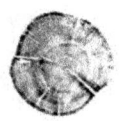

AUTHOR'S NOTE

THE TRAVELER SERIES, BOOK FOUR

THE CHANGELING

I haven't told most people how this series came about, and what I have learned that led to the start of it all. Almost twenty years ago.

I dreamed I was a fair man, seated opposite one who was dark. On the floor upstairs from a rave party. He was angrier than anyone I have (almost) ever known and, as is true most times I have been yelled at, I didn't, or couldn't, understand a word. We were both cross-legged on the floor. He pulled a stub of chalk from the pocket of his jacket and drew what I presumed was a circle of protection around his seated body. Uh-oh, I thought, this is sorta war. And, as is the nature of dreams, I also happened to have chalk in my clothing so I did the same as him. As he yelled he spat. I was aware that was not his intention, that he just wanted to get a serious point across to me but was not averse to a rammy (fight).

Then I seemed to fall. Metaphor, yes, but into his head. And I was in an incalculably enormous underground carpark. Was it a carpark? Pillars as far as I could see in the strange buttery amber light. No one. No vehicles. Just maybe two or ten acres of concrete with pylons supporting a ceiling too high for me to see. On the ground was an object. A base of old gold about twenty centimeters high and the same around. Crusted with rubies and garnets. From which a central, slim pillar rising to the height of my thighs, four serpents wound upwards, their heads, faces, to the unseen ceiling, ecstatic. The whole was turning as though a carousel, the rare metal and the gemstones catching that butter light reflecting and refracting it almost blindingly. I had never seen anything so beautiful.

I fell out of his head and was back in the room with the spitting and the yelling. 'I just saw you,' I said.

He continued the rant for maybe ten seconds before he faltered, his brow scrunching. 'What did you say?'

'I just saw you.'

It was though all the hatred and all the futility and all the unfulfilled despair in him melted. And then I woke up.

I went downtown for a covening of coffee and chat. I thought no more about the dream. One doesn't, yes? Until I returned home. I walked through the back gate and flatlined. As a stolen child I have lived within the shadow of depression (whatever that is; the inability to achieve resolution, perhaps? Rage slowly breaking down resolve but, with nowhere to go, toppling. An avalanche-like destruction of inner space, perhaps? The closing off of escape?).

I did what I have taught myself to do, a mental scan to ascertain whether the mood was due to some slight of my attention, and there was nothing. A flatline, then, always indicates a psychic thing that I wait for. That will always expose itself. A tickle of words slid along the left side of my head. They said:

The power's been going on and off all day. It's a good thing the boss decided the open fire look would please the customers. Pub's been packed all night, everybody trying to keep warm. 'Lot of people gonna freeze in this weather.'

I went into my cottage and took up the notebook and pen from beside the bed. I sat in the wicker chair in the garden and wrote. All day. Until around six. Eighteen A 4 pages. I didn't know what I'd done. It was the story of how the Rowan first met Hunter and what it was to be witness to an event of such profundity that normal people were likely to think he maybe made it up.

He says: *I'm freaked. I look up into coal-black eyes, pinning me to the spot. He's easy six-two, six-three, bundled in a big old army greatcoat. I can't figure out if he's got layers and layers of clothes underneath or whether he's just plain huge. Dark skin, little plaited beard, no hat, ragged dreds studded all through with black feathers hanging to his waist.*

I read it to my daughter. She normally cringes when I try to do that but didn't, so I figured it was significant. Then nothing. Not the next day, at least. The day after was Thursday and I went to the gym, worked upper body, was home by nine that morning, and wham. More tickle of words. Same timing, same number of pages. And after a while When I See the Wild God ended up on Natalie Harter's desk, my editor, at Llewellyn Worldwide, on Turtle Island.

Natalie said to me, *if you write a whole book on this lot we'll publish it.* I did.

That was *The Quickening* which was published there in 2005. There's a but. In 2003 I traveled to Ireland and into strangeness. I cannot explain without an entire book. I wrote as I moved from town to town and ended up in Roundstone, just up the road from Galway. I think the mysteries, the fáidh, commonly and disrespectfully called fairies, stuck to me like the fluff of a white cat on black jeans because of almost legendary events that followed.

That book was pre-released in Ireland and it's also where I lived a while with a family of na lucht siúil. Indigenous Irish gypsies, called walking people, despite the horses and the remnants of bright wagons. Forced off the roads by the government. I stayed near them, in their shed. They taught me enough that I was altered by the words. English. No one had taught them Shelta.

The Quickening won an accolade. It was followed by *The Shining Isle* because the Travelers had not done with me yet. Had not done fixing me, an insect in amber, as their messenger to mortals other than me.

I learned that indigenous people the world over are subdued by poverty, indifference, brutality, poison, rape, loss of culture for the so-called illegitimate children, or annihilation of identity, and destruction of language. How colonialism and religion exert a right that cannot be justified, but is cruelly enforced, and an agreement made with something parasitic, the Monstrum, that got away, literally, not only with murder but with genocide.

Studying anthropology and the etymology of words and language I had a kazillion lightbulbs burning brightly as I realized that most indigenous peoples anthropomorphize landscape, weather, wind, ice, the movement of water, and an understanding of travel and the ley of environment but that so-called civilized people do not realize this, because they are afraid they might not be seen as top doggie, and so they invent things, small things, easy to crush or spray with pesticides, or simply scoff at: leprechauns, fairies, elves, manitou, ghosts, demons, you name it, and then proceed to metaphorically shit on them, ridicule them or turn them into Little Golden Books painted winged caricatures. Only *god*, one, not many, and looking decidedly like an old bloke living in the clouds with just the ghosts of once-living humans who agreed with everything he said, knelt heaps and never questioned, now with their harps and white, white, whiteness, *him* with an upper case G, like a name, since ideology became acceptable. Eye-watering and mind-numbingly dumbly and misguidedly acceptable.

Sometimes, after years, I thought the Travelers and the Great Mystery gone. But they were not.

Inspired by a page of prose written by Serenity de Angeles, I reopened whatever track these pieces of you and me and land and forever had carved, and the third in the series, featuring Hunter and Puck's son Robin, and how he loves, and how utterly enchanting, became the third book in the Traveler Series: *Under Snow*. Because of love. The Lady of Shalot; Rose. My daughter and I wrote this together. Ancestry, it turns out is bone-deep.

I, like my ancestors, am Albion, Éire, Scandinavia, and what is now called France, and my grandmother's mother was also a Traveler. A bootlegger I have learned.

In the last decade of the current era, the Icelandic Road and Coastal Administration, and the huge Kárahnjúkastífla dam project, have been thwarted to protect the very soul of the land. A wayshower known as Ófeigskirkja (ancient guardian rock) was uprooted and moved so that the álfur (an Old Norse word translated to elves, and so are/is diminished in the face of such weirdness as christianity) could retain themselves/itself. The singular/plural aspect of this word and the words related to the diminishment of memory, fairies, gives multinationals and capitalist greed big fat feet in the door. The reductionism, to a point of ridicule, is a ploy. A game upon some unseen Monopoly board. Chess is, then, more honest. It does not kill the spirit of place. And yet, álfur also means white.

Briefly: fáidh, faerie, fair, faith, fair (as in a joyous event), fate, and fear all derive from knowledge almost written out of consciousness. To our ominous and looming detriment.

Yes, I am an environmentalist, an ecologist a lover, and respecter of place. I do not get upset when outdoor plans must necessarily be changed to indoors due to an impending hurricane. Recently what was home for twenty nine years, the Northern Rivers of New South Wales (nothing like South Wales, I discovered whilst traveling), has been utterly transformed by what was originally called an historic, once-in-a-lifetime, unprecedented flood. Mother Water moved the land. Created new rivers and changed the coastline. Did a LOT. Then, within a month, the flood has been repeated, so "once-in-a-lifetime" became an oopsie.

How many chances do we have to stop relegating fact to

fallacy? Mystery to obscurity? Words like pendragon is supposed to be the title of a man, a king, and not a track, traveled by critters including humans for untold eons, ending in a headland on a Cornish coast? That cailleach is not some old ugly woman but a full 360 circle view from a high up vantage point, like Hag's Head on the east coast of Ireland, except *hag* is a Saxon word so what's it doing in such an outpost unless the language was taken there by either trade or harm? Mórrígan, two words, *mór*: great or large and *rí* translated into English, the language of the "butcher's apron", as some ruling monarch, when sovereign territory is both kindred and tribe. Never a war goddess with large breasts and no waist, depicted like a Marvel character with a bow or a spear, posing in a short, ripped skirt with long bare legs and a raven on her shoulder. Mother-as-map, like standing stones and impossible rock circles. Look what has been done. Is modernity responsible for reducing vast tracts of indigenous lands to "a goddess of battle"? I shudder.

I once knew a scholar (or so I thought) of Egyptology. She contacted me with some huge awakening of consciousness. She said words to the effect of *My god! Do you know that Ireland and Egypt must once have been connected because 'Tara' includes the name of the Egyptian hawk god, Ra?* She was disillusioned when I patiently explained that the seat of árdrí (translated as high king), and the Lia Fáil is spelled Teamhair.

The etymology of words allows us to trace the movement of us as a species from one place to another. If we look with sufficient objectivity, we can understand what the conqueror's history books don't tell. This seeking homogeny is rude. It kills story-sharing. It denies a deeper understanding of who we are and how we are conquered. How tired we become. There's a but (so often there is a but).

Every Irish person I have known who hasn't been cruelly dislocated by christianity, fears the Travelers because they can drown a body in a bog, kill a crop, bewitch cattle, scuttle a ship and drive the fish away. Nowadays they can burn an oil rig to ashes, killing all on board for drilling into the sub-layers of earth so deeply it could be considered some archaic rite of rape. Albion, or alba, means white. This has nothing to do with a human animal's pelt color but the wisdom, almost lost, of what white is safe to travel in or walk upon and what white will kill. What we need to remember is that we are place. Not only are we place we are weather and sea and kindred to all who live with the shapes and movements of place, whether they be volcanic, earthquake, foot-blistering desert sand, blizzard, creek, mountain presence, cobbled back streets in a dirty city, animal intestine and, well, all of the above. I am first generation human of my (for lack of a less personal term) family lines to be born in this vast landscape called, erroneously and rather unimaginatively, Australia. I have no right to be here.

I, therefore, pay my respects to the people where I am living, the Wurundjeri, Boon Wurrung, and Wathawurrung people of the Kulin

Nation, and up north, the Bundjalung people of the Arakwal Nation, and I bend the knee in respect to their Elders past, present and emerging.

NO ANSWERS

I intentionally don't give all the answers in this book. I don't explain everything because to do so would be to trap questions in cages. I won't do that. I could not, anyway. Or I'd be agreeing to the very process that is destroying habitat and species cousins worldwide.

I trust in people's intelligence. I also am aware that if only one person 'gets' what I am doing with this, the fourth and final book in the Traveler Series they will understand what draíocht, magic, is and how to be a spell.

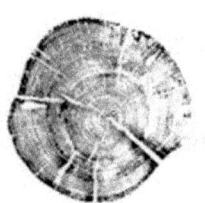

DEDICATION

This work is not only dedicated to the three babies, now adults, expelled from my body but to the ancestors whose names I seek to breathe life into, and theirs. It is also for the children thrown into the sewers in Tuam, Ireland, the children in mass graves of Canada, Turtle Island, the land called by English invaders Australia, and wherever else their unrequited souls haunt for justice. This is not nearly over.

For all the women, living and dead, denied their dignity when pregnant, told they are dirty; to the fathers whose names were not recorded because they either did not care, were kept from the truth, wept, shot themselves, or ran, in hopes they would not be tainted by a living bastard.

To all the incorrigible rebels who have worked with me, tirelessly, in Australia, Ireland, and other parts of what is now called Europe and Scandinavia, to get me, finally, to that court and have the cruelty of the Monstrum exposed and undone, thank you.

Respect to Lynne Kelly, Robert Macfarlane, Robin Wall Kimmerer, Martin Shaw, Paul Kingsnorth, Kim Scott, Lisa Carey, for your books, the work of Kahlil Gibran, Nan Shepherd and Wendell Berry. The Dark Mountain Project, for an alternative way of wording. Respectfully and lacking the crudity of objectification. You change people. That is magic. Oh, yes, and W. B. Yeats.

And because, then, she chose not to, rebel that she is, a major hubbub broke out across sky and sea, mountain and mythworld. A mighty council convened: Night Mares came. Pleasant Dreams ceased sanguinity and took a serious turn, Enbarr de Manannán, the white horse from the sea, from the wild west coast off Weary Bay, sent envoys, night owls known to call a body's name, predicting their death a week or two before (so's to give them a chance to make peace), turning when into resolution. Well, they came as thick as crows, and as murderous as ravens. People of every species, conspiring with mist and fog and hoarfrost giants who have heard tell of this one little chit of a woman, her drawings and her rebellion all potentially damaging to their hiddenness. The conjecture about what would happen if predestination was actually realized as real—

It is real.

All real.

Folk tales are not fairytales. That's just rude.

ABOUT THE AUTHOR

2022

Lore de Angeles has written under the name *Ly de Angeles* since *Witchcraft Theory and Practice* was published, by Llewellyn Worldwide, USA, in 2000. She is also a teacher, storyteller, mystic, has been in print since 1987.

An award-winning author and short film maker, a director and producer of stage, screen and street, mother, grandmother, scholar, deep ecologist, mythographer, feminist, consultant, psychic and is currently deeply engrossed in anglo-linguistic anthropology, the psychology of words and a hunter of repetitious metaphor. She trained as a silversmith, an archer, fought with a crew named Clan Fianna with staff and broadsword (she made her own) and is accomplished in Hapkido, MMA, a smattering of Aikido, free- weights and healing.

She is a 3rd Dan Iaido sensei.

De Angeles was taken from her mother, at birth, and was denied all knowledge of ancestry and heritage for more than fifty years. She has since received justice for herself, her children and theirs. As much as anyone can.

GLOSSARY

PRONUNCIATION

A cara	a cara (love)
Alba	alapah (white, as in landscape)
Anam cara	anam kara (soul friend)
Annis	annish (look up Wild Hunt)
Ban-nighe	banny (woman sídhe)
Bogle	bowgul (baddy)
Calléach	(circle, 360° visuals)
Coutie	cootee (a spell rag tied to a tree)
Craic	crack (good time)
Deartháir	dehar (depending on place, brother)
Déjàvu	day ja voo (to see again)
Draíocht	dree-ucht (magic)
Fáidh	fay (faerie)
Gabhdán	gavahn (gullible person)
Golem	golum (am undead entity)
Inishrún	inish-roon (isle of secrets)
Lia Fáil	lee-ya fahl (ardrí stone)
Meagín	mijun (magpie)
Mo chroí	mow cree (my love)
Mulo	moo-low (ghost)
Moddy Dhoo	moddy-doo (death)
Ogham	och-am (druidic lettering)

Púka	pooka (see fáidh)
Seelie	sheelee (see fáidh)
Shine	(a bright essence)
Sídhe	shee (faerie, landscape, weather)
Slúagh	shlooah (enemy)
Temhair	tara (place of ardrí)
Tír na nÓg	teer na noch (land of the ever young)
Ulchabhán	ool-ha-van (owl)
Úllcran Ciallmhar	oolcra cialvar (apple tree)
Unseelie	(see sídhe)
Yr Angau	er anga (servant of death)